falling out of HATE *with* YOU

USA Today and International Bestselling Author

Lauren Rowe

Published by SoCoRo Publishing

Cover design © Letitia Hasser, RBA Designs

ONE

SAVAGE

Hollywood Hills, California

Music is blaring around me as I wade through the packed party, precariously balancing six shot glasses filled to their brims. I come to a stop when I reach my four bandmates—Kendrick, Kai, Ruby, and Titus—plus, our manager, Eli.

"Grab 'em, quick!" I call out over the loud music, and, thankfully, my friends immediately relieve me of the tequila-laden Jenga tower in my palms. Once all glasses have been distributed, I raise mine to our band's drummer and beat-maker, my best friend in the world, Kendrick Cook. "Happy twenty-fifth!" I shout. And, of course, everyone joins me in wishing Kendrick a great one.

According to Reed Rivers' party invitation, we're at his hilltop mansion tonight to celebrate an upcoming issue of *Rock 'n' Roll* magazine—a special issue that's going to feature nothing but the top artists from his record label, an elite group that thankfully includes our band, Fugitive Summer. But since nobody throws a better bash than our label owner—or, as my band has dubbed Reed Rivers, "The Prick"—and since most of the people we would have invited to a separate birthday party for Kendrick are here, anyway—we decided to hijack Reed's fancy shindig to celebrate our boy's birth.

"Do I have drool on my chin?" Kai Cook, our bass player and Kendrick's older brother, shouts above the music, as one of the most head-turning women at the party, a reporter for *Rock 'n' Roll* named Georgina, walks by and waves as she goes.

Our other guitarist, Titus, nudges my shoulder. "The reporter winked at you, Savage! Go get her, Player!"

I roll my eyes. I hate that my bandmates still call me "Player," the same way they've been doing since the beginning, when I was admittedly drunk on all the attention our band—and especially *me*—had started getting. But these days, the nickname isn't nearly as accurate as it once was, not since an "influencer" in Barcelona made my dick the top trending topic on Twitter last year.

Immediately after sex with that spicy little Spaniard, I hopped into the shower in my hotel room, thinking she'd fallen asleep. And that's when she snagged my wallet, snapped some surreptitious photos of me cluelessly washing up, and then promptly posted the shots, along with a detailed play-by-play of our night together. And off she went, into the Spanish night, while I continued singing a happy tune, literally, in the shower. And I swear, I haven't been the same "player," ever since.

It wasn't that I was upset about the wallet. While on tour, I barely ever have anything in it. Condoms, a credit card that was easy to cancel, and my ID. Also, I wasn't all that bent out of shape about the world seeing my naked dong or finding out, through the Spaniard's posted commentary, that I'm a rabid fan of oral sex.

No, as cliché as it sounds, the thing that threw me for a loop was the shocking breach of trust. The realization that nobody out there is trustworthy, no matter how much it feels like they might be, in the moment. It was the realization that anything I might say or do in private, no matter how intimate it might feel in the moment, could end up as a meme on the internet.

In that moment, I knew whatever genuine connection I'd thought the woman and I had shared that night was an illusion. Or worse, if it had been real, she was willing to sacrifice it on the altar of snagging my wallet and her fifteen minutes of fame.

It was the first time I truly understood the downside of this crazy life. The loneliness and eternal separation from normalcy that's inherent in the gig. And it changed me. I've never been a guy who wears his heart on his sleeve, anyway. I don't trust easily and never have. But after that experience, I felt even more closed off and determined to keep myself under wraps.

Kai grabs my arm, like he thinks he's keeping me from chasing after the hot reporter, Georgina. But I'm not even tempted to run after her. Kai yells above the blasting music, "I call dibs on the reporter! And you know I *never* do that, dude! So, you'd better respect The Dibs!"

I'm offended. Why does Kai feel the need to say that to me? I *always* respect The Dibs, more than anyone else in the band, other than Kendrick. Kai should know by now I don't give a fuck which gorgeous woman I wind up with, if any. There are far too many of them in this world, and, certainly, at this party, and I'm far too good at getting whoever I want, to chase after someone who's caught the eye of one of my best friends. Especially when I barely know the woman in question.

I'd call my general mindset in this regard "bros before hoes" or "dicks before chicks," if our bandmate, Ruby, not to mention, my cousin, Sasha, hadn't both made a thing about the words "ho" and "chick" being derogatory. So, maybe "brovaries before ovaries" would be the better bet? The point is that I *always* respect The Dibs. Although, in this instance, Kai probably shouldn't pursue the reporter, anyway. Not because *I* want her. But because I've surmised there are extenuating circumstances.

I reply to Kai, "You never need to 'call dibs' with me. Just tell me you're in hot pursuit and that's that. But I think you're gonna need to set your sights on someone else this time, brother. When I played ping pong with Georgina earlier to talk about my interview, I got the solid vibe she's already with Reed. Or if not, she's definitely at the top of his To Do List."

"*Reed*?" Kai bellows, like that's a preposterous notion. Like every woman at this party wouldn't give her left tit to get with Reed. The guy with the big house, the fit body, the garage full of sports cars, and a bank account that puts every band member here to shame. But, whatever. My bandmates and I are drinking and having fun tonight, and roasting the bastard who takes way too big a cut of our royalties, thanks to the shitty contract we signed as puppies, before Eli started repping us, is one of our favorite drinking games.

Titus and Kai continue roasting Reed for a bit. And as they banter, I reach for my phone when it buzzes in my pocket. I wouldn't normally check my phone at a party. But only my inner circle has this particular number, and almost all of them are here tonight.

When I check my screen, it's a text from my cousin, Sasha, as suspected, regarding our grandma.

. . .

Sasha: Are you available to FaceTime, by any chance? Mimi had a nightmare you died in a plane crash. She wants to see your face.

Me: Can't FT. I'm at a noisy party and kinda drunk. How about a quick video?

Sasha: Awesome.

I shoot a brief selfie video in which I smile, make silly faces, and blow kisses to my grandma amid the noisy throng around me. And after I press send, Sasha quickly replies in all caps.

Sasha: IS THAT ISABEL RANDOLPH BEHIND YOU?!?

I turn around, and, I'll be damned, one of the most famous movie stars on the planet is standing directly behind me, chatting with a group of suits I don't recognize.

Me: It is, indeed.

Sasha: HOLY SHIT. Do you know her?

Me: Nope.

Sasha: Go meet her and send me a photo for my birff-day! Pleeeeease!

Me: Your birthday isn't for two months. But more importantly, doing that for you would require me to speak to a new person, which, as you know, I try to avoid at all costs.

Sasha: Why do you go to so many parties, if you hate talking to new people so much?

Me: Because I like talking to MY people while surrounded by new people I can gawk at but NOT talk to. Especially tonight, when we're celebrating KC's bday.

Sasha: Aw, wish KC happy birthday for me! Have you performed a birthday dare for him yet?

Me: Not yet. He's still deciding what brand of humiliation to inflict upon me.

Sasha: LOL. Don't do anything dangerous.

Me: It's always all in good fun. Give Mimi a hug for me.

Sasha: Already did. She loves the video. Says she loves you and stay safe.

Me: Love her, too, and you. Tell her I'm fine and mostly traveling by bus on the next leg of the tour.

Sasha: Will do. Goodnight. Have a blast.

My cousin is being sincere when she tells me to have fun. But I can't help feeling guilty she's there on a Saturday night, hanging out with our grandma and one of the nighttime care-givers I've bankrolled, while I'm at a star-studded party in LA. Not to mention that Sasha works hard at a real job in Chicago—she's a massage therapist—while I traipse around the world and swoop into town for occasional visits, when-ever convenient, like I'm Weekend Daddy after a divorce.

Sasha always says she wouldn't have it any other way. She's ten years my senior and always says she's gotten her partying out of her system. Plus, she always reminds me, she's a homebody by nature, anyway. "I'm happiest when I'm hanging out with Mimi, reading or knitting," she always says. "I like sitting still and watching TV." And so, I bought my beloved homebody her own home last year, where she now takes care of our beloved grandma, along with the caregivers, and mostly believe my cousin when she says she's truly not the least bit angry with me for continuing to play rockstar.

I send a quick goodnight text to my cousin, stuff my phone into my pocket, and tune back into my bandmates' conversation, just in time to hear Titus saying, "I think it's bullshit. I mean, yes, if you'd already gotten to know the reporter, and had done more than spot her across a crowded room, then, okay, calling dibs on her makes sense. But I certainly wouldn't back off a woman, simply because you *spotted* her. And I sure as hell wouldn't back off just because Reed *might* be interested. Would he extend the same courtesy to any of us? Fuck no!"

"Reed's more than 'possibly' interested," I interject. "During my ping pong game with Georgina, I noticed Reed spying on her the whole time from behind a bush."

Everyone laughs at the imagery, except for Titus, who's shaking his head.

"No way," Titus says. "Reed must have been standing near a bush, looking at his phone or talking to someone you couldn't see. I love roasting The Prick as much as anyone, but there's no way Reed Rivers would hide behind a bush, at his *own* party, while surrounded by some of the world's hottest women, in order to keep tabs on a summer intern at *Rock 'n' Roll*."

My eyebrows shoot up. "Georgina's an *intern* at the magazine?"

Titus gestures to his pink-haired twin sister, Ruby, our keyboardist, who's standing nearby talking to our manager, Eli. "When Ruby and I played cornhole with the reporter, she said she'd just graduated from UCLA and that her 'internship' with *Rock 'n' Roll* is her first professional gig."

"I never would have guessed that," I say.

Titus nods. "Georgina is just a baby. She said she's turning twenty-two next month."

I'm floored. I glance at her across the packed room, where Georgina is presently talking to the bass player of 22

Goats—a sweetheart of a guy named Fish. "I never would have guessed she's that green," I say. "With all that swagger, I would have thought she's large and in charge at *Rock 'n' Roll*." I chuckle. "Well, either way, I know what I saw. Reed was *definitely* spying on Georgina, from behind a bush, like a goddamned stalker."

Titus nudges Kai's shoulder. "Did Reed spy on you when you talked to Georgina?"

"No. Not that I noticed."

"And he didn't spy on Ruby and me playing cornhole with her, either. Huh. I wonder why Reed felt the need to spy on her with *you,* Player."

I wink. "I guess he's only worried about the good lookin' ones, eh?"

Titus flips me off as Kai flags down a cocktail server who's walking by with a slew of margaritas, and we quickly relieve her of her entire burden. His new drink in hand, our trusty manager, Eli, bids the group farewell, saying he's going to "schmooze" for a bit. Ruby joins our conversation, and we continue bantering and people-watching as a full band.

"So, have you decided on Savage's birthday dare yet?" Kai asks his younger brother, Kendrick. Earlier tonight, Kendrick made Kai fanboy all over some blonde actor on a Netflix show I've never heard of. And ever since, Kai has been dying to watch me get equally humiliated.

For the past ten years, on each of our respective birthdays, Kendrick, Kai, and I have played a shitfaced game of "Birthday Truth or Dare." Although calling it that is a misnomer by now, since we've long since taken the "truth" option off the table in our game. Why waste the chance to inflict humiliation in order to ask some stupid question we probably already know the answer to? Kai and Kendrick are brothers, after all, and I've known them both for well over ten years.

"Not yet," Kendrick says, answering his brother's question about my dare. "I'm still weighing my options."

"Oh my gosh!" Ruby blurts. "Savage was right about Reed and the reporter! Look at Reed now, guys! He's totally spying on her from across the room!" We look to where Ruby is indicating and discover Reed covertly staring at Georgina while she chats with the guys from Watch Party. Almost certainly, it's Zach Rosendo—their frontman whom everyone calls Endo—who's attracted Reed's eagle eye this time. That dude's definitely got a reputation as a lady killer.

"I just decided on my dare," Kendrick declares, his mischievous gaze trained on Reed. He looks at me, smiling wickedly and rubbing his palms together. And, instantly, I know what's coming.

"Aw, fuck. *No*," I mutter.

"You're not allowed to say no," Kendrick reminds me.

"I know the rules, motherfucker. Do *you*?" I'm referring to rule number one of our game. Namely, that the birthday boy can't pick a dare that's likely to maim, kill, or send his victim to prison. Rule number two is that the birthday boy is king—a deity whose dare can't be refused, as long as it complies with rule number one. And, finally, rule number three is that the dare has to be something that can be performed on the spot. In other words, birthday dares can't be some elaborate prank or hoax that would require weeks of planning.

Kendrick smiles. "Yeah, I know the rules. And I promise no bodily harm will come to you. The only thing that could possibly happen to you, in theory, is that you'd get onto Reed's shit list. But you're already there. So, really, there's no downside."

He's right. I've been on Reed's shit list for a while now, despite all the money my band makes him—powered in large part by me, personally. All because, years ago, I hit on his little sister, Violet, at my first Reed Rivers party, without having a clue who she was. This was long before Violet met her husband, Dax, the lead singer of 22 Goats. And, frankly, she seemed pretty receptive to my flirting, as I recall. And yet, Reed's held it against me, ever since.

"I don't get it," Ruby interjects. "What's the dare, Kendrick?"

Kendrick motions to me, like he's inviting me to enlighten Ruby.

Rolling my eyes, I say, "I'm assuming he wants me to hit on the hot reporter in front of Reed."

"Bingo," Kendrick says. "Let's test your theory that he's been sleeping with her, or wants to. I want you to hit on her, really obviously in front of him. With enough fuckboy heat you'll lure Reed out of his proverbial bush this time. But not with so much heat he lurches at you like a cheetah and smashes your face against a wall."

I grimace, as everyone else laughs.

"Why on earth would you force me to walk this tightrope?" I say. "You were there when C-Bomb told us that crazy story about what Reed did to the dude who'd fucked his ex."

"What did Reed do?" Ruby asks, her eyebrows shooting up.

But, unfortunately for Ruby, she's asking her question as Kendrick is saying, "Reed would never beat the shit out of you, simply for *flirting* with his woman. Flirting is way less a crime than fucking. Plus, your face makes him way too much money to smash it into a wall, regardless."

"What the hell did Reed do?" Ruby shouts, this time cutting through the din. She looks at her twin brother, Titus, who's laughing along with Kendrick and Kai. "You know this story?"

Titus nods. "I heard it from C-Bomb." He's referring to

the iconic drummer of Red Card Riot—Caleb Baumgarten—who's a good friend to our band.

"Well, he didn't tell *me*," Ruby says.

"You weren't there," Titus replies to his sister.

"Well, tell me the damned story already!" Ruby blurts. "It sounds juicy."

Without further ado, Kendrick launches into telling the tale, which, in summary, is that, in the earliest days of River Records, Reed went batshit crazy after discovering the lead singer of one of his earliest bands had fucked his unnamed ex. Apparently, upon discovering the news, Reed beelined to a party at C-Bomb's house, where the lead singer was hanging out, and promptly smashed the guy's face into a wall. Not content to stop there, however, Reed also dropped the guy's band from his label the next day and permanently shelved their debut album, which, C-Bomb said, was due to release within weeks. "And Reed did all this," Kendrick says, "despite the fact that he'd already invested tens of thousands of dollars into developing the band's music and marketing."

Ruby explodes with shocked comments and questions, which the guys answer with relish. But since I've already heard this story, I let my mind and attention wander. I check out the movie star, Isabel Randolph, for a bit, admittedly feeling star-struck. As a guy with some fame myself, albeit not at Isabel's level, I understand the inner workings of the cult of celebrity and consciously try not to let it seduce me. But, still, I can't deny it's kind of cool to see such a world-famous face, in person.

After a bit, however, when my interest in Isabel flags, I continue surveying the packed, noisy room. I check out several friends as they laugh and chat in nearby groups, noting, in particular, that my buddy, Fish, seems particularly smitten with his cute date. And that she looks absolutely enthralled with him. Good for Fish. Couldn't happen to a nicer guy.

I keep scanning and people-watching. Sipping my drink. But when my gaze lands on Laila Fitzgerald, it stays put.

Laila Fitzgerald.

She's another River Records artist. One I've been dying to meet for some time. And by "meet" I mean "meet, seduce, and, God willing, fuck." When I first saw Laila's most recent scorching-hot music video, that sucker immediately went into my spank bank, where it's been in heavy rotation ever since —and, surprisingly, it hasn't lost a bit of its effectiveness on me over time. In fact, repeat viewings have only made me more appreciative of Laila's sex appeal.

At the moment, Laila is standing in a far corner of Reed's palatial living room, chatting animatedly with two beautiful women. One of them, I know—fellow artist, Aloha Carmichael. The other one, I don't. A Black woman with confidence and high cheekbones. Someone I'd probably consider hitting on, if I hadn't spotted Laila. As it is, though, now that I know Laila is here, there's no other woman in the room.

With her long, sandy hair, light eyes, and peaches-and-cream complexion, Laila isn't my usual type. On paper, she's far more Kendrick's type than mine. Kendrick likes girls who look like they were cheerleaders in high school. Or maybe foreign exchange students from Sweden or Russia.

But, see, the thing about Laila that makes her so uniquely appealing to me, despite her "cheerleader" packaging, is her exquisite and undeniable "fuck you" charisma. Thanks to her full lips, which she wears in a perma-pout, and the persistently naughty look in her gorgeous blue eyes that practically screams "I'm a freak in the sheets!", Laila comes off like a first-class sex kitten. A bombshell. A siren. Which means, when it comes to Laila Fitzgerald, the phrase "not my usual type" isn't in my vocabulary.

As I'm staring at Laila from across the room, admiring every inch of her, she jolts me by glancing over her friend's shoulder and looking straight at me. We're nowhere close to each other in this huge room, so, in theory, she could be looking elsewhere. But I know she's not. I know, without a doubt, she's staring at me with lust in her eyes, the same way I'm staring at her.

When our gazes meet, I feel an instant electricity, coursing all the way down into my balls. And by the look on Laila's face, she feels something similar on her end.

Ruby blurts, "Reed's a psychopath! Are you sure you want to throw Savage to the wolf like that?"

But, still, I stare at Laila, biting my lower lip seductively.

Kendrick says, "Are you kidding? It'll be the best birthday dare, ever." He slides his arm around my shoulders, forcing me to end my staring contest with Laila. He says, "Are you ready to entertain me for my birthday, brother?"

I clear my throat and shift my weight, trying to ease the pressure on the hard-on that's started gaining momentum in my pants. "If you're hell-bent on making me do this, then, yeah, of course, I'm in. Your dare is my command, birthday boy."

Kendrick is giddy. "Where's Reed?" He drops his arm and excitedly peers around the party, like a meerkat on a prairie. "We have to make sure he can see *everything.*" Kendrick gasps. "Whoa! Laila Fitzgerald is here!" He flails his arms. "I call dibs! I hereby call dibs on Laila Fitzgerald!"

No.

I follow Kendrick's gaze to Laila, just in time to see Reed walking up to her.

Kendrick sighs. "I've had the biggest crush on Laila

Fitzgerald *forever*." He looks at the group. "Do any of you know her? Can you introduce me?"

Please, God, no. This can't be happening. Kendrick and I *never* set our sights on the same woman. Ever. I'd expect to run into this problem with Titus. We're both attracted to women who look like they could commit murder without the slightest crisis of conscience. But not *Kendrick*. He likes his women sweet. He likes women who aren't fucked up and toxic and crazy. Unlike me. I mean, yes, I realize Laila is *exactly* Kendrick's *physical* type. But can't he sniff the crazy, sassy little freak beneath her girl-next-door exterior? Because I sure can. And I'm digging it.

Everyone around me is saying they've never met Laila.

"It doesn't matter," Kendrick says, his resolve written all over his face. "With Reed over there, I can act like I need to talk to him about the tour." He's referring to the fact that we just got back from the eight-month-long international leg of our world tour and will be heading back out onto the road in a few weeks for the three-month-long domestic leg.

"Yeah, I don't think . . ." I begin to say. But I'm saying it to Kendrick's back. He's already on the move. Walking directly toward Laila Fitzgerald. "Hey, KC!" I shout. "Wait up, Kendrick!"

But it's no use. The music is too loud for my best friend to hear me. Or maybe he's hearing me just fine and doesn't give a shit. Something tells me it's Door Number Two—that wild horses couldn't stop Kendrick from heading over to meet Laila right now.

Shit.

For the first time in my life, I don't feel like standing aside when a bandmate has called dibs. For the first time in my life, I feel like running after my friend, tackling him to the ground, and shouting, "I saw her first! I call dibs! *She's mine*."

But since Kendrick's already halfway there, and it's not my style to seem overeager, and since it *is* his birthday, after all, I force myself to stay put. I tell myself not to panic. Instead, I calmly throw back the rest of my drink and tell myself another gorgeous woman who interests me even more than Laila will cross my path, any minute now. Her friend, for instance. She's hot as hell. The one with the dark skin, lush Afro, and banging body. But, no. Even as I try to talk myself into not giving a shit, I can feel my sights setting on Laila and nobody else.

A cocktail waitress walks by and I grab another drink. Ruby has started telling a story, so I try to focus firmly on that and try my damnedest not to obsess about what might be happening across the room. But it's no use. I can't think of anything else but my sincere desire and hope that my best friend in the world, the guy who'd throw himself in front of a bus for me, is, right at this moment, miserably striking out.

Unable to resist any longer, I sneak a peek across the party, just in time to witness Kendrick getting a huge hug from Laila. Reed is still there, but Aloha and the other woman are gone. And, damn, it looks like Laila is full-blown fangirling over Kendrick. *Whoa.* That's not a normal introductory greeting! That's the sort of hug fans give us during meet and greets. The kind women give their lovers when greeting them at the airport. Jesus Christ. Did I imagine that smoldering, come-hither look Laila flashed me a few minutes ago? Obviously, I did. Was she looking at Kendrick standing next to me the whole time?

I should be happy for my best friend, and I know it. But that's not what I'm feeling. In fact, what I'm feeling is something quite the opposite of that. Something I never feel. *Jealousy.*

When Laila finally breaks free of Kendrick, animated conversation between Laila, Reed, and Kendrick ensues. As the trio talks, Laila's eyes suddenly shift to me. And this time, when our eyes lock, when Laila discovers I'm already staring at her, *again,* she flashes me a wide, beaming smile that simultaneously takes my breath away and kind of pisses me off. She just hugged the crap out of Kendrick and now she's trying to knock me onto my ass with that dazzling smile of hers? For fuck's sake, Kendrick is standing right there, obviously still flirting his ass off with her, and she's ignoring him to smile at me?

My brain feels like it's toggling between primal desire, deep confusion, and downright anger, even as every fiber of my body yearns to return Laila's beaming smile—to let her know I'm interested. Ready to go. *Let's do it, baby*. Ultimately, however, my primary emotions seem to be protectiveness of Kendrick and annoyance at Laila for flirting with both of us. And so, ultimately, I do the thing Kendrick would surely do for me, if the situation were reversed: I clench my jaw, press my lips together, and look away, ceding the runway, free and clear, to my best friend. The birthday boy.

TWO

LAILA

When I enter the party, I'm blasted with blaring music combined with the loud din of laughter and chatter. I take in the grandeur sprawling before me, my lips parted in awe. Reed's house is magnificent—a modern-day palace. Which makes sense, since Reed Rivers is the King of LA—a music mogul known in the industry as "The Man with the Midas Touch."

I scan the expansive room, looking for any sign of my good friend, Aloha. A few minutes ago, she texted she'd find me near Reed's front door when I arrived, but I don't see any sign of her. What I do see, however, is wall-to-wall glamour and hotness. It's silly for me to feel this way, given how much awesomeness has happened in relation to my debut album this past year and a half, but finally getting to attend one of Reed's legendary parties makes me feel like I've really and truly arrived, every bit as much as attending the Grammys earlier this year.

My eyes drift as I await Aloha and stop short when I spot my celebrity crush across the large, crowded room. He's Adrian Savage from Fugitive Summer. If you ask me, Savage is the hottest man alive. Dark hair and eyes. A jawline that could cut glass. A chiseled physique that looks like it was forged in tan marble. And all of it made especially panty melting by his omnipresent "big dick energy." An attitude that apparently isn't false advertising, based on those notoriously mouthwatering photos of him in the shower.

At present, Mr. Donkey Dick is throwing back shots with his bandmates, all of whom I recognize but haven't met. And I must say, he's every bit as gorgeous in person as in his leaked photos and music videos and promo. Even more so, actually. Because, in person, I can physically *feel* Savage's undeniable charisma, even from across a crowded room.

"Laila!"

I wrench my eyes off Mr. Perfect and discover Aloha walking toward me with our mutual agent, Daria Brown. When Aloha and I returned from our tour last year, she generously introduced me to Daria, her hot-shot agent, one of the best in the business—and then proceeded to convince Daria she'd be a fool not to take me on as a client, despite the fact that I'm still a relative newbie in this industry. But that's Aloha for you. From day one of our friendship, when I was nothing but an opener with a debut album to promote, she's never once hesitated to help me out and cheer me on and show me the ropes.

After hugging me in greeting, Daria says, "I've got some exciting news for you, Little Miss Laila!" Her smile widens with excitement, revealing white teeth that gleam against her beautiful dark skin. "I sealed the deal! You're going to be a mentor on the eighteenth season of *Sing Your Heart Out*!"

I gasp in disbelief, slapping my palm to my cheek. "I don't believe it!"

"Believe it, girl. It's official."

I launch myself at Daria and wrap her in a grateful hug. "This is a dream come true!"

When we disengage from our hug, Daria tells me the basics of the deal. I'll be assigned to Aloha's team of contestants, thankfully. That's exciting. Also, per usual for mentors, I'll only appear in one episode, but Daria assures me even *one* episode on a juggernaut like *Sing Your Heart Out* will introduce me to *millions* of new fans. I ask a few questions and find out my shooting schedule won't be set for several months yet, since the show is currently shooting the season prior to mine. "The pay is basically nothing," Daria explains. "Union scale. But I *promise* the exposure will be well worth it."

"Oh, I don't care what they pay me," I say. "I'd pay *them* to get to be on the show."

Daria flags down a roving server and the three of us grab flutes of champagne. With a loud whoop, we clink and drink and talk excitedly about the amazing news. But when the topic of conversation shifts, and Aloha and Daria fall into a conversation about a career decision for Aloha, I can't resist sneaking a peek at Mr. Perfect across the party again.

This time, when I peep Savage, I'm shocked and thrilled to discover he's not focused on his friends, like last time. This time, he's looking straight at *me*. My heart stops as Savage's dark eyes fix on mine, but I try to play it off like I'm totally unfazed and only vaguely interested, if at all. I know full well what I'm dealing with here—the kind of guy who can get *any* woman at this party. Actually, in the world. So, of course, on pure instinct, I'm instantly hell-bent on making him think he can't get *me*.

To my surprise, Savage doesn't look away, but continues brazenly staring at me, his dark eyes smoldering and his jaw set. Until . . . Oh, no! Shit! I waited too long to look away and let him do it first. *Stupid Laila*. Talk about a rookie mistake.

Granted, Savage's buddy—the drummer in the band, I think?—put his arm around Savage's shoulders, diverting his attention. So, I don't think Savage looked away from me out of a lack of interest. But, *still*, it was a dumb error by me, all the same. With players like Adrian Savage, a girl should *always* be the first to look away. *Always.* She needs to be the one who couldn't care less. Now that Savage knows he's got me hooked on his line—which is *exactly* the opposite of what I should let him think—who knows if I'll be able to attract his attention again tonight. *Damn.*

"Laila?"

I return to Aloha and Daria to find it's Daria who's spoken my name.

Daria continues, "When does Reed plan to release your second album?"

I'm flustered. Still reeling from the exciting news about the show. Feeling aroused by that sexy smolder Savage flashed me. Also, pissed as hell I've stumbled so stupidly in my effort to ensnare him.

"Oh. Uh." I take a deep breath, collecting myself. "We're not finished recording, but close. We only have a few more minor things to add before sending it off to mixing and mastering. At that point, we'll set the schedule for release, promo, and a tour."

Aloha smirks. "Who were you looking at, babe?"

"Huh? Me? Nobody. When?"

"Just now." Aloha flashes me a side-eye. "Who was it, honey? I know you. Somebody's got you all worked up."

I blush. On tour, Aloha teased me all the time for being attracted to players and fuckboys. The ones who are the most fun to bring to their knees—but the least likely to stay there for long. "Yeah, I was being true to form. Having a staring contest with Savage from Fugitive Summer."

Aloha giggles. "Oh, God, Laila. You're so predictable. Didn't you learn your lesson with Shawn?" She's talking about my last boyfriend—a rookie basketball player for the

Clippers I dated about six months ago. Shawn pursued me relentlessly, at first, and said all the right things . . . before turning out to be the world's biggest *d-o-g* when he finally felt certain he had me.

Aloha looks at Daria. "Poor Laila has the worst taste in men. They're always gorgeous. The hottest guys in the room. But nice boys need not apply."

"Ugh. I can relate," Daria says. She winks at me. "It's a sickness, isn't it? Pure insanity, in the true sense of the word, to think, over and over again, we can be the ones to tame them."

"Exactly," I murmur, rolling my eyes at myself. "The problem is . . . it's so damned fun bringing a cocky bastard to his knees. Truly, my favorite past-time, though I haven't had the pleasure in a while."

Daria laughs. "Girl, you're my spirit animal. Oh, by the way, honey, don't post about being on the show yet, okay? The deal is done and official. But they're not promoting the next season until this one wraps up. I'm sure they'll want to be the one to announce all new cast members for the next season."

"Is it okay if I tell my mom and sister?"

"Only if you're *positive* they won't blab about it to *anyone,* even unintentionally. The producers are insane about controlling all promo."

"I'll wait, then. Better safe than sorry. My mom would never purposefully let the cat out of the bag, but who knows what she might say, unintentionally, while drinking wine with her best friends." I sigh happily. "My mom will be so excited when she hears the news. We never missed *Sing Your Heart Out* in my house. Every week, my family watched and dreamed of me being on the show one day."

It's a true statement, although, technically, we dreamed of me being the *winner* of the singing competition. Or, better yet, a full-time judge on the show, like Aloha is now. But there's no reason for me to say any of that to Daria, after she's secured such an amazing windfall for me, this early in my career. The singing competition attracts icons to its ranks, even as mentors. The fact that Daria secured a spot for me at all is close to a miracle.

"I truly can't thank you enough, Daria," I say. "This is the chance of a lifetime."

"It's Aloha who deserves most of the credit," Daria replies. "She joined me on the conference call with the producers and convinced them they'd be stupid not to hire you."

I clutch my heart. "Aloha! You did not! *Thank you*!"

Aloha shrugs. "You were a tough sell, dude. They were *convinced* you're a raving bitch who'd be a nightmare to work with, thanks to your face."

I burst out laughing at the inside joke. During our tour together, Aloha and I teased each other constantly about our resting bitch faces. For both of us, unless we're literally smiling from ear to ear, we look like we're sulking or plotting murder. As a child star on the Disney channel for a decade, Aloha expertly learned to mask her resting bitch face with a perma-smile. But me? Not so much. On a daily basis, *someone* who doesn't know me will undoubtedly ask, "Are you okay, Laila? Is something wrong?" Even when I'm feeling light as a feather and happy as a clam.

Aloha sips her drink. "No, actually, you were an easy sell, Laila. I told them you're the perfect combination of sassy and sweet. The kind of person who'll give the sweetest encouragement to the contestants while doling out unparalleled death glares to Hugh, whenever he acts like a jackass blowhard during the all-cast round table. Which, of course, he will. And, *voila*, the producers were sold."

I giggle and raise my glass. "To aud-sassity!" It's what

Aloha and I have coined our special brand of badassery. *Audacious sassiness*. And Aloha and Daria clink my glass and whoop, just as the host of the party, Reed Rivers, walks up.

"Wow, looks like I've found the epicenter of the party," he says. He greets everyone, and we quickly tell him the reason for our toast. Of course, Reed congratulates me on the amazing news and we chat about it for a bit. But when Aloha's darling husband, Zander, the sweetest guy in the world, appears, Aloha excuses herself to meet some friends outside. And just like that, I'm alone with Daria and Reed, two of the biggest power brokers in the music industry, and neither of them is telling me to "scram, kid." Seriously, how did I get here?

Reed says, "When it rains it pours, Laila. I've got some exciting news for you, too." He pauses for effect, his dark eyebrow raised. "The opener for Fugitive Summer's domestic leg had to bow out, unexpectedly, for personal reasons. So, I've decided to push up the release of your album and send *you* in their place."

I gasp. "Are you serious?"

"Very serious," Reed says, just as none other than the drummer of Fugitive Summer approaches the group.

"Hey, Reed," he says. "Oh, Laila Fitzgerald!"

And before he says another word, I throw myself into his muscled arms and thank him, profusely, for the amazing opportunity. "I'm so excited!" I shriek. "I *love* Fugitive Summer!"

"Wow," the drummer says, laughing. "Good to meet you, too."

Reed says, "I just told Laila the exciting news that she's joining your tour. You know, because Alexa Play Music had to bow out?"

"Aaah," the drummer says, returning my hug. "That's

awesome. I'm so glad you told her the news, Reed. That's actually what I was coming over to do."

"Oh, I'm sure."

I pull away from the drummer, laughing. "Sorry. Did I hurt you?"

"Not at all." He smiles adorably and puts out his hand. "I'm Kendrick Cook, by the way."

I shake his hand maniacally. "I know! I'm so glad to meet you. Thank you so much for coming over here to welcome me to the tour! That was incredibly sweet of you, Kendrick!"

Kendrick looks at Reed and smiles. "Of course, Laila. We're all *super* excited to have you aboard."

"You *are*? Oh my gosh! What an honor! *Thank you*!" My heart racing, I glance excitedly across the room toward Savage, all prior "I don't give a shit" pretense impossible now. And once again, I'm ecstatic to find him already staring at me. Which makes perfect sense now. Obviously, the band has been sitting on this thrilling news, waiting to see my reaction when Reed finally let the cat out of the bag.

Practically bursting with excitement, I smile broadly at Savage, letting him know, yes, Reed and Kendrick have delivered the amazing, exciting, shocking, thrilling news to me—although, I'm sure Savage has already surmised that fact, given the way I hugged his drummer just now. But to my dismay and acute humiliation, Savage doesn't return my goofy, no-holds-barred smile. Instead, on the contrary, he frowns in the face of my exuberance and immediately looks away like I've greatly offended him. Like he's *pissed* about me joining the tour.

And suddenly, I know the heated staring contest we had a few moments ago wasn't proof of our mutual attraction, like I thought. It was evidence of Savage's disdain for me. His objection to me joining his band on tour. Clearly, Mr. Rockstar doesn't think I'm worthy of the opportunity, but Reed is calling the shots, against his will. I've heard rumors that sometimes happens in the world of River Records—Reed calling the shots against an artist's will. And now I know the rumors are true.

Shit.

I'm going to be stuck on tour with a guy who's not happy I'm there. A guy who's not only gorgeous and brooding and talented and hot . . . but also a flaming fucking *dick*.

THREE
SAVAGE

When Kendrick returns to our group, he's got none other than The Prick in tow. We greet our lord and master, half-heartedly, before Reed says, "I've got some bad news, guys. Cooper went into rehab this morning, so Alexa Play Music won't be able to finish the tour."

Ruby looks distraught, which isn't a surprise. During the international leg of our tour, Ruby became good friends with the talented but tortured lead singer of the opening band. Reed assures everyone Cooper is safe and sound, but definitely out of commission for the foreseeable future, as he confronts his demons, head-on.

"The good news," Reed says, "is that I've already found a new opener who's thrilled to join the tour. Laila Fitzgerald. The timing is perfect. I can push up release of her sophomore album, pretty easily, and make it a win-win."

Everyone but me reacts favorably. They say Laila is incredibly talented and that her debut album was fantastic. They mention the fact that Zeke, our producer, also produced

Laila's debut, which is kind of cool. And through it all, I feel like my cells are physically vibrating.

Reed says, "Laila wanted to come over here to meet everyone and thank you for the opportunity." He rolls his eyes. "But I told her we had a few things to discuss and you'd find her later to say hello."

"I was so relieved you said that," Kendrick chimes in. "I didn't want her coming over here and figuring out the band had no idea."

Everyone laughs at the notion, but I clench my jaw, feeling annoyed. It irks me to no end that Reed has full discretion to slot our tours, without even asking our opinion, thanks to our shitty contract. Yes, Reed's *technically* got full control in these matters, but, still, as a matter of professional courtesy, it's my opinion he should have discussed this with our band before telling Laila. Especially since, if you ask me, Laila's not even a good fit, musically, with our band and brand. Is Laila talented? Absolutely. But that doesn't mean she should be opening for Fugitive Summer. Reed should put her with Aloha. Or maybe 2Real.

And yet, everyone around me continues reacting enthusiastically, like this is the best idea, ever. My aggravation ratcheting up with each passing second, I look across the room. And this time, when my eyes meet Laila's, she's got no beaming smile for me. No lustful stare. This time, the only thing on Laila's face is a death glare. And I must admit, it's a good look on her.

"She's not a good fit," I declare, turning away from Laila's blue daggers. And everyone stops talking and looks at me like I've yelled the earth is flat. "You should put her with 2Real," I suggest. "He's going out soon, isn't he?"

Reed's face contorts into an expression of pure disdain, the likes of which I've seen many times from him. "Thanks so much for your opinion, Savage," he says, his tone dripping with sarcasm. "The thing is . . ." He leans forward. "I don't actually give a flying shit what you think about this decision. I wasn't asking for *permission* to put Laila on the tour. I was merely informing you, as a courtesy, that I've already done it, so you won't wonder what the hell she's doing there when she shows up at her first soundcheck." With that, he flashes me a nonverbal "fuck you" before smiling at Kendrick. "I hear it's your birthday, KC?"

"Yep. The big two-five."

"Wow. A quarter century. You can rent a car now." He chuckles. "Feel free to take home any bottle you want from any of the bars. There's some pretty expensive Scotch behind that one . . ." He points across the room, to a bar located near a set of French doors, and names the brand. "Tell the bartender I said you can have the whole bottle."

"Thanks, Reed. I'll take you up on that."

"Please do." He smiles at Ruby, his favorite in our band, by far, and wishes her a good time. And then, with a quick nod to Titus and Kai, he heads off without even a cursory glance at me.

"Fuck you, too," I murmur to Reed's departing frame.

"I'll catch ya later, guys," Kendrick says. "I'm gonna get that bottle of Scotch and ask Laila if she wants to—" He gasps. "No! Fuck my life. Nooo!"

"Well, that was fast," Kai says to his younger brother. And when I follow their mutual gaze, I see Laila in conversation with a good friend of ours—a guy named Cash who plays guitar for another River Records band, Danger Doctor Jones. Cash is in profile to us and standing all the way on the other side of the party, but, even so, it's clear he's currently hitting on Laila with everything he's got.

"Motherfucker," Kendrick declares.

"You snooze, you lose, baby brother," Kai says, whacking Kendrick's broad shoulder.

"It's probably for the best," I say, surprising myself. "Now that Laila is our opener, I think we can all agree she's off-limits." I'm grasping at straws here. Being a manipulative dick. Because, even as the words leave my mouth, I know I'd fuck Laila raw, to within an inch of her life, whether during the tour or at this party tonight in the nearest bathroom, if given half a chance.

"No, I don't agree to that," Kendrick says.

"Come on," I say, forging ahead with my bullshit. With my testosterone-driven gaslighting. "It's a weird dynamic, KC. It's like we're her boss, sort of. Plus, don't forget, you're gonna be stuck with Laila for *months*. Once things go south between you, which they will, you'll be stuck hanging around with her for however long. Sounds horrible to me."

"I'll risk it."

Shit.

I glance at Laila again. She's still talking to Cash across the room. But after a moment, her gaze flickers to mine, and this time, she flashes me an especially murderous glare that sends tingles shooting straight into my dick. In reply, I flash her a look of total impenetrability, letting her know her daggers have no effect on me. That in fact, they've bounced right off my steel chest, baby. And she reacts by turning to Cash and smiling at him like she wants to suck his dick. The little vixen. I gotta say, I'm digging it.

"Yo, birthday boy!" I shout to Kendrick, over the music in the room, my gaze finally leaving the bombshell who's making my blood simmer inside my veins. "I think I'm ready to do that birthday dare now. Let's do it, brother . . ." I peek at Laila again, making sure she's still looking, before adding, "Let's make *Reed* jealous as shit."

FOUR
SAVAGE

Why hasn't Reed come over here yet? I feel like I've been hitting on Georgina pretty damned aggressively for the past five minutes, mere feet away from him. Giving it my best fuckboy effort. And yet, he's still keeping his distance. Hiding behind his proverbial bush. Is Reed embarrassed to pursue Georgina in front of all these bigwigs, for some reason? Is it because of their age difference? What am I missing? The Reed Rivers I know stops at nothing to get whatever he wants. And there's no doubt in my mind he wants Georgina.

"That's so interesting, Savage," Georgina says. "I'll definitely want to explore that further during our actual interview. Do you find that songwriting is a cathartic process for you?"

I look at her with so much heat, I feel like a parody of my younger self. My eyes smoldering, I lean in and say, "Wow, that's a great question, Georgina." I'm trying to make it sound like I've never heard her question before, despite it being pretty standard fare. "Hmm. Yes. Now that you mention it, I think songwriting *is* a deeply cathartic process for me. I'm not the best at expressing myself, sometimes, in my daily life. Oftentimes, I don't even know what I think or feel about something. But then, I start writing a song, and my true feelings pour out of me like a confession."

Georgina gasps and holds up her arm. "*Goosebumps*!" Her beautiful face aglow, she grabs her phone. "Do you mind if I jot that down? I don't want to risk you forgetting that wording when it's time for your actual interview."

Well, that's adorable. I've said that exact thing at least ten million times in interviews over the past four years. But, obviously, a summer intern for *Rock 'n' Roll* wouldn't know that. I sneak a peek at my buddies over Georgina's shoulder to find them red-faced and holding back laughter. Which means Reed, who was standing behind me the last time I checked, must still be there. And not only that, he must look like a volcano about to blow.

I touch Georgina's hand, signaling she doesn't need her phone. "No need to write that down. I promise, I'll remember it during the actual interview." With the touch of my hand to Georgina's, I sneak a peek at Laila to my right, hoping she's still rooted to her spot next to Cash, shooting me daggers. And to my sizzling delight, she is. In fact, if looks could kill, I'd be splattered all over the walls of Reed's massive living room right now.

Holding back a smile, I return to Georgina, lick my lips like I've just devoured her pussy, and brush a lock of dark hair off her shoulder. "So, hey, Georgina, when do you think we should—"

And that's it. Reed's seen enough.

"I need to speak with you," he barks out, appearing out of nowhere at my shoulder like The Flash.

"Can it wait?" I say. "Georgina and I—"

"*It can't wait,*" Reed snaps. "Follow me."

Without waiting for my reply, Reed grips my sleeve and physically drags me across the room and around a corner into a short hallway, leaving Georgina with her hazel eyes wide and her mouth hanging open.

"Reed, come on, man," I say, smiling broadly at my friends as Reed drags me toward my certain doom. "*You're cock-blocking me.*"

Reed's entire body shudders at my words, but he continues dragging me until we're away from the party. Once safely outside of Georgina's sightline, Reed whirls around, his dark eyes aflame, and spits out, "Do *not* hit on the *Rock 'n' Roll* reporter!"

I shake my arm free of Reed's vise-like grip. It's a tragedy Kendrick isn't here to witness this moment, but, by God, when I recount the story to him later, I want him to be duly impressed with me. Never let it be said I don't give Birthday Truth or Dare my all.

Leaning my shoulder against the wall, I whine, "But, Reed, she's hot as hell."

Reed's jaw pulses. "*She's hands-off.*"

"Who says?"

Reed pauses, his nostrils flaring and his dark eyes on fire. And against all odds, I feel a tiny pang of compassion for the bastard. I don't know why he's been stalking Georgina from afar tonight. What dynamic, real or imagined, has kept him from making his intentions clear to the world? Whatever the hell is going on, Reed is clearly flustered in a way I've never seen him before.

Reed opens and closes his mouth, searching for his response, before finally blurting—and not convincingly, I might add, "She's here to do a job, not to get hit on." When I raise my eyebrows, conveying my skepticism, Reed adds, "I promised her boss nobody would hit on her."

Well, that's ludicrous. Since when does Reed let anything or anyone get in the way of something, or someone, he wants? Could it be Reed promised Georgina's boss *he* wouldn't hit on her, for some reason? Which I suppose is possible, given her age and inexperience and his position of power and reputation as a womanizer. But even then, I can't imagine Reed would uphold a promise like that for long, if he really wanted Georgina.

I languidly pull a box of cigarettes out of my pocket. I only smoke when I've been drinking. And I couldn't be happier to have a box with me now, given how much Reed notoriously despises cigarettes. Casually, I stick an unlit cigarette between my lips and say, "I think we should let *her* decide if she wants to get hit on or not."

Well, that does it. Reed can't keep it together another minute. His dark eyes blazing, he points toward the end of the hallway, like he's commanding a misbehaving dog into a doghouse. He shouts, "Go find the other writer! Her name is Zasu. She's been assigned to do your interview."

I can't believe my ears. Reed is going to make poor Georgina, a summer intern with stars in her eyes, give up a solo interview with *me*—one of the hottest commodities on the planet right now—solely because, *waah, waah*, Reed doesn't want to risk me seducing her?

I say, "Georgie and I have great chemistry." I heard Fish's date call Georgina that nickname earlier tonight, during our ping pong game, so I'm assuming it'll piss Reed off if I use it, too. I add, "We already have the whole thing figured out."

"You're doing an interview with Zasu," Reed commands vehemently. "*It's not a request.*"

I remove my unlit cigarette from my lips, unable to locate my lighter. "You want Georgina for yourself, don't you?"

Bingo. From Reed's facial expression, it's clear I've hit the nail on the head.

His voice tight, Reed grits out, "My motivations don't matter. The only thing you need to know is the owner of your label is telling you she's off-limits. *Now, go find Zasu.*"

I slip the cigarette back between my lips. "Got a light?"

"No!" Reed booms. He points again, nonverbally ordering me away, and I know I've reached the finish line—the point where there's nothing more I can say or do in this passion play. I pull the unlit cigarette out of my mouth again, wink at Reed, and saunter away, but not before tossing over my shoulder, "You're too old for her, anyway, man. She's only twenty-one."

Ha. That ought to sting.

When I re-enter the main room of the party, I discover my friends buckled over with laughter at my performance. I walk toward them, my arms outstretched like, "Did you expect anything less from the master?" and then, instinctively, glance toward Laila. But, damn, she's not there. As I look around, I don't see her anywhere. Did she storm out, too disgusted by my fuckboy display to stick around? Or, worse, did my aggressive flirting with Georgina prompt her to go into a dark corner . . . with *Cash*?

My heart strumming against my sternum, I look around the large room again, to no avail, suddenly regretting my decision to try to piss her off. Why do I always do shit like this? Why do I always self-sabotage? I thought we were playing a sexy game of "fuck you" with each other. A game of "*I'm* not jealous, *you're* jealous!" You know, lobbing fastballs at each other and daring the other to try to hit it out of the park. But now I'm thinking I miscalculated and totally turned her off.

When I reach my friends, they demand a play-by-play. Which, of course, I give them, eliciting even more raucous laughter, especially from the birthday boy. After a while, Reed comes by and berates me for not following his direct orders and finding Zasu. And so, reluctantly, I leave my friends and take a lap of the massive downstairs area, looking for this Zasu chick—even though I wouldn't put it past Reed to send me on a wild goose chase, solely to get me away from Georgina. But, whatever. Whether Zasu actually exists or not, I'm more than happy to take a lap of the party to pretend to look for her, if only to give me a believable excuse to look high and low for the woman I'm actually interested in finding: *Little Miss Death Daggers Laila Fitzgerald.*

FIVE

SAVAGE

Would it have killed Reed to *describe* this mythical Zasu person to me, if it was so damned important to him that I find her? Fucking prick. As I've rambled around the packed party, I've asked a couple people, half-heartedly, if they know someone named "Zasu," who's supposedly a reporter for *Rock 'n' Roll,* and each and every one of them describes Georgina.

"No, no. Not *her,*" I keep saying.

To which they reply, "Oh. Then . . . I dunno."

Of course, throughout my quest, I've kept my eyes peeled for Laila the whole time. So far, no luck. Not knowing what else to do, I head outside to continue my search in Reed's expansive backyard. If Laila is outside with Cash, or, worse, if she's already left the party with him, I'll be so pissed at myself. It's one thing for me to have refrained from hitting on Laila for my best friend in the world—the guy who's more responsible than anyone else for my current lot in life. But as friendly as I am with Cash, I'd *never* in a million years step aside from hitting on Laila for *him*. No fucking way.

Becoming increasingly frustrated, I wander into the pool

area and immediately stop dead in my tracks, and then sigh with relief, when I spot Laila in the far distance, bopping around happily on Reed's basketball court, looking like a kid on a playground during recess. There's a large group on the court along with Laila that includes Aloha Carmichael and the guys from 22 Goats and their dates. *But no Cash.*

I smile to myself. Did Naughty Little Laila ditch Cash's ass the minute he was no longer useful to her—the minute she no longer needed him to make me jealous? I bet she did. Which means I'm still in the hunt, baby. That is, if Kendrick strikes out with her, of course. Obviously. I owe him at least that much.

I watch Laila and her friends for a moment, and quickly discern the group is playing HORSE, based on the way everyone keeps taking the same shots in rotation. And the minute I realize the game, I feel oddly invested in standing here long enough to find out if Laila makes her shot. I make a bet with myself: "If Laila makes her shot, I'll head over there and welcome her to the tour. If she doesn't, I'll head inside and make her come to me."

Fish from 22 Goats takes his shot and makes it and his cute date jumps for joy like he's won a Grammy. Next up, Fish's girlfriend takes her shot and whiffs so badly, I laugh out loud. Immediately, Fish and Laila console her and the girlfriend slinks into Fish's waiting arms.

Finally, after a few other players take their shots, it's Laila's turn. She gets the ball from Aloha's husband, Zander, a buff Black dude I've met here and there, and then heads to the designated spot on the court—a location a few feet behind the three-point line. After taking a ridiculously long time to gather herself, as if the fate of the world depends on her making the shot, Laila bends her knees, exhales, and flings her arms upward, releasing the ball into the air.

And . . . it's a brick. A clunker that thuds to the ground a few feet from the rim.

Confronted with her abject failure, Laila shrieks before peeling off a glorious streak of laughter I can hear all the way over here. Finally, she drops to the ground, dramatically, and writhes around like she's been shot, making her friends guffaw.

As Laila is writhing on the ground, a couple of tall, muscular guys reach the court. They high-five Aloha's husband, Zander, before standing over Laila and laughing along with everyone else. And that's when I realize one of the guys is the pro basketball player, Malik Wallace of The Knicks. The NBA's Rookie of the Year last year, who led his team, singlehandedly, to win the Eastern Conference Finals. Jesus Christ. Reed's contact list really is the coolest in LA.

As a fan of The Bulls, I should probably hate Malik Wallace, given how much he bitch-slapped my team last season. But it's impossible not to respect such rarified talent and skill.

Heeeey, I think. *Malik would be a perfect cover for me*! I suddenly realize I could walk over there to the court and act like I came to meet Malik, thereby giving Laila the chance to introduce herself to me and thank me for letting her join the tour. Laila doesn't know I had nothing to do with her getting the gig, after all. So why not walk over there to "meet Malik" and let Laila kiss my ass while I'm there, as any grateful opener would do? It's pure genius.

I start walking, feeling pretty damned good about my strategy. It's critical with a woman like Laila Fitzgerald—the kind who can get any man she wants—not to let her know how much I'm drooling over her. I can't let her think she has the upper hand. Otherwise, she'll surely ditch me as fast as she ditched Cash. And maybe Kendrick, too? That remains to be seen.

Fuck.

No.

I stop walking, the hair on the back of my neck standing up.

Of all the people on that court right now, the last one I'd want to be talking to Laila is Malik Wallace. But he's doing just that. And not only talking to her, but brazenly *flirting* with her. She's off the ground now and the pair has drifted off to the side to talk one-on-one.

Crap.

She's laughing now. Swatting flirtatiously at Malik's muscular arm.

Fuck.

Laila calls for the ball from one of her friends, and when she gets it, she hands it to Malik, clearly being sassy with him. She points. And he laughingly steps to the spot where she just airballed her latest attempt. Gracefully, Malik releases the ball and sinks it with nothing but net. And when he's done making his shot—and, presumably, his point—he beelines back to Laila . . . and she gives him an exuberant high-five.

Fuck, fuck, fuck.

They're obviously bonding over there—in record speed.

The pair continues talking as the game continues around them. But, soon, their conversation is interrupted when Dax Morgan, the lead singer of 22 Goats, says something to the group that makes his bandmates—Fish and Colin—huddle up. My guess, based on the way the night has been going, is that Dax just received word that it's 22 Goats' turn to take the large stage in the main room of the party, along with whatever combination of musician-friends they want to invite. My band already played earlier in the night with our selected group of friends, so it makes sense to me that's what I'm seeing.

"Hey, Savage!" a female voice says to my right. And

when I turn my head, there's a beautiful Asian woman standing before me. She extends her hand with a bright smile. "I'm Zasu, one of the writers for *Rock 'n' Roll*. Reed sent me to find you to talk about your upcoming interview."

Well, I'll be damned. By now, I'd convinced myself Zasu didn't actually exist.

I shake her hand and say it's good to meet her and she flushes visibly at my touch.

"I'm a *huge* fan," she gushes. "I was elated to find out you'd been assigned to me for the special issue."

"Thanks." I glance at the basketball court again. And fuck my life, Laila is still talking to Malik.

Zasu says something, forcing me to return my attention to her. She's flustered. Blushing. Fanning herself like I've seen many, many fans do over the past few years. And so, I wait, feeling vaguely annoyed. Women react like this upon meeting me all the time. Which is fine, but weird. I mean, I'm the same guy I've always been, yet nobody reacted like this when I worked at a supermarket in Chicago. But, okay. I get it. I'm famous now. And this is part of the gig when I meet fans. But when I meet a *reporter*? Come on.

Zasu laughs at herself and sighs. "Forgive me. This never happens to me. I'm being so unprofessional." She shakes it off, pulls herself together, and starts explaining the general game plan for the one-on-one interviews. Specifically, she says they're going to be different, and more fun, than the typical sit-down.

But since I've already heard this exact spiel from Georgina earlier, I tune her out. By the end of my ping pong game with Georgina, she'd convinced me to go ATVing with her on the day of my interview, since it's something I've never done. Something I've never wanted to do, honestly, but I wasn't going to say no to Georgina. There are worse things than spending the day with a gorgeous woman, watching her ride a fast machine.

As Zasu continues talking, I gaze toward the basketball court again, just in time to see Kendrick and Kai arrive. There are some hugs and handshakes. Some introductions. Kendrick and Kai both visibly recognize Malik Wallace. And, not surprisingly, they stride up to him and Laila and strike up an animated conversation.

Finally, Dax and his bandmates break from their huddle. Dax announces something that wrangles the cats around him, and the entire group begins walking toward the house, with Laila falling into step between Malik and Kendrick.

"So, do you have any ideas about an activity you might like to do?" the reporter, Zasu, asks me. "Maybe something you've never done before?"

The group is even with Zasu and me now, about thirty yards away behind Zasu's back. Kendrick hasn't noticed me because his head is turned toward Laila. But Laila, who's looking at Kendrick as he speaks sure as hell sees me standing over here in a dark corner with Zasu. How do I know that? Because she's rolling her eyes at me, as if to say, *Again*? And I can't help winking at her in reply. Dude, she's the one who was flirting with Cash earlier, and is now the cream filling between Malik and Kendrick. If Laila's annoyed that I've bounced from one hot woman to the next at this party, then maybe she should look in the mirror and be pissed at herself.

"Savage?" the reporter says.

But my eyes are tracking Laila's movement like a hawk tracking a mouse in a field. With a death glare to me, Laila turns her head and says something to Malik before finally walking far enough forward that I'm now looking at her back. I crane my neck, still watching, as Laila, and everyone she's with, including Malik and Kendrick, disappear through a set of double doors into the house.

"Um. Savage?"

My heart racing, I look at the reporter but say nothing.

"I was asking if you have any ideas for an activity we could do on the day of your interview?"

"No. I have no idea."

"Oh. Okay. Well . . . I can send you a list of ideas, maybe?"

"You know what? I'd rather do the interview by phone. My band will be heading out on tour soon and I'd like to have as few obligations between now and then as possible."

Zasu's shoulders sink with disappointment. "Oh."

A collective roar of excitement blasts from inside the house, followed by the amplified sounds of an electric guitar and Dax Morgan's voice, greeting the crowd.

"*Oooh*!" Zasu shouts. "It's 22 Goats!"

"Go on," I say, gesturing toward the house. "You don't want to miss this."

"That's okay. I can listen from out here, so we can finish our conversation."

"I'm not really up for this right now, actually," I reply, just as the band begins playing one of 22 Goats' biggest hits —a mid-tempo love song called "Fireflies."

"Okay. No worries. Thanks for your time, Savage. I'll be in touch." Zasu pauses, apparently expecting me to respond. And when I don't, she sprints toward the house.

For a long moment, I stand alone in the shadows, trying to decide what to do.

Dax is singing the lyrics to his famous song. But, suddenly, a female voice takes over. It's Aloha. Followed immediately by another female voice taking the next line. *Laila.* The sound of her distinctive voice makes me close my eyes. *Damn, she's good.*

I run my hand through my hair, feeling a rush of adrenaline and yearning. Knowing Laila is in there, dazzling the crowd with her talent and beauty and sultry stage presence is almost too much for me to bear. I want to head in there and watch, more than I want to breathe. But not when I know Kendrick is in there, watching and wanting her. Probably Malik Wallace, too.

Jealousy floods me again. Which makes no sense, given that I've never even spoken to the girl. She's just another hot woman at a party. Another vixen in a music video. A gorgeous artist with astounding talent, yes. But, still, someone I've never even met. So, why should I care if she's off-limits to me, when another woman, just as alluring and desirable, will surely cross my path in a matter of minutes? I need to let Kendrick have her. And that's that.

Several voices launch into singing the famous sing-along chorus of "Fireflies." Yet, the only voice my brain can hear is Laila's. And, suddenly, I feel the urgent need to get the hell out of here. If I don't, I'm going to do something I'll regret. I'll fuck over Kendrick. Or I'll pick a fight with Malik Wallace, of all people. Or, God help me, I'll pick a fight with Laila herself, just to prove to myself I don't want her.

Exhaling loudly, I grab my phone and tap out a message to Kendrick:

Me: Yo, KC. I'm gonna dip. Not feeling great. Happy 25th. I love you, brother. Have a blast tonight. Good luck with Laila.

After pressing send, I shove my phone into my pocket, grab a cigarette and light it—and then stride with purpose toward a faraway set of French doors. They're a different set than the ones Laila and her group walked through several minutes ago. I don't know where they lead, exactly, but I'm thinking the odds are high they won't take me directly through the main room of the party, where Laila is currently onstage, gracing the world with her insane talent and sex appeal.

Happy Birthday, Kendrick, I think. *For the love of fuck, don't let her leave with Malik Wallace.*

SIX

LAILA

One month later

Well, *there's no turning back now.*

Not that I'd want to turn back. I'm just saying I couldn't, even if I wanted to. Today is the start of my tour with Fugitive Summer. One of my favorite bands. And the beginning of a whole new, exciting chapter of my career.

I'm sitting in the backseat of a large SUV with tinted windows, alongside my assistant, Katrina, plus the security guy assigned to me for the tour. Which is super fancy. We're driving to Van Nuys Airport outside of LA, rather than LAX, because we're flying private. Also, super fancy. At the airport, I'll board a private jet headed for Philadelphia, where the tour will kick off tomorrow night. After that, we'll spend three months zigzagging the entire country in a fleet of buses before ultimately winding up back in our hometown of LA.

Shortly after that, the new season of *Sing Your Heart Out*

will begin shooting, at which point I'll find out when my one-episode stint as Aloha's mentor will begin. And once that happens, all bets will be off. According to Reed and Daria, the one-two-three punch of my second album, this tour, and, ultimately, my stint on the show, will catapult my career to staggering new heights. Fingers crossed, anyway. I've learned that "success" is out of my control. All I can do is work hard, do my very best, remain professional and humble at all times, and let the universe take it from there.

My phone buzzes with an incoming text from Malik. He's wishing me safe travels and says he hopes it'll work out he'll be able to catch my show in New York. I reply and tell him, "Yeah, I hope it works out! Have a great game tonight!" And leave it at that.

Malik's been fairly persistent since Reed's party. But I've been super busy and also wary of his reputation as a manwhore. So, nothing much has happened between us this past month, since he slid into my DMs immediately after Reed's party. At Malik's invitation, I did go to one of his games a few weeks ago—the hometown Lakers vs. Malik's team, The Knicks. I sat courtside at The Staples Center, in the front row, and cheered Malik on. Which meant I was cheering *a lot,* since he was the high scorer in the game.

But afterwards, I only kissed Malik and thanked him for having me, at which point it became clear he'd been assuming we'd go back to his place to bang after the game. I didn't see the point in pursuing something with him, though. Not with me leaving for three months and Malik's schedule being packed with games and events. Not to mention, Malik is based in New York and I'm in LA. Even if Malik does wind up coming to my show in New York, what could really happen between us, after that? The whole thing seems point-less to me.

I shove my phone in my purse as the SUV stops at a security kiosk at the airport entrance. The driver shows his credentials to the guard, along with mine, my assistant's, and the bodyguard's, and then, away we go, toward a private jet parked on the tarmac.

"Are you *so* excited?" my assistant, Katrina, asks, poking my arm.

"*So* excited," I confirm. But that's all I can muster, thanks to the pounding of my heart. I'd never admit this to Katrina, or to anyone. But I'm almost as excited about finally getting to meet Adrian Savage as I am about starting the actual tour.

By now, I've met all the other members of Fugitive Summer. Two of them—brothers Kendrick and Kai—approached me at the party. The other two—twin siblings, Titus and Ruby—were more than gracious and welcoming when I approached *them.* Also, Kendrick and Ruby both gave me their numbers at the party and told me to contact them if I had any questions before the tour. I never did initiate any texting with either of them, however. First off, I wanted to play it cool. But, also, I've been crazy busy this past month, finalizing my album for a rush release in time for the tour and rehearsing with my backing band. But, still, it was incredibly sweet of both of them to make me feel so welcomed and appreciated. Especially Kendrick, who was sweet enough to reach out a couple times to ask about the progress of my album.

And then there's Savage, who didn't speak to me at the party, even once. But, rather, made it abundantly clear, through his glares and body language, he was a) not happy about me joining the tour, and b) way too busy chasing tail to stop and say a single word to me.

During my performance with the Goats and Aloha, I looked for Savage in the audience, but didn't see him. And that pissed me off. Everyone else at the party had the decency to watch our performance, as a show of camaraderie. But Savage couldn't be bothered?

When I got offstage and looked around for Savage, I realized he hadn't seen the performance because he'd already left. My guess? He cut out the nano-second he settled on whichever lucky lady he was going to bang that night. Predictable.

It was in that moment I made a vow to myself: I wouldn't speak a single word to Savage during the tour, unless and until *he* spoke to me *first*. Which means this five-hour flight I'm about to take with him could turn out to be an interesting, and extremely quiet, standoff between us.

The SUV parks on the tarmac. My door flies open. And a blonde woman greets me with a big smile. "Welcome, Laila!" she says. She introduces herself as Tracy, our tour manager, and says she's thrilled I'm here. I thank her and express my excitement, as someone swiftly attends to my luggage in the trunk.

A moment later, I'm climbing the staircase of the private jet, alongside my assistant and bodyguard, while preparing myself mentally to maintain a poker face when I see Savage for the first time. *Don't stare at him,* I tell myself. *Don't drool. Don't blush. And for God's sake, Laila, look away first.*

I enter the plane, my heart crashing, and I'm immediately greeted by a flight attendant who smells like roses. A staffer whose name I don't catch introduces himself. And then another.

As I speak to everyone, I look around but don't see the members of Fugitive Summer. Which makes sense, now that I think about it. Surely, I was given the first arrival time, to minimize their waiting-around time. Because that's how it works in this business. Everything is geared toward the headliner's comfort and convenience. Aloha never treated me like an underling on our tour. She always treated me like an equal, from day one. But I have to remind myself Aloha is the outlier in this industry. Maybe, one day, I'll be the headliner who'll treat my opener the way Aloha treated me. But in the meantime, I'm happy to be here on Fugitive Summer's tour, and to wait around for them, whenever necessary.

I get settled into a window seat, while my assistant heads to the back to chat with an assistant for Fugitive Summer. I check my phone and find out my band of musicians are already in Philadelphia, since they're based out of New York. I text excitedly with them for a bit, saying I can't wait to see them soon. After that, I text with my mom and sister, with lots of emojis, about how excited I am. And, finally, when there's a commotion at the front of the plane, I look up to find the famous faces of Fugitive Summer boarding the aircraft. There's Kendrick, Kai, Titus, Ruby, and . . . some body-guards. Some staffers. And that's it. *No Savage?*

Fuck a duck, man. I've been girding my proverbial loins all morning in anticipation. No, all week. All month! *And he's not here?*

The famous foursome heads into the heart of the aircraft, each one saying hello to everyone they pass. When they get to me, they're gracious, but polite and calm, with nobody mentioning Savage. And that makes me lose my freaking mind. Is *nobody* going to mention the fact that the most famous face in Fugitive Summer isn't here? Because . . . he's kind of important.

"Do you mind if I sit here?" Ruby asks, motioning to the empty seat next to me.

"Please do."

Ruby flops down next to me, her pink hair tied into two adorable buns on top of her head. She says, "I'm so excited to finally have another girl on tour with me!"

"I couldn't be more excited," I reply. And it's the truth.

Ruby begins pulling items out of a backpack, getting

herself settled with various devices and chargers. A pillow. Some fluffy socks. And as she does her thing, I admire her adorableness. She's attempted to harden her pixie vibe with piercings and tattoos. But somehow, on Ruby, all of her adornments only accentuate her innate sweetness. The tougher she tries to look, the sweeter she appears.

After shoving her backpack underneath her seat, Ruby leans back and exhales loudly like she's in a Jacuzzi at the spa. Her eyes closed and her head pressing against a pillow, she says, "And so it begins."

I laugh. "And so it does."

She opens her eyes. "During the international leg, Alexa Play Music opened for us. Do you know them?"

"I know of them."

"Four more boys," she says. "So, with our boys and theirs, it was *eight* boys and me. Good God, I'm a saint."

We both laugh.

"What I'm trying to say, Laila, is I'm elated you're here."

"I'm elated I'm here, too. I've never toured with boys. My last tour was with Aloha. So, you'll have to show me the ropes."

"Just don't let them steam-roll you. They don't even realize they're doing it."

"Good advice. But I'm the opener, so I kind of have to let them steam-roll me a bit. It's part of the gig. Or so I've heard. Aloha never hazed me. But I've heard stories about head-liners doing that to their openers, as a regular thing."

"Yeah, the guys did some of that to Alexa Play Music. They tend to feel like openers need to know their place in the pecking order, you know? It's stupid, but whatever." She rolls her eyes. "Something tells me that won't happen to you. You've got a knack for making people want to roll out the red carpet for you, Laila."

"I don't expect any special treatment," I say. "I'm just happy to be here."

"I don't think the boys will be able to keep themselves from treating you with kid gloves." She flashes me a snarky look. "Boys are very visual creatures, Laila. And you're a very pretty visual."

I laugh. "Well, thank you. So are you."

She smiles. "It kind of sucks, though, doesn't it? Everyone should be treated with respect, no matter what. Not just pretty girls."

"I agree."

"Good. I'll let the guys know you insist on being treated exactly the same as any other opener."

"Well . . . I don't know if *that's* necessary."

She laughs, and I join her. And just this fast, I know we're going to be great friends.

A noise at the front of the plane attracts my attention and makes my heart lurch. Is Savage here? But, no. The sound is the front door of the plane closing, without Savage appearing. And even though I swore to myself Savage's name wouldn't pass my lips during this entire tour unless he broke the seal and spoke to me *first,* I can't resist asking Ruby what's going on.

"No Savage?" I ask.

Ruby shakes her pink head. "He's been in Chicago this week, visiting family. He's flying to Philadelphia today on his own."

"Ooooh." I smile. "That's good news. This whole time, I was thinking he was pulling a 'rockstar' by making an entire flight of people wait on him."

"Oh, trust me, Savage is perfectly capable of doing that. That boy is many, many things, but *punctual* certainly isn't one of them. It's really annoying, so brace yourself."

"If you're constantly annoyed by his lateness, why don't

you ever slap the shit out of him for it? You're not the opener."

"Meh. We pick our battles with him. In the end, it's hard to say which parts of Savage's personality contribute to his mad genius. So, we let him be, in case messing with the shitty stuff will mess with the amazing stuff. We all benefit from Savage being happy and carefree and left alone. That's when he's at his best."

"So, you think if you slap the shit out of him, you might slap some of his genius out of him?"

"Exactly."

I smile and nod. But I'm not sure I could hold my tongue like that with a bandmate. Aloha is a genius in her own right, too. An icon in the music industry. But during my tour with her, she *never* kept anyone waiting. In fact, she was usually early for everything. I remember Aloha telling me, early on, "We're the lucky ones who get to go onstage and experience all the adulation and praise, but never forget it takes a village of crew and staff and musicians to make a tour happen for the thousands of fans who pay their hard-earned money to watch you perform. So, in the end, even if it feels sometimes like it's all about *you,* never forget you're there to create happiness for your fans and hundreds of jobs for your crew and staff. Make art when you make your album, Laila. Make happiness for the fans and *money* for the machine when you're on tour."

I distinctly remember Aloha's words blowing me away. They were a revelation to me. A whole new way of looking at things. And to this day, I've kept them close to my heart at all times. Has nobody ever sat down Adrian Savage to give him a similar speech? Obviously not, based on what Ruby said a moment ago. And that's a shame. I bet Savage would benefit from hearing Aloha's thoughts on the importance of humility and professionalism in our industry.

About twenty minutes after the plane takes off, as drinks and food are served, Ruby and I settle into an easy, interesting conversation.

"Is it weird being the only girl in your band?" I ask.

"Nah," Ruby replies. "You know Titus is my twin brother, right? So, being in a band with him feels totally natural to me. And then, with Kai and Kendrick being brothers, they feel like a single unit, too. So, I don't really feel outnumbered there. And then there's Savage, who feels like an extension of Kai and Kendrick, because he grew up with them. So, I guess I don't often feel like *one* girl in a band with *four* boys. I feel more like part of a duo that's merged with a trio." She makes a cute face. "Does that make sense?"

"It makes perfect sense. Does Savage have any siblings?"

"No, he's an only child." She snorts. "Which, trust me, will make *perfect* sense to you once you get to know him. *If* you get to know him. He's a tough nut to crack."

I bite my lip. I haven't exchanged a single word with the man and I already knew that. Which, unfortunately, is only making him more intriguing to me. Savage is a tough nut to crack? Well, guess what? I just so happen to consider myself an expert at busting balls and cracking nuts.

"Hey, ladies." It's Kendrick. With a huge, handsome grin on his face, he plops himself down across the aisle from Ruby.

I take in his surfer-boy handsomeness, his wavy blonde hair and bright eyes, and, immediately, I'm filled with warmth and happiness at the sight of him. It's the same way I felt when I met Kendrick weeks ago at Reed's party. Warm and safe. The same way I felt when we exchanged texts these past few weeks, regarding the progress on my album.

"I hope you don't mind me hanging out here with you ladies," Kendrick says. "Kai's already annoying the fuck out of me."

"We're happy to have you," I say.

"Speak for yourself," Ruby says. But it's clear she's joking.

"So, Miss Fitzgerald," Kendrick says. "Congrats on the release of your album last night."

"Thank you. Phew! It was a tall order, but we did it."

"I've already listened to it twice and it's a-maaaazing."

I'm floored. "You *bought* it? You didn't need to do that! I have it on my laptop."

"Of course, I bought it. And then, I stayed up late listening to it, twice. And I can honestly say it's a masterpiece. I loved your first album, but this one is next level."

Squealing happily, I get up from my seat and give Kendrick's neck a little hug, making him chuckle. "That means so much to me, coming from you," I say. "*Thank you.*"

He talks into my shoulder. "I'll be shocked if you don't win a bucketful of awards this time. Not just nominations, but *wins.*"

Flushed and smiling, I return to my seat, where I proceed to talk excitedly with Kendrick for the next twenty minutes about the album. And, quickly, it's clear Kendrick is anything but a bullshitter. Based on his questions and comments, it's obvious he really *did* listen to my musical baby *twice*—and genuinely believes every word of praise he's giving me. As the conversation progresses, however, I begin to realize something I hadn't understood before. Specifically, that I think Kendrick is . . . *into me*. Like, totally flirting with me. And not just being welcoming and friendly. Shit.

The thought is flattering to me, of course. Kendrick is a beautiful, talented, lovely person. Truly, he's as sweet as can be. But, the thing is . . . if I'm going to sleep with someone in the headliner during this tour—which Aloha has repeatedly advised me against doing, by the way—then it's not going to be Kendrick Cook. Or Kai Cook. Or Titus Connolly. Obviously, I'm not proud to admit this, but if I'm going to sleep with anyone, it's going to be Adrian Savage. *Obviously.* I've had a crush on him forever. As wonderful as Kendrick is, I'd never blow my chances with Savage by sleeping with his bandmate, let alone the one who's apparently his very best friend.

"So, when will the world have *your* next album, guys?" I ask, trying to change the subject and deflect from the flirtatious vibe I'm feeling.

"We'll probably start recording in earnest right after the tour," Kendrick replies. "We've all been on fire writing new songs during the tour. Savage, especially. He's been churning out some amazing stuff—pure gold. So, I'm sure we'll jump straight into the studio when we get back."

"That's so exciting," I say. "If you guys ever give friends 'early listener' copies of your albums, I'd love to be on that list."

"Hell yeah," Kendrick says. "It'd be great to get your feedback. I loved the mix on your new album."

"Thanks so much."

Kendrick smiles broadly, and I return the gesture, simply because that's what Kendrick Cook does to a person. He makes them want to smile. But a little piece of me knows I'm playing with fire here. Is Kendrick interpreting this smile as encouragement of something more than friendship? Because, if so, I've got to figure out a way to tactfully steer him into my friend zone, as soon as possible.

"So, I saw a photo of you at a basketball game recently," Kendrick ventures. "It was a Lakers game in LA, but you were cheering on Malik Wallace?"

And there it is. The look in his eyes that confirms he's interested in me romantically. No doubt about it. "Yeah, Malik invited me to the game. You were there when I met him at Reed's party, right? You met Malik, too?"

Kendrick nods. "Strangely, Malik didn't invite *me* to sit courtside at a Lakers game."

I chuckle, not knowing what else to do. "It was a last minute thing. He slid into my DMs, and asked me, so . . ."

"Are you guys dating, or . . .?" Kendrick asks tentatively.

I don't know why I do it, but I reply, yes, I'm dating Malik. In fact, I use the word "boyfriend." Even though, in reality, that's a massive overstatement. In truth, Malik is nothing to me, really. He's been pursuing me, and I went on a date with him, but we've made no promises, to put it mildly. For all I know, he's screwing someone else right now, and that's perfectly fine with me. But the thing is, I don't want to have to tell Kendrick, point blank, I'm simply not interested in him. I don't want to hurt his feelings or make things weird, especially not on day one of the tour. So, I take the easy way out, when it's offered to me.

"Cool," Kendrick says. "He's a . . ." He sighs. "Cool."

"I barely saw him this past month," I add quickly, not wanting Kendrick to get the impression Malik is the great love of my life or something. "I was so busy expediting the album, and rehearsing for the tour, I barely had time to eat or sleep, let alone see him."

Kendrick tries to smile. "Yeah, well, your hard work really paid off. Seriously, Laila, the album is incredible."

"Thank you so much, Kendrick. You're a great friend."

At that last word, Kendrick looks like he wants to scream. There's an awkward pause as he bites the inside of his cheek before finally puffing out his cheeks in resignation and whispering, "Cool."

I look at Ruby and she's grimacing compassionately, not even trying to hide her awareness of what just happened.

"Hey, asshole," Kai says, appearing out of nowhere and, thankfully, filling the awkward silence. Kai flops into a seat next to his brother and demands Kendrick watch the next episode in some series they've been binge-watching together.

"As long as you ply me with alcohol," Kendrick says.

"You don't need to ask me twice." Kai flags down a flight attendant and we all place orders. As we're doing that, Titus comes over and joins the party. And soon, our whole group is drinking and talking, laughing and swapping stories. Even Kendrick, much to my relief, seems like he's back to himself.

A few times during the conversation, Savage's name comes up, organically, and I feel myself perk up every time his name is mentioned—every time I get a new scrap of insider information about him. I hate that I'm constantly drawn to Savage, considering his obviously oversized ego, but I can't help myself. Not only is he gorgeous and talented, by all accounts he's closed off and prickly, too. Which, unfortunately, I must admit, makes him *exactly* my type.

SEVEN

SAVAGE

Chicago, Illinois

Me: *Yo, KC. I decided to fly into Philly tomorrow morning, instead of tonight. Mimi asked me to come to her treatment this afternoon, and I couldn't say no. Don't worry, I'll be there in plenty of time for soundcheck tomorrow.*

Kendrick: Does Tracy know?

Me: Yeah. She's pissed. Says I'm cutting it too close. I told her not to stress. It'll work out just fine.

Kendrick: How is Mimi doing?

I look at my grandmother sitting next to me on the couch, looking like a little hummingbird. She's flanked by me on one side and my cousin, Sasha, on the other, as we watch the season finale of Mimi's favorite show, *Sing Your Heart Out.*

. . .

Me: She's good. Feisty and funny, as always. Just really tired. Today's treatment kicked her tiny ass pretty hard.

Kendrick: Give her a big hug for me.

Me: Will do. How's tricks on your end?

Kendrick: Good. We're at the hotel, chilling before tomorrow.

Me: Chilling how?

Kendrick: The usual. Watching Netflix with Kai and Titus. Smoking a blunt. Eating way too much pizza. Be jealous.

I sigh with relief. Call me paranoid, but all day long I've been imagining Kendrick and Laila hitting it off on the plane by day, and then fucking like rabbits in Kendrick's hotel room by night. Thanks to Kendrick's response, I'm highly relieved and cautiously optimistic. But, still, I can't help probing a bit more. This time, I get straight to the point.

Me: How'd it go with Laila today?

Kendrick: FUCK MY LIFE, DUDE! SHE'S GOT A BOYFRIEND AND HE'S MALIK FUCKING WALLACE!!!!

No.

My heart is sinking. But not for Kendrick. For *myself.* But why do I even care? I don't know Laila. She's nothing to me but a sexpot in a music video. A pair of blue eyes shooting daggers at me from across a crowded party. A pair of perfect tits. Plush lips I'd do anything to kiss . . .

Fuck!

What's wrong with me? Why do I feel this primal desire to fuck the living hell out of that woman, above all others? It's insane. I know I'm having a classic "celebrity crush," like a teenager with a wall full of posters. Which is so unlike me, it's ridiculous. And yet, I can't help it. From the moment I saw her in that music video, I wanted to fuck her. And not in a fantasy. I wanted to hunt her down, maybe through Reed, or her agent, and meet, seduce, and fuck her. Unfortunately, I was on tour at the time, so it wasn't in the cards . . . and now, she's magically the opener on the rest of our tour, and I'm supposed to hang back and do nothing while Kendrick pines for her and she has FaceTime sex with Malik Wallace, of all people?

Me: I think I saw Laila with Malik at Reed's party.
Kendrick: Yeah, that's where they met. Can you believe it? I missed my chance by minutes. If I'd walked onto that basketball court five minutes earlier and invited Laila to get a drink, she never even would have met Malik.

And if I'd disregarded Kendrick calling dibs an hour before that, and beelined over to Laila when I first saw her across the party, I'd already have banged her a hundred times by now.

Me: It's probably for the best, KC. Like I said before, messing with an opener is a bad idea.

Okay, it's now official. I'm going to hell. Because even as I press send on my latest text, I know I'd fuck Laila, whether she's our opener or not, if only Kendrick wouldn't hate me for it. And maybe even if he would.

Kendrick: You're probably right. I've heard horror stories about guys messing around with openers and living to regret it.

Me: Exactly. It would have gone all kinds of bad in the end.

Kendrick: I'm sure the middle part would have made the bad ending well worth it, though.

I exhale a long breath, not knowing what to reply to that. As I ponder my response, my eyes drift to the TV as Hugh Delaney, the crusty old country star who's been a judge on *Sing Your Heart Out* since its inception, tells a wide-eyed contestant what he thought of her second of three performances in the finale show. Shaking his head, Hugh says, "Honestly, Deanna, I was expecting more from you tonight. This is the finale! And yet, I didn't see your usual sparkle. Hopefully, you'll pull a rabbit out of your hat for your final song."

The audience boos, as Aloha leans into her microphone. "I couldn't disagree with you more, Hugh," she says, eliciting rousing applause from the crowd. "Deanna's performance was far more subtle than her prior ones. But that's what made it so moving to me. Sometimes, less is more, Hugh." Aloha looks straight at him. "Try it sometime."

The audience roars its approval of Aloha's assessment—and, even more, her zinger to Hugh. The man everyone loves to hate.

My cousin, Sasha, yells from her end of the couch, "You tell him, Aloha! *Boom*!"

Chuckling, I look at our grandmother between us to see her reaction to Aloha's zinger, as well as Sasha's effusive support of it, and discover our little hummingbird is fast asleep, her tiny body looking peaceful and painless in repose.

"Aw, Mimi," I murmur. "Sweetheart." With a little wink to Sasha, I get up and scoop our grandmother into my arms, bring her into her bedroom, and carefully lay her down. I tuck her in and head to the kitchen, where her regular nighttime caregiver, Stuart, is sitting at the table, eating a bowl of soup. I tell him Mimi is down for the count, and Stuart says he'll take it from here.

I head back into the family room and sit back down next to Sasha, just as my phone buzzes in my pocket. It's another text from Kendrick.

Kendrick: JESUS CHRIST!!!! I just researched Malik Wallace. He's total trash to women, dude. Look him up. Reddit is full of women who say he's a DOG. Which means I'm back in the hunt with Laila, baby! I'm gonna build the friendship during the tour. Become her bestie. Her confidante. Her soulmate. And when her asshole boyfriend fucks it up—which he WILL, mark my words—and she's looking for a broad shoulder to cry on, I'll be the one she turns to. Genius, right?

Seriously? Goddammit. I tap out my reply:

Me: I'd think Ruby would be her shoulder to cry on, don't you? Ruby's great at that.
Kendrick: FUCK RUBY!!!! LOL. Laila's all mine. Ha!

. . .

Well, there's no way out. I can't keep this up. Obviously, Kendrick wants Laila and he's willing to play the long game to get her. It's time for me to step aside and forget this stupid fantasy. Because that's all it is. A stupid fantasy. When I actually meet the woman, I bet she'll quickly bore me to tears.

Me: You're a genius, KC. Go get her, tiger. See you tomorrow.

Kendrick: Try really hard not to be late, okay? Opening shows are always extra crazy. First soundchecks always take twice as long to get everything dialed in.

Me: I'm insulted. When am I not on time? Haha! Gotta go. Sleep tight.

"Who are you rooting for?" Sasha says.

I look up from my phone.

Sasha points to the TV. "Are you rooting for the woman or the man to win tomorrow night?"

"I'm rooting for an asteroid to crash into the studio and kill everyone associated with the show, except Aloha."

"Lovely."

Sasha picks up the remote and turns off the TV. "Well, I'm rooting for Deanna. She's improved, week after week, and she's sweet as can be."

"Good luck to her. I don't care. You wanna smoke a joint on the porch?"

"Hell yeah."

I sit on the porch with my cousin, smoking and shooting the shit. Sasha's a massage therapist, so she tells me a couple stories about her recent interactions with clients at the spa where she works, including a recent story of a guy who wrongly assumed he'd be getting a happy ending from my cousin. We're having a normal, amusing conversation. Nothing earth-shattering. But comfortable and calm. And that's exactly what I want. I know I'm about to re-enter the Twilight Zone for three months, beginning tomorrow—a world where I'm a god among men and nobody but my band ever treats me like a normal human. So, I sit and listen and smoke and enjoy the peaceful moment with someone I trust completely.

After a bit, Sasha does what she always does at times like this. She stands and says, with a gleam in her eye, "Now, let me at that famous body."

It's an inside joke. She's mocking the fact that my body is now a hot commodity around the world. That I've become a product, as much as the music. A piece of meat half the world would die, cheat, or kill to get with. I'm not complaining about it, by the way. This strategy has served me and my band well. But, still, it's a weird thing to think about, and particularly hilarious to Sasha, who still thinks of me as the dorky and angry twelve-year-old who, out of the blue one day about thirteen years ago, showed up on our grandma's doorstep, needing a place to live.

And, of course, as a massage therapist, Sasha is always bizarrely excited to get to work on the ever-present knots clustered stubbornly in my shoulders and neck. Sasha's weird like that. Her favorite thing in the world, literally, is massaging muscles that are especially knotted and stubborn, and to get to experience the satisfaction of coaxing them into a state of smoothness and relaxation, however temporary. Apparently, from what my cousin has told me, my knotted muscles are among her favorites to knead and coax into serenity, because they're almost always in a state of extreme tightness.

It's funny. The world thinks I'm a rockstar with zero

fucks to give at all times. A guy who floats through life, care-free and light as a feather. And I think that way about myself, too, in certain situations. And yet, at least according to Sasha, my muscles tell a very different tale about what's hiding underneath my apparently relaxed exterior.

"Knock yourself out, Sasha," I say. It's the same thing I always say to my cousin when she gets that crazy gleam in her eyes about unleashing her magic hands on me.

Gleefully, Sasha comes around to the back of my chair and gets to work on the mountains of knots and clusters in my shoulders and neck. And as she works miracles on my body, we talk about nothing particularly important for another fifteen minutes or so. But with the weed in my system, that's all the time I can handle of Sasha's magic hands before I'm too relaxed to remain upright in my chair.

"I gotta get to bed," I say. "Big day tomorrow."

"I can give you a full-body massage while you're lying down, if you need some help drifting off to sleep," she offers. "You're pretty tense, Adrian."

"Nah. I'm good. Go finish your book. I'm just gonna knot right back up again on the plane tomorrow, anyway."

I thank my cousin for everything she does for me and Mimi, kiss her on the cheek, and head off to my room. First off, I hop into a hot shower and jack off, thinking, yet again, about Laila. It's the last time I'm going to fantasize about Laila, I decide. Starting tomorrow, she's off-limits to me, even in my mind. Kendrick is obviously *really* into her. And he's the one, unlike me, who actually knows the woman. I've never even said two words to her, for fuck's sake! So, that's it. I'm moving on.

When I'm done with my shower, I slide on a pair of sweats, set my alarm, and reply to a text from my assistant about my travel schedule for tomorrow.

"Back to the grind," I murmur softly, closing my eyes.

But, unfortunately, sleep doesn't come to me, despite the weed in my system.

Finally, I give up. I grab my phone and google "Malik Wallace" and "cheater" and "Reddit," and quickly discern Kendrick was absolutely right. The dude is trash. I guess it's possible some of these stories about his assholery aren't true. There are definitely lots of stories online about me that are pure fiction. But, come on, not *all* of these stories can possibly be fake. Obviously, Malik's not a guy who keeps his word when it comes to women. Which means Laila won't put up with him for long. I don't know the woman, granted. But I know enough to know a firecracker like her, the woman who wanted to murder me for seemingly flirting with Georgina, and then Zasu, at Reed's party, doesn't put up with a guy's shit for very long.

I can't help smiling to myself at the realization that Laila will almost certainly wind up kicking Malik to the curb during the tour. Will she be looking to have a little revenge sex after Malik fucks around on her? Because, if so, I'll be right there to volunteer as tribute.

No.

Stop it, man.

That's Kendrick's plan. You can't steal it.

I take a long, deep breath and exhale slowly.

Actually, I think it's good Laila has a boyfriend. This way, I won't immediately succumb to temptation and betray Kendrick, or otherwise cockblock him. Because a woman having a boyfriend is a boundary I can respect.

Sort of.

Okay, not at all.

But, at least, I can tell myself I respect it. I can tell myself there's double the reason to stay away from Laila. This way, I don't have to resist her, based solely on Kendrick calling dibs. Which, admittedly, is a tall order for me. This way, with Laila dating a guy with as much clout as me, probably even more, I've got double the chances of *not* betraying my very best friend.

EIGHT

LAILA

Philadelphia, Pennsylvania

"They haven't even *started* yet?" I say, feeling flabbergasted. According to today's itinerary, Fugitive Summer should have finished their soundcheck a half hour ago. Which is why I *prematurely* wrapped up an interview in my dressing room to race down here to the stage area, right on time, to begin *my* soundcheck. And now I find out Fugitive Summer hasn't even *begun*? I know the headliner *always* soundchecks first, and takes as long as needed. And delays can happen. But would it have killed our tour manager, Tracy, to let me know the itinerary is no longer accurate, so I didn't miss out on the rest of my interview?

Tracy says, "Savage took a later flight from Chicago than originally planned. But no worries, he's on his way from the airport now and should be here any minute."

She's calm and cool. Which I can't fathom. Savage isn't

even in the building yet? Because he didn't fly last night, as planned—as any sane and responsible person would do, when literally *thousands* of people are depending on him? What the ever-loving rockstar cliché is wrong with that man? Who else but him, in his shoes, would travel on the day of any show— let alone the tour opener? It's not like Savage's fans would be perfectly fine to watch a replacement singer tonight, the way audiences accept understudies on Broadway. People pay a lot of money to watch *Savage*, and only Savage, sing, play his guitar, and shake his famous ass! And yet, Savage felt it was a perfectly reasonable thing to risk letting *thousands* of people wait tonight—or maybe even risk letting them down completely? All I can say is that boy had better have a damned good reason for cutting it this close.

I look at my assistant, Katrina, my aggravation probably written all over my face. But I don't care if our tour manager knows I'm pissed. In fact, I want her to know. Now that my soundcheck has been delayed by at least an hour and a half, my assistant will need to reschedule a ton of stuff for me. My hair and makeup. Another interview. Plus, call me crazy, but I was hoping to have a moment to eat and relax before show-time. To call my mom and sister before going onstage. But now, thanks to Savage, I won't be able to do all of it.

"Why don't you take a seat and relax, rather than going back to your dressing room?" Tracy says, emphasizing the word *relax* in a way that tells me she already thinks I'm a raving bitch. She motions toward the front row of seats. "This way, you'll be ready to hop onstage the moment they're done."

"That's a great idea," I say, trying to sound super chill and easygoing. But I don't think I'm fooling her.

Both of us smiling serenely, my assistant and I take our seats . . . and then proceed to quietly gripe about the situation between ourselves for the next several minutes. In the middle of our bitch-fest, however, a male voice behind us takes us by surprise.

"Yeah, I vote we kill him. He's such a dick."

I turn around to find Kendrick sitting behind us, looking highly amused.

"Hello, ladies," he says. "Sorry we're running late. Savage was visiting his family and got delayed."

"Oh no," I say. "I hope everything is okay."

"It's fine. He's on his way now."

"Great," I say brightly, my cheeks turning red. "How long have you been sitting back there, Kendrick?"

His smile broadens. "Long enough to know you've been plotting Savage's murder. But don't worry. You're not the first, and you won't be the last."

My shoulders soften under his warm smile. Clearly, he's not holding whatever he heard against me. But it's a good lesson for me. From now on, I need to keep my nose down and my big mouth shut.

For the next few minutes, Kendrick and I chat breezily as we await Mr. Rockstar's arrival.

And finally it happens. Adrian Savage enters the building. Which I know even before I've seen him, thanks to the sudden shift in the air. The electricity instantly coursing through the building. All at once, crew members who've been working calmly suddenly spaz out. And Kendrick rises from his chair.

"Talk to you later, Laila," he says. "Come eat with us after your soundcheck. We'll be in Greenroom 2 with a full spread. Plenty for you and your band."

"Thanks so much."

Kendrick heads toward a far door, just as Savage's striking face comes into view. He strides into the large venue and toward the stage, and Kendrick greets him warmly and then falls into step with him. At the same time, the rest of the band converges on the stage and gets settled with their instruments in a way that suggests they've all done this before. Many, many times—and on a very tight schedule. When Savage and Kendrick walk onstage to join the rest of their band, everyone waves curtly at Savage. But they don't scold him or otherwise freak out. They just get down to business.

Savage slides the strap of his guitar over his shoulder. "Has this been tuned?"

"Yes," a nearby roadie confirms. "All three are ready to go."

"Thanks." Savage steps up to his mic and taps on it, quickly discerning it's not live. He waves his arm and the soundman at the back of the venue flips a switch. "Hello, Philadelphia," Savage booms when the mic is live. "1-2, 1-2." *Boom.* Savage's eyes land on me. And there it is, again. That same crazy electricity I felt every time my eyes met his at Reed's party. A kind of double-ovarian explosion I've never felt before. "Hello, Laila," Savage says calmly into his microphone, a smirk on his handsome face.

But that's all I get. Without even waiting for me to mouth "hello" in reply, Savage looks down and rips off the opening guitar riff from one of Fugitive Summer's biggest hits—the sexiest song in their catalog, by far—a song filled with double *entendres* about orgasms and oral sex called "Come with Me."

Did Savage just now dedicate this song to me, by saying my name before launching into it? Or am I connecting dots that simply aren't there?

Of course, the full band expertly follows Savage's lead, right on cue, and, soon, he leans into his microphone and begins to sing. And just like that, even during a soundcheck, Savage transforms from a mere mortal into a god before my eyes. Even when there's no audience cheering him on, no collective hysteria to elevate him to superhuman status,

Savage nonetheless looks supernatural in this moment. The perfect representation of a man doing what he was divinely created to do. And whether I want to think it or not, despite me actively *not* wanting to think it, as I watch Savage performing onstage, I find myself thinking, on a running loop: *I. Want. That.*

NINE

LAILA

"All I'm saying is it's a lucky thing you've got bodyguards," Kendrick is saying to Savage as I enter the greenroom with my musicians after our soundcheck. "Or else Laila would have murdered you in there."

Crap.

Fugitive Summer is sitting at a large table, eating a meal. And based on what Kendrick just said, it seems Kendrick has been telling his band the story of my earlier bitchfest, the one in which I complained to my assistant about Savage traveling on the day of the opening show.

At the sound of my band entering the room, Fugitive Summer collectively turns their heads toward the door.

"Hey, guys," I say awkwardly, my cheeks blooming. "Have you met my band?"

My heart racing, I introduce everyone—two guys and two women—trying to sound light and bright. And through it all, I steadfastly avoid Savage's gaze.

Kendrick enthusiastically invites us to fill our plates from a buffet at a nearby table. So, we all head over there and begin doing just that, exchanging small talk with Fugitive Summer as we do. We talk about the venue. The acoustics. The amazing sound crew. My musicians compliment Fugitive Summer on their soundcheck, and several of them compliment my band in return, saying they heard our two songs from in here and we sounded great.

As I walk to the dining table with my meal in hand, I feel eyes on me. And when I finally muster the courage to look up, I discover I'm right. But the eyes don't belong to Savage. They belong to Kendrick. He's looking at me apologetically. Like he feels bad he just ratted me out to his friends.

I shoot him a warm smile to let him know I'm not offended in the least. That in fact, I'm well aware I deserved it. Actually, although I'd never admit this to Kendrick or anyone else, I'm kind of glad Savage knows my thoughts about his lateness, albeit not directly from me. Someone needs to tell that boy the truth—that the entire world doesn't revolve around him. It might as well be me.

As conversation at the table between the two bands becomes easier and gains momentum, I muster the courage to peek at Savage, and find him already staring at me. Or, more accurately, *glaring* at me. Glowering, like he wants to beat the hell out of me.

Oh, dear. Is Mister Rockstar pissed about what Kendrick just now revealed? Because, if so, I'm not sorry. The man made me have to reschedule half the stuff on my calendar and cancel the rest. So, I think I'm allowed to be a tiny bit annoyed. Lesson learned, though. Annoyed or not, I'll shut my trap going forward.

Savage slowly slides a bite of food into his gorgeous mouth and chews, not taking his eyes off me.

So, I arch my eyebrow, and do the same.

He subtly mimics my facial expression, like he's mocking me.

So I shoot him a look that says, *Come at me, bro.*

He doesn't hesitate. He makes a face that says, *Oh, I will . . .* and then looks away.

Damn it! When will I learn to look away *first*?

Feeling pissed at myself, I take a big bite of food and tune into the conversation happening around me. It seems Kai and one of my musicians went to the same music school and have several mutual friends.

"I had classes with your older brother, Sebastian!" Kai says to my musician, Tate, connecting the dots.

"No way!" Tate replies.

"Is Sebastian still playing for Alicia Keys?" Kai asks.

"No, not anymore. Right now, he's playing in the house band for *Sing Your Heart Out.* He's been doing that for the past three seasons."

Kai laughs. "Holy shit! Is that a cushy gig?"

"*Super* cushy. No travel. Easy songs and arrangements. Sebastian could do it in his sleep."

"I bet."

Everyone at the table joins in with questions and comments about the show, with Titus rolling his eyes and calling it the most "cringey-ass show ever."

"Yeah, it's cringey as hell," Tate, my musician, agrees. "But a massive gravy train. My brother's salary from the show itself is shit, total shit, but he gets so many side gigs from the contacts he makes on the show, it's turned out to be a goldmine. Now that the show had its season finale last night, he's getting ready to go on tour with Hugh Delaney's band. Who, of course, he met on the show."

"Good for him," Kai says. "Although I'd sooner shoot myself than play Hugh Delaney songs, night after night."

"Hey, it's a steady job," Tate says. "They're not always easy to come by for a musician."

"Oh, of course," Kai says, quickly backtracking. "I know

it's tough out there. Any musician would leap at a regular gig on a popular TV show. Good for him."

"I watched the final performances last night," Ruby interjects. "I can't wait to find out who won in the big reveal tonight. I'm hoping Deanna."

"I saw the finale, too," my musician, Tate, says. "Did you see Aloha kick the crap out of Hugh?"

"I saw that!" Ruby says, laughing. "I thought both contestants did such a great job. I think it's so fun to watch people trying to make their dreams come true, any way they can."

"I agree," I say, my heart thumping. As this conversation has worn on, I've felt internal pressure to mention I'm going to be on the next season of the show. The lineup hasn't been announced yet, but that's not why I haven't mentioned it to this group. Obviously, this is a highly trustworthy crowd. I think I've held off because I'm a little embarrassed to admit I'll be appearing on a show half these people think is "cringey-ass." Testing the waters, I say, "In my opinion, the only thing that's really cringey about the show is Hugh Delaney."

"I agree completely," Ruby says. "But even then, watching Hugh *pretend* to be some kind of down to earth everyman, when everyone knows he's secretly the biggest prima donna on the show, is super entertaining to me."

"To me, too!" I say, laughing.

"What does your brother say about Hugh?" Kai asks.

Tate chuckles. "My brother says Hugh is a flaming cunt."

Everyone laughs uproariously while I shift my weight in my chair. If I don't say something now, I feel like it will seem weird later, when my name is announced and everyone realizes I sat here and said nothing.

"Titus and I used to watch the show every week with our mom," Ruby says.

"*You* watched with Mom," Titus says. "I never did."

"Yes, you did. Remember, you were obsessed with that one contestant . . . *Kikuko*?"

Titus grins. "Oh, yeah. *Kikuko*. She was hot."

Everyone laughs, except Savage, who hasn't laughed once during this entire conversation. At this point, I'm not sure if he's even capable of laughing.

I clear my throat, still mustering my courage. "I used to watch with my mom and sister every week," I say, looking at Ruby. "And guess who's always been my mom's favorite?" I snort. "*Hugh*."

Everyone chuckles. Again, everyone except Savage. And I suddenly realize this is it. My last chance to mention that I'm going to be appearing as a mentor on the next season. If I don't say it now, the conversation will shift and I'll lose my chance. I take a deep breath. "I'm actually going to be on the show next season. Just one episode, as a mentor for Aloha's team."

The table explodes with congratulations and reactions from everyone except Savage. Most notably, Titus apologizes for calling the show "cringey-ass" earlier.

"No need to apologize," I say. "It *is* cringey-ass."

"But that's its charm," Ruby interjects. "Congrats, Laila. That's *awesome*."

"Thank you. The best part was telling my mom. She shrieked with joy when she found out."

"Yeah, and I bet the paycheck won't suck, either," Titus says.

"Actually, the pay for mentors is almost nothing," I admit. "Only a couple thousand bucks—just enough to meet union minimums."

My musician, Tate, says, "Yeah, my brother says they're cheap-ass bastards to everyone but the judges. The judges make millions per season, while everyone else makes peanuts." He smiles at me. "I'm sure it'll be well worth your while, for reasons other than the salary."

"My label head and agent both think so. Honestly, I'd have said yes for no money at all. Just for the exposure."

Savage scoffs and, for the first time, deigns to enter the conversation. "Never do *anything* for free, unless it's for charity. But definitely not for a cringey-ass TV show that's making money, hand over fist, for everyone but the talent. Always know your worth, Laila. If you don't, nobody else will."

I furrow my brow in surprise. I'm not certain if he was intending to compliment me, or chastise me, with that comment. All I know is it felt like the latter. "There was no way to push back on the money," I insist. "They've got a waiting list a mile long of people wanting to be a mentor. Plus, like I said, Reed and my agent, who's one of the best in the business, *both* said it was worth it to take the gig, so that's what I did. But, regardless, it's one day of work to make my mom extremely happy. And that's enough for me."

Savage rolls his eyes. "Never mix emotion and business, Laila. That's a recipe for disaster."

What the fuck? Who does he think he is? I pull a face that hopefully expresses my extreme annoyance. "I don't know why you think it's your place to offer me unsolicited business advice," I say. "Especially when I've already signed the contract and can't do anything about it now. I had one of the top agents in LA, plus Reed, both *adamantly* advising me to take the deal, so I did."

"I don't know your agent, but I know Reed is always looking out for *Reed*."

"Good, because our interests are perfectly aligned. The show will boost my music sales and profile, so I can make big money down the line, both for Reed and myself. Not everything is about instant gratification, Savage, contrary to what you might think."

He smirks but says nothing . . . but the air between us suddenly feels like it's crackling with electricity.

"Sounds like you made a great decision to me!" Ruby chirps, her eyes telling Savage not to say another word.

Slowly, Savage picks up his water bottle and takes a long, languid sip, his eyes trained on mine and his body language oozing with disdain.

I shouldn't do it. I shouldn't care about his opinion, but I do. My breathing stilted, I say, "So, I take it you agree the show is cringey-ass?"

"I do. My grandmother loves it, so I've seen it a few times. And it gives me hives every time."

I tighten my jaw. "Well, thank goodness, you're not the one they've asked to be on it, then."

"Thank goodness for small mercies." He puts his water bottle down. "Obviously, you're happy about this, so I'm happy for you. Congrats."

I shoot him daggers. Even while saying all the right words, his tone is infuriating. Doesn't he realize my career is at a totally different level than his, and almost certainly will *never* reach the towering heights of his? So excuse me if I've taken a job he considers beneath him. A job I'm honestly really excited about.

Out of nowhere, Savage bites back a smile in reaction to whatever he's seeing on my face. He licks his lips, suggestively, and, suddenly, despite my annoyance with him, I'm feeling highly aroused. Without warning, warmth oozes into my core and between my legs, making me pulse and tingle. And that's how I know there's something *really* wrong with me . . . because being angry with this man only makes me want to fuck him, all the more.

I stand, suddenly feeling the need to get away from him.

To save myself. I announce, awkwardly, "I think it's time for me to meet my hair and makeup woman in my dressing room." It's not true. It's not even close to time for that. But that's what came out of my mouth. My gaze still holding Savage's and my cheeks burning, I add, "I'll probably call my mom, too, for a little pre-show pep talk." Why am I saying that? These people don't care about my To Do List. My face blooming, I peel my eyes off Savage's to address the rest of his band. "Have a great show, guys. I'll watch from the wings."

They wish me a great show, too, and I thank them, before turning on my heel and striding out of the greenroom as fast as my legs will carry me, feeling Savage's dark eyes on my backside as I go.

TEN
LAILA

Providence, Rhode Island

There's music blaring in Titus' hotel suite. Drunk, stoned people are all around me, laughing and playing drinking games. Beer pong and Drunk Jenga, mainly. We're celebrating Titus' and Ruby's joint twenty-fifth birthday tonight at a post-show party. All the musicians from both bands are here, plus, a select group of staffers and crew. And, glory be, I'm the perfect level of drunk. Still totally coherent and in control of myself, but feeling fine as wine and *invincible*.

For what feels like the hundredth time tonight, my eyes drift to Savage across the crowded suite to find him already looking at me like he wants to murder me. Or fuck me. Or fuck my face. With him, I'm never sure which is which.

I should look away, I think. But the second I think it, Savage looks away first. Dammit! The only reason I held

Savage's gaze in the first place was so *I* could look away *first*!

It's par for the course between us. The way it's been since Philadelphia, two weeks ago. We stare and glare and have lengthy nonverbal conversations. But we don't talk. Ever. So, tonight, I've decided to reset the game clock, meaning I'm never going to speak to Adrian Savage again, *ever*, unless *he* speaks to me *first*. Is he *still* pissed about the little bitchfest I had with my assistant about his lateness on day one? Or has he simply decided he doesn't like me because I pushed back on his unsolicited career advice? Either way, he can kiss my ass.

Oh, God. I wish Savage would kiss my ass. And then, the rest of me.

Stop, Laila.

Ha.

I take a long swig from my bottle of whiskey and lean my back against a wall in a corner of the crowded hotel suite. I'm acting like an antisocial weirdo at this party, which is totally unlike me. But I've reached my breaking point with Savage and his constant brooding and glaring. I don't expect him to treat me with the kind of warmth Ruby and Kendrick always do, obviously. Those two are sunshine in human form. But I can't stand this constant tension between us. Something's gotta give. Somehow, I've got to shake things up and force Savage to make the first move. *But how?*

My phone buzzes in my free hand, and when I look at the screen it's a text from Malik, asking me if I'm available to FaceTime.

> **Me: Sorry, no. At a noisy bday party. What's up?**
> **Tall_Man: I'm coming to your show in NYC!**
> **Me: Which one? Friday night regular show at Radio**

City or Sat night charity concert with lots of bands at The Garden?

Tall_Man: Sat night at The Garden. I'd come to both but I've got a game on Friday. I'll come backstage to say hi and take you out for late dinner afterwards. Yes?

Me: Gotta do a dinner thing after the show with Reed and all the other artists on the bill. You can come as my guest, if you want. We're allowed a plus one.

Tall_Man: Hell yeah. See you then, beautiful.

Me: See ya then, dude. Good luck in your game(s)!

I smile wickedly to myself and take a long slug of my whiskey. Well, damn, if I'm looking to shake things up, I think that might very well do the trick.

After putting my phone away, I look across the crowded suite at Savage again. This time, he's looking at something on Kai's phone. So, I scan the party again, this time landing on darling Kendrick, who's already looking at me. When my eyes meet Kendrick's, the smile he beams at me would light up the darkest night.

Aw, Kendrick. I think he's still got a crush on me. In fact, I know he does. If I gave him the green light, he'd throw away our budding friendship in a heartbeat for something more. But, unfortunately, I'm just not feeling that way for him. I wish I were. What sane, functional, self-respecting woman *wouldn't* want a guy like Kendrick Cook? Ergo, I'm a nut job.

I take another long slug from my bottle, just as Savage and Kai approach Kendrick and divert his attention from me. Kendrick says something to Savage that makes him throw his head back and laugh from the depths of his soul. And my jaw practically clanks to the floor. I've never seen that before. Savage can laugh? And like that? Holy shit.

All of a sudden, I'm flooded with a weird cocktail of emotions. A thumping attraction to Savage that physically takes my breath away. And, weirdly, jealousy because I wasn't the one who elicited that laugh from Mr. Pouty Face.

When Savage comes down from laughing, he pulls out a box of cigarettes and holds it up to his two besties. And then, off he goes, straight out the door of Titus' suite, obviously intending to smoke a cigarette outside.

I don't hesitate. My chest heaving, I march toward the door, eager to seize this unique opportunity to talk to Savage alone. We've never had a private conversation before. Never been in a room alone. And I must admit I'm dying to have his full attention. To get to know him. Maybe even find out what kinds of things make him belly laugh, against all odds. But, mostly, I want to find out why the hell he hates me so much, and has since day one.

When I get outside, the night air is brisk but not uncomfortable. I wander around, briefly, before locating Savage around a corner. He's sitting on the ground in the dark with his back against a building, looking out at the dark ocean below while smoking a cigarette.

As I approach, Savage blows out a long plume of smoke into the night. And I can't help thinking the moment feels like a painting that'd hang in a contemporary art museum: "Moody Demi-God in Contemplation."

"Mind if I join you?" I ask, coming to a stop over him.

Savage pats the ground. "I saved you a seat."

I get settled next to him and he holds up his box of cigarettes, offering me one.

I shake my head. "I don't smoke. I hate the taste, actually." I offer him my bottle of whiskey and he takes a long, greedy sip.

"I don't think I knew you smoked," I say.

He returns the bottle to me. "I only smoke when I'm

drunk, which doesn't happen very often." He licks his lips, slowly. Suggestively. "I've got a big-time oral fixation. When I get drunk, it becomes overpowering to me . . ." He licks his lips again. "And I feel like I *have* to put something in my mouth."

Oh, Jesus Christ. The boy just flash-melted my panties.

I clear my throat, pretending I didn't understand the sexual innuendo dripping from his comment. "I noticed you doing shots at Reed's party. I assumed you get drunk regularly, like the Rockstar Manual requires."

"Actually, that was the last time I got shitfaced. It was Kendrick's birthday. In my band, we always get shitfaced on each other's birthdays. It's not optional."

"That was the last time you drank?"

"No. I'll have a beer or whatever. But I won't get *drunk.* I've got a rule I never 'drown my sorrows.' Drinking has to be about having fun for me. Otherwise, if I drink when I'm angry or upset in any way, I wind up being a huge asshole." He shrugs. "Plus, I have to eat and drink fairly clean most of the time to keep myself in shape . . ." He lifts his shirt, haphazardly, momentarily revealing the jaw-dropping grooves in his abs. "Looking like this is a big part of the job. And I can't do it, unless I stay disciplined and committed."

I lift my eyebrows in surprise. "Huh. I think 'Rockstar Cliché Bingo' requires you to drink like a fish, *especially* to drown your sorrows. The last time I checked, there were no bingo squares labeled 'eat clean and stay disciplined and committed to maintain abs of steel.'"

Savage chuckles and takes the bottle from me. "Meh. I already check plenty of boxes in 'Rockstar Cliché Bingo.' No need to check them *all* off, right?"

"You think you're a rockstar cliché?" I ask.

He looks at me, as if to say, *Well, obviously.* But he says, "If I'm not already, then I'm well on my way." He takes a long drag of his cigarette. "Honestly, one of my biggest fears is that I'll become so beholden to the money and fame and all the . . . *expectation*, I'll forget who I am and why I do this. I'll become exactly that—a cliché. A parody of myself." He looks out at the dark ocean. "I mean, come on, I've got to think 'dick pic trending on Twitter' is at the center square on *every* 'Rockstar Cliché Bingo' card, right? So, I'm probably already fucked."

I stare at his exquisite profile for a long moment, overcome by my attraction to him, and finally say, "I heard a rumor you posted that shot yourself—for publicity or whatever. True?"

He scoffs. "Not true." He flicks some ash from his cigarette onto the ground. "I had nothing to do with it, other than I was stupid enough to take a shower after sex with someone I barely knew, without locking the door."

I contemplate that response for a moment, while, again, admiring his gorgeous profile. His lips as he sucks on his cigarette. I hate cigarettes and don't find them sexy. But I must admit the way Savage is sucking on that thing, and licking his lips in between, makes me wonder what it would be like to kiss him. To have him perform oral sex on me. *Sex, sex, sex.* Suddenly, that's all I'm thinking about. Sex with Adrian Savage.

I clear my throat and motion to the cigarette between his lips. "Aren't you worried you're gonna get addicted? Nicotine is supposedly more addictive than cocaine."

Savage shrugs. "Like I said, I only smoke when I'm drunk and feel the overwhelming urge to put something in my mouth." He licks his lips again, this time even more suggestively than before. And, right on cue, I'm feeling the beginning stirrings of arousal again.

I shift my position on the ground, trying to alleviate the faint pulsing between my legs. "My dad was a heavy smoker and my sister and I once stole one of his cigarettes, when we were, like, nine and twelve. And the minute I inhaled, I thought I was going to die. I thought it was the most disgusting thing I'd ever tasted in my life."

"And you've never tried it again?"

I shake my head. "Why would I, when I know how bad it is for me? Plus, I associate smoking with my father, and he's not a good memory."

"Is he dead?"

"No. Just out of my life. And good riddance."

He holds up the bottle. "Cheers to that." He takes a swig and hands it to me.

"Cheers to that," I echo, before taking a long guzzle. "Uh oh," I say. "Does this qualify as me drowning my sorrows, now that I've mentioned my asshole father?"

He chuckles. "Yeah. Probably."

"You seriously *never* drown your sorrows?"

He shrugs. "You associate cigarettes with your asshole father. I associate being an angry, pissed off drunk with mine. Good riddance."

"Cheers to that." I take a swig and hand him the bottle.

"Cheers to that," he echoes, before taking a long sip.

My heart is thundering at this unexpectedly amazing conversation. I don't know how I thought this "confrontation" was going to go when I marched out here . . . but never in a million years did I think it would go like *this*. Savage seems almost normal. Likeable and friendly. And insanely, irresistibly hot.

"So, what do you do whenever you feel like drowning your sorrows, if you don't drink?" I ask.

Savage blows a stream of smoke into the air, but this time, pointedly, away from me. "Various things. I work out. Write a song. Jack off. Or, if convenient, I fuck."

A soft whimper escapes my lips, so I press them together

and look out at the ocean to gather myself. Well, that was a fascinating answer.

"You still dating the basketball player?" he asks, out of nowhere. And I'm shocked he knows that false fact about me. Kendrick told him about that? Now, why would he do that?

I pause, not sure how to play this. Should I come clean and admit I lied to Kendrick, because I didn't want to hurt his feelings? Or should I lean into the lie?

Before I've decided, Savage says, "I overheard Tracy putting Malik's name onto the VIP list for the New York charity show."

There's jealousy glinting in his dark eyes, as plain as day. He's trying to hide it, but it's there. The same way it was there when I flirted with Cash in front of him at Reed's party. And, suddenly, I know exactly how to play this. *Lean into the lie.*

"Yeah, he's coming," I reply casually. "He wanted to come to both nights, but he's playing a game on Friday night."

A scornful puff of air escapes Savage's nose. "Have you never googled him, for fuck's sake? Look at the Reddit boards about him, Laila! I wouldn't call him 'boyfriend material.'"

I'm flabbergasted. What an unexpected burst of passion from Mr. I Don't Give a Fuck! "Of course, I've googled him," I retort. "And it ain't pretty. But guess who else I've googled? *You.* And that shit ain't any prettier, Mr. Dick Pic. So, I'd advise you not to throw stones from your glass house."

"The difference is I don't *pretend* to be boyfriend material."

"People change and grow. They learn from their mistakes. Malik swears he's learned from his mistakes, and I believe him."

The first part of my statement is true. Malik has, indeed, sworn up and down he's a changed man who's now looking for a committed relationship. The second part, however—that I'm stupid enough to actually believe what Malik told me—is a bald-face lie. In fact, it's my firm belief Malik only said he's looking for a committed relationship because I told him that's what I'd need to sleep with him. I actually only said that to Malik to torture him. I've certainly had sex outside of a committed relationship in my life. But I won't do that with Malik Wallace. Hell no. There's no way I'm going to be nothing but another notch on that bad boy's belt.

Shaking his head, Savage takes a long slug from the bottle before saying, "Chris Rock once famously said men are only as faithful as their options. Looks like you're going to be putting that theory to the test with your 'boyfriend,' especially in a long distance relationship. Open your eyes, Fitzy. Basketball isn't that guy's only game."

Fitzy? I've never heard that before. It sounds to me like the name of a very tiny dog in a very fluffy tutu. I'm not sure I like it. But I decide, rather than mention this new, surprising nickname he's concocted for me, to call him something I've never called him, in return. "I find it perplexing you've gone to the trouble of googling Malik and his track record with women, *Adrian*. What a strange thing for you to be wasting your time doing."

Savage scowls when I call him Adrian, and then says, "I didn't google him, *Fitzy*. Kendrick did and then wouldn't shut the fuck up about what he'd found."

I feel my shoulders droop with disappointment. But why? I should have known. Savage had the chance to hit on me at Reed's party, every bit as much as Malik did. And Savage chose to hit on everyone else *but* me, and then leave early with whoever he'd settled on, while I was performing onstage. "Not that it's any of your business," I say, "but

Malik and I have had some detailed conversations about his past behavior and I've told him I won't put up with that kind of shit." *True.* "He's assured me he's a new man." Also, true. "I believe in second chances." Again, true, although I'm not sure Malik Wallace is deserving of one. "So, I've decided to believe what Malik has told me, unless and until he proves me wrong." *Lies, lies, lies.* I'm stupid when it comes to men, but I'm not a damned fool.

Savage rolls his eyes, looking remarkably, exquisitely pissed off. "A leopard doesn't change his spots, Laila. Don't be stupid."

"You think maybe you're projecting, *Adrian*? I've googled you, remember? And it looks to me like *you're* the one who's only as faithful as your options."

"That's *false.* I'm one hundred percent faithful, if I've made a commitment." He winks. "Which is why I rarely make one."

I scoff. "You want a medal for that?"

"No. I'm just defending myself. I'm a man of my word, if I've given it."

"So, obviously, you don't give your word regarding *punctuality*, huh?"

Savage's face ignites. "I knew it!" he shouts gleefully. "I knew you've been secretly losing your mind whenever I'm late and biting your tongue about it until it bleeds."

He's right. He's driven me bonkers these past two weeks with his perpetual lateness. Since that first time in Philadelphia, Savage was late for two additional sound-checks, as well as one early-morning departure on the buses. But all three times, I kept my mouth shut and my face neutral, even though I was annoyed as hell to witness him behaving so unprofessionally. I bat my eyelashes at him. "You've been late for something since Philly? I hadn't noticed."

Savage's nostrils flare as he hands the bottle back to me. But he says nothing.

For a long moment, we sit in silence, both of us biting back smiles. Until finally, Savage sighs and says, "Seriously, Fitzy. Dump the basketball player. If your kink is trying to be the one woman a cheater doesn't cheat on, then I've got news for you, baby. You need to find a new kink."

"Oh, yeah? Well, guess what, Adrian? If your kink is doling out unsolicited advice to me, then I've got news for you, baby. You need to shut the fuck up, motherfucker."

He bursts out laughing. I mean, the dude *belly* laughs. And I can't help feeling like I've accomplished something amazing.

His laughter subsiding, Savage brings the bottle to his lips and mutters, "Touché, Fitzy. Too-fucking-shay." I watch him sip and swallow, once again imagining his sensuous lips performing oral sex on me. It's impossible *not* to imagine it. Everything about his song "Come with Me" suggests he's an enthusiastic fan of that particular sex act. And the way he's moving his mouth right now is insanely sexy.

Suddenly, I find myself wondering how the groupie thing works with him. On the one hand, I know his reputation. When I said I've googled him, it was the truth. Not that I needed to google him. Everything about him screams "man-whore." Plus, I saw his reputation in action at Reed's party, firsthand, so I know the dude's got no qualms about hitting on women, one after another, until he gets what he wants.

On the other hand, I haven't actually seen Savage with a single woman during this tour. Do his handlers quietly bring groupies to his room in every new city? I've noticed he doesn't hang out and party nearly as much as his bandmates. Is that because he's typically otherwise engaged in his room?

"Call me *Savage*, by the way," he says, out of nowhere. "Only my family calls me Adrian."

"Only if you agree not to call me 'Fitzy' again."

"You don't like Fitzy?"

"It sounds like the name of a white fluffy dog wearing a tutu."

Savage chuckles. "Well, shit, now I've got no choice. You're Fitzy for life."

"Okay, then you're Adrian."

He pauses like he's weighing his options, and finally says, "Yeah, it's totally worth it."

I roll my eyes. "So, anyway, *Adrian,* the whole reason I came out here was to clear the air with you. I think maybe you've been pissed about me trash-talking you in Philly for being late, and I—"

"I'm not pissed about that."

"No?"

He pulls a face like that's a ridiculous notion. "Why would I give a flying fuck what you think?"

My lips part and my brow furrows. Did this motherfucker just *insult* me while forgiving me for insulting him? But before I've responded, the sound of sharp laughter and familiar voices cuts through the darkness and causes both of us to jolt and lean back like we've been doing something wrong over here.

The voices belong to Ruby, a couple people from my band, and *Kendrick.* And the minute Kendrick's voice becomes identifiable, Savage's entire body stiffens. He hastily stubs out his cigarette, clears his throat, and pops up, looking very much like a kid who's just been caught with his hand in a cookie jar.

"I think I'm gonna crash in my room now," he murmurs. And for a split-second, I think he's inviting me to join him. But, no. He quickly adds, "Do me a favor and tell Ruby and Titus I left the party and said happy birthday, okay?"

"Uh, sure," I reply, feeling vaguely disappointed. But I'm

speaking to Savage's back. He's already on the move. High-tailing it out of here like a bank robber on the run. "Don't be late for the buses tomorrow!" I call out. And then add, pointedly, "*Adrian*."

Just before his frame disappears into the dark night, Savage turns around, so that he's walking backward. Facing me now, he flashes me an impish grin and says, "I'm never late, *Fitzy*. Everyone else is just . . . *early*."

ELEVEN

SAVAGE

New York, New York

My band and everyone else who played at tonight's charity concert at Madison Square Garden are seated at a long table in a swanky restaurant in Midtown, courtesy of our host, Reed Rivers. *And I'm shitfaced.* Breaking my hard and fast rule about never drinking to drown my sorrows. Because . . . Malik Wallace.

To anyone watching me drinking like a fish tonight, I'm sure I look like I'm merely celebrating tonight's amazing show, along with everyone else at this table. But I'm not. In reality, I'm fixated on that bastard's every movement. His every flirtatious smile, aimed directly at Laila. Basically, I've been drinking while trying to figure out how I can murder that motherfucker and get away with it.

"You called it at Reed's party," Kendrick says next to me,

jutting his chin at Reed and his date on the far end of the table. Who's Reed's date tonight? Well, none other than Georgina, the sultry reporter I hit on as Kendrick's birthday present. The fact that Georgina is at Reed's side at all, a full two months later, is shocking enough. But factor in that Reed's brought her as his date to a work event, which isn't Reed's style, *and* that he's been packing on the PDA with her throughout the entire dinner, and I'm thinking this woman has cast a spell on The Prick, the likes of which I never would have believed.

But, whatever. I don't have the bandwidth to focus on Reed and his love life for very long. I'm too fixated on Laila and *hers*. Fucking Malik! When he walked into the green-room at The Garden earlier tonight, I felt an almost primal desire to pummel his face. And the impulse has only grown as the evening, and my alcohol consumption, has worn on.

Unfortunately, the happy couple—Laila and her handsy MVP—is sitting immediately across from Kendrick and me at this long, crowded table, so I can't avoid constantly staring at them. And guess what? The fucker *never* stops touching Laila with his huge hands. *Ever.* At any given moment, Mr. Basketball's got his arm around Laila's shoulders, or a hand covering hers. Or maybe he's got his hand under the table, doing God knows what to her under there. Or if not any of that, he's touching her hair or leaning in to whisper into her ear—oftentimes, immediately after glowering at *me*.

Actually, I don't know if I'm imagining that last part. The glowering. Is Malik Wallace a mind reader? Or is the booze making my face a whole lot more readable than usual? Either way, the man clearly wants me, and everyone in this restaurant, to know the magnificent, sultry, talented Laila Fitzgerald is *his*.

The crazy thing is I don't get jealous, except when it

comes to Laila. Why should I, when there are unlimited fish in the sea? And yet, here I am, contemplating physically attacking a professional athlete, despite my brain knowing, logically, he'd almost certainly beat my ass. Also, logically speaking, I know Malik's got every right to drape himself over his *own* girlfriend. I'm nobody to Laila, after all. If Malik were out of the picture, she'd be in Kendrick's arms. Not mine. And yet, I can't stop staring and plotting Malik's untimely demise.

I think the part that burns me the most is knowing Laila hooked up with Malik after meeting him at Reed's party. If I hadn't left when I did that night, if I'd sucked it up and walked over to her to welcome her to the tour the way my bandmates did, would everything be different now? I thought I was stepping aside for my best friend, which is something I can stomach, though not happily. But it turns out, I was stepping aside for Malik Wallace. And realizing that feels like a special kind of torture.

Kendrick leans into me, just as Malik whispers something to Laila that makes her giggle. "Fuck my life," Kendrick mutters. "Sitting across from them is my personal version of hell."

"Sorry, brother. That sucks. Let's drink another round."

I flag a server—a young woman I'd guess is an aspiring actress or model or dancer, given that this is Manhattan and she's lithe and stunning. And she immediately strides over to me with a big smile on her face.

"Another round," I say, motioning to my empty glass and Kendrick's. "Make 'em both doubles this time."

"Triples," Kendrick says.

"You got it, boys," she says with a wink. She bites her lower lip and leans into me. "If this is inappropriate, I'm sorry. But would you and Kendrick mind taking a selfie with me? I'm a huge fan."

Kendrick agrees, of course, because he's much nicer than me, and she pokes her head between us and snaps the photo. But when that task is done, she doesn't leave. Rather, she turns her attention on me, specifically, in a way I've seen many times, and whispers, "I'm a *huge* fan, Savage."

Well, that's not subtle. If history has taught me anything, she's telling me she's down to sleep with me tonight. If I'm right about that, I'm not interested. However, I couldn't help noticing, as we took that selfie, Laila was watching the interaction with blazing eyes. So, I decide, interested or not, to let Laila think she's not the only one who'll be getting laid tonight.

"Come here," I say to the waitress. I motion to her to lean closer, like I'm going to tell her a secret, and she follows my command with obvious excitement. I lean in, my body language shifting into fuckboy mode, the same way it did when I hit on Georgina at Reed's party. "What's your name, beautiful?"

"Desiree," she replies breathlessly. And I can almost see her heart pounding against her sternum.

"That's a sexy name. What's your favorite Fugitive Summer song?"

She doesn't hesitate. "'Come with Me.'"

It's not a surprise. I don't know if that song is genuinely a top favorite for all the women who've claimed as much. All I know is that song has gotten me laid more times than I can count. Whenever they say they love that one, in particular— my band's most brazenly sexual song—and then look at me the way this waitress is looking at me now—I can pretty much count on the next thing the woman says making it clear she's down to fuck.

The waitress licks her lips and adds, "I listen to that song *a lot,* Savage. *A lot, a lot.*"

It's been a while since I've had this particular conversation, simply because I grew tired of leading women down this predictable path. But I guess it's like riding a bike. You never truly forget how to ride, no matter how long it's been. Especially when you're trying to make a certain pop star with blazing blue eyes and sensual lips feel the same thing you've been feeling all night. *Seething jealousy.*

I glance at Laila to make sure she's still watching the show. She is. So, I decide to turn up the heat. Raising my voice a bit, for Laila's benefit, of course, I ask the waitress, "What are you doing later tonight, Desiree?"

"Nothing at all. I get off at midnight and don't work again until four tomorrow."

"That's convenient," I say. "As luck would have it, we've got a free day tomorrow. No travel. No show. I was planning to chill in my hotel room tomorrow."

Her ample chest heaves with excitement. "If you'd like some company, I could give you my number . . ."

"Sounds good." I glance at Laila again as I pull out my phone, and her face is a forest fire. At my prompting, the waitress tells me her number, and I make a big show of making sure I've entered it correctly.

"Yep, that's it," the waitress says. "I hope you call me tonight."

"I will," I say, although I'm not sure that's true. As long as I get her to sign an NDA, like Eli keeps telling me to do these days, then there's no reason for me *not* to call her. Fucking this waitress for ten hours straight would be a whole lot better than tossing and turning all night, imagining Malik fucking Laila. And yet, for some reason, I don't feel enthusiastic about the idea. In fact, the thought only makes me want to drink some more.

The waitress straightens up. "Crap. My manager is mad at me. I've got to get back to work. I'll get those drinks for you, gentlemen."

"Tequila shots, too!" Kendrick shouts.

"Got it!"

As the waitress strides away, I return my attention to Laila, eager to flash her a smug smile, but to my extreme disappointment, Laila isn't watching me any longer. She's standing and engaged in conversation with Reed.

"Thanks so much, Laila," Reed is saying. "I really appreciate this."

"I'm happy to do it," Laila replies. "Alessandra is adorable, and you know I adore Fish."

Reed says something I don't catch, due to some laughter at the far end of our table, and they wrap up their conversation.

Laila sits back down and immediately fields some seriously angry energy from Malik. I can't hear what he says to her, but, clearly, he's not happy with her.

"*Seriously*?" Laila replies sharply to Malik. She whisper-shouts, "I couldn't say no. Reed's the head of my label! And Alessandra is a brand-new artist who's really sweet. And her boyfriend, Fish, is a good friend of mine. You think, despite all that, I should have said no, so we could 'hang out' tomorrow?"

Malik snaps, "Don't get all pissy with me. You should be happy I wanted you to spend your free day with me."

"Keep your voice down," Laila says, before leaning in and whisper-shouting something I can't make out. Whatever it is, Malik doesn't like it.

"Thank you, Baby Jesus, there's *finally* trouble in paradise," Kendrick whispers to me.

"Sure looks like it," I say. "What did Reed ask Laila to do tomorrow? I couldn't hear."

"You know Fish's girlfriend, Alessandra?"

He motions to the end of the table, but I nod without looking. Everyone here knows Fish's girlfriend, Alessandra, at this point. Not only is she the same girl who looked so smitten with Fish at Reed's party two months ago, not only is she sitting next to Fish at the table now, Fish gave that girl a whopper of a kiss in the middle of the greenroom earlier, in front of *everyone,* and then proceeded to sing to her onstage during the concert. So, yeah, to put it mildly, I know Fish's girlfriend, Alessandra. In fact, so does everyone in the world by now.

Kendrick continues, "Alessandra has a one-song deal with River Records and her music video is shooting tomorrow in Brooklyn. From what I've gathered, it sounds like Reed and the director down there . . . That woman there." He points to a cute brunette who's sitting next to Reed. "Reed and the director came up with some complicated new storyline for the music video, just now, and Reed asked Laila to play a big part in it. Which means she'll be busy shooting all day tomorrow." Kendrick smiles wickedly. "Rather than hanging out with Malik."

I snicker. "What a cry baby."

Kendrick nods. "Hopefully, he'll keep crying until she's pissed enough to dump his ass tonight." He smiles. "And when she needs a shoulder to cry on tomorrow night, I'll be Johnny on the Spot."

Our server, Desiree, arrives with our new drinks and shots —plus, a flirtatious smile for me—and we dig in. We watch Reed making his way around the table, talking to every band, one by one, until, finally, reaching our band. After greeting all five of us, Reed tell us everything Kendrick has already told me about Alessandra's video shoot tomorrow. Except Reed doesn't ask us to come down for the whole day, as he asked Laila to do. He requests we drop by, at any convenient time, to shoot quick cameos. "I know it's your free day tomorrow," Reed says. "But I'll owe you guys a favor if you stop by. The cameos will take no more than fifteen minutes to shoot. You'd sit at a table in a coffeehouse and pretend to watch Alessandra playing her guitar onstage. We'll stitch it all together later in post-production."

Everyone in my band, other than me, says they'll try but can't promise anything. They're not trying to be jerks. It's just that everyone looks forward to those rare days off on the schedule, when we can crash and burn and not have a single obligation.

Reed looks at me, clearly most interested in securing my face, above all others, for the video. "I'd consider it a personal favor to me if you'd come tomorrow, Savage," he says. "It's important to me, for personal reasons, to make this song a huge hit for Alessandra. As big as I can make it." He pauses and it's clear it's going to pain him to say whatever's on his tongue. But he says it, anyway. "Please."

Whoa. That was as close to groveling as I've ever heard from Reed. Even so, I don't care about making Reed happy, or having him owe me a favor. What I *do* care about, however, is that Laila has already committed to being there tomorrow, all day—and, apparently, *without* Malik. Also, that she's looking at me right now, awaiting my response with bated breath.

"Yeah, I'm down," I say. "As long as I don't need to get there until the afternoon." I look at Laila and smirk. "It sounds like I'm gonna be pretty busy tonight and into the first part of the morning."

Laila snarls before looking away and I can't help smiling broadly at her reaction. God, she's fun. Wind her up and watch her go.

Reed claps my shoulder and thanks me effusively, before moving along to the next band at the table, the guys from Watch Party.

Biting back my smile, I return my attention to Laila across the table and discover she's gotten up and is talking to

Fish and Alessandra and Georgina. But guess who's looking straight at me right now? *Malik*. With eyes like laser beams.

I rise, flip him off, and stride to the bathroom on the far side of the restaurant. After taking a piss, I wash my hands and face and stare at myself in the mirror for a moment. "Pull yourself together," I whisper. "If you had her, you wouldn't even want her. You only want what you can't have." Satisfied with my pep talk, I open the door to the bathroom and enter the short hallway, and immediately get slammed, rather forcefully, into a wall.

"Are you fucking her?" Malik whisper-shouts, his large body pinning mine into the wall.

"Fuck off," I say, pushing against his hulking frame. But it's no use. As fit as I am, his body is a brick wall.

He grabs my shirt. "Are you the reason she never answers my calls?"

"Let go of me unless you want to hear from my lawyers, Malik."

He exhales a warm breath on my face and lets me go. Which is a damned good thing because, now that I'm here, I'm realizing my fantasy about strangling him was a pipe dream.

I lean into Malik's angry face. "If I were fucking Laila, trust me, you wouldn't be here tonight to ask me about it. One taste of me, and she'd ditch your ass in a heartbeat."

Without warning, he shoves me again, crashing my back into the wall—although, thankfully, I'm way too drunk to feel it. Immediately, a nearby waiter appears in the hallway and frantically orders Malik to leave the area.

As Malik walks back to the table, I yell to his back, "If you can't keep your woman satisfied, don't blame me!"

"Mr. Savage, please," the waiter says. "Cool off outside. *Please.*"

"Gladly."

My veins flooded with adrenaline and my breathing ragged and hot, I stalk across the restaurant and straight outside into the crisp night, mustering every drop of willpower along the way not to punch a hole in a fucking wall.

TWELVE
SAVAGE

Once outside in front of the restaurant, I bum a cigarette off one of the valet parkers and then pace back and forth, inhaling on it like a lifeline, until, a moment later, Laila bursts outside and marches up to me.

"What the hell is wrong with you?" she shouts. "Malik said you *attacked* him outside the bathrooms?"

I roll my eyes. "Wow, you've got yourself a real gem there, Laila. What are you doing with a psychopath like him?"

Her nostrils flare. "What's it to you?"

My body feels alive with adrenaline and booze—jealousy and lust. "You can get any man you want and you know it. You've got the nicest guy in the world, practically throwing himself at you—which, by the way, he *never* does for *anyone* —and you'd rather be with an asshole like *Malik*?"

She looks at me blankly.

"Kendrick!" I shout, enraged at her lack of comprehension. "Don't pretend you don't know he's totally into you."

Now it's Laila's turn to be enraged. "That's what you

want to say to me right now?" she yells. "The most pressing thing you want to tell me in this moment is that you're pissed I haven't given *Kendrick* a shot?" She pulls on her hair and screams at the top of her lungs. "God, I hate you! You're so infuriating!"

I blow smoke in her face and she coughs and sputters and waves at the air.

"Put that thing out!" she screams. "Kill yourself, if you must. But leave me out of it!"

I drop the cigarette onto the sidewalk and stub it out angrily with my shoe. "Your boyfriend is the one who attacked me, Laila. Not the other way around. He's convinced you've been sleeping with me."

She looks genuinely concerned. "Are you hurt?"

"Not at all, unless you count the fact that I'm pained you've got such bad taste in men."

Her chest heaves sharply. "Why do you care, Savage? You want me to break up with him, so you can pimp me out to *Kendrick*?" She waits a beat for my reply and when it doesn't come, she turns into a goddamned demon before my eyes. "You'd sleep better at night knowing *Kendrick* was the one fucking me, instead of *Malik*? Huh? Is that what you want? Or is there someone else you'd prefer to do the fucking?"

Oh, God, I want her. I want to pull her to me and press my lips to hers and claim her right here and now. I want to take her back to my hotel room and rip off her clothes and eat her pussy and do every filthy thing imaginable to her. But before I've figured out if I'm willing to betray Kendrick, without first speaking to him about it, a group that includes Kendrick emerges from the restaurant. Besides my best friend, there's Ruby and Kai, Reed and Georgina, the guys from 22 Goats and their dates, and more.

"Come with us, Laila," Kendrick says. "We're going to

Times Square to see a billboard of Colin in his underwear." He's talking about Colin Beretta, the drummer of 22 Goats—a tatted badass who hates my guts because I fucked his on-again-off-again girlfriend last year while they were on a break.

"I can't make it," Laila says curtly. "But, thanks."

Kendrick looks at me. "I didn't bother asking you because I know you've got plans with the waitress. Have fun!" With that, he jogs to catch up to the group, and when I return to Laila, or at least, to the spot where she was standing a minute ago, she's gone—angrily stomping toward the front door of the restaurant.

"Laila!" I shout at the top of my lungs. And she turns around in front of the doorway, breathing hard.

"Break up with him."

She swallows hard. "And then what, Savage? You'd fuck me like one of your groupies? Like that waitress inside? Wow, lucky me! Or would you pimp me out to *Kendrick*? Either way, no thanks." With that, she turns on her heel and marches into the restaurant. And the minute she's gone, some fans who've been standing on the sidelines of our screaming match descend on me, apparently unbothered by my obvious personal turmoil.

The bodyguard assigned to me appears, out of nowhere, and helps me negotiate the onslaught. With his help, I briefly go through the motions, giving a few selfies, until Laila emerges from the restaurant with Malik in tow, both of them looking somber. Quickly, they dip into a dark SUV that's been awaiting them at the curb. And just like that, they're gone. Heading back to the hotel to fight or fuck or both.

And I'm distraught.

I mumble my goodbyes to the remaining fans and quickly take off down the street, with my bodyguard keeping pace behind me. A couple blocks into my journey, I dip into a liquor store and buy a large bottle of vodka, which I drink like Gatorade throughout the remainder of my journey.

Not surprisingly, by the time I arrive at my hotel, I'm not only blitzed out of my mind, I'm also beside myself with rage and regret. By now, I've relived my fight with Laila a hundred times, each time wishing I'd played it differently. Let down my guard. Figured out my feelings in time to say them out loud to her. Whatever those feelings might be. Honestly, I'm still not entirely sure.

I slide the keycard in my door and hurtle myself into my suite and immediately do the thing I've been aching to do all night: I punch a hole in the wall. Because that's what rockstar clichés do, right? They have drunken temper tantrums and trash their hotel rooms.

I can't believe I've been jacking off, alone in my room, every night of this goddamned tour, foregoing every woman who's slipped me her number, all because I've been waiting like a puppy for Laila to be single. For Kendrick to grow tired of waiting for Laila to be single. For Kendrick to do what he always does on every tour—slide into a tour "relationship" with some staffer or crew member—and thereby leave me to finally seduce Laila, boyfriend or not, without worrying that I'm betraying my best friend. The guy who believed in me, when nobody else did, changing my life forever.

My knuckles throbbing from punching the wall, I grab my phone and swipe into my contacts, looking for that waitress' number. But, quickly, I realize I don't want her. If Laila hadn't been sitting there tonight, watching me flirt, I never would have bothered to get that number at all. The waitress was too thirsty for my taste. Just like that model in Barcelona who fucked me and kissed me and said all the right things on a night when I was feeling particularly lonely . . . and then took off with my wallet and made my dick an internet star.

I toss my phone onto the nightstand with a loud grunt, just

before a wave of nausea seizes me. I stumble into the bath-room and wash my face with cold water, trying to stave off the inevitable. But it's no use. *Fuck.*

I drop to my knees at the toilet and lose my fancy dinner and drinks into the bowl. When I'm finally empty, I wash my face again, brush my teeth, strip off my clothes, and stagger, naked, into the bedroom. I flop onto the bed, groaning as the room spins around me. As visions of Laila getting fucked by Malik ravage my drunken brain.

Ever since Philly, I've been busting my ass to be on time for Laila—to soundchecks and buses. As much as possible, anyway. Have I been perfect? No. Because, unfortunately, I get easily distracted sometimes. While, other times, I get hyper-fixated. Especially when writing a song, time ceases to exist for me. Which isn't a great thing for time management. Plus, I try to say yes whenever Mimi wants to talk to me, even if the timing is terrible. So, yeah, I admit I'm not going to win any prizes for punctuality. But I have genuinely tried my best, and for only one reason: *to make Laila like me.*

But now, I realize I never should have bothered. No matter what I do, she's always going to hate me and think I'm a selfish rockstar cliché—an asshole who doesn't give a shit about anyone but himself. Well, fuck Laila Fitzgerald. If she thinks she's already got plenty of reasons to hate me, then she ain't seen nothing yet.

"Cut!" Maddy, the director of the music video, calls out. "That was perfect, ladies! Great job."

I straighten up and let the baseball bat in my hand dangle at my side, as Reed's girlfriend, Georgina, my co-star in this scene, does the same. We're shooting on the street in front of the coffeehouse where we've been shooting throughout the day—a scene featuring Georgina and me bashing the hell out of an old sedan that's supposedly owned by our two-timing boyfriend, played by hunky actor Keane Morgan.

Throughout this particular scene, Keane's been looking on, horrified and helpless, as Georgina and I have smashed his car to smithereens. It's the climactic final scene of our "love triangle" storyline. And I must say, it's been my favorite to shoot. Talk about cathartic! The perfect release after my two fights last night. First, the one I had with Savage in front of the restaurant. And, later, the one I had with Malik in the car, when I soundly told him to fuck right off and never, ever call me again.

As it's turned out, shooting this video was the perfect way

to spend the day. The song is fantastic. The artist, Alessandra, sweet and talented. And the video concept is hilarious and adorable. Plus, it's been fun seeing all the River Records artists who've dropped by to shoot their cameos. Surely, with everything this video has going for it, it's going to become a viral sensation.

Not surprisingly, Savage was too busy banging his waitress to keep his word and come down here today. But, luckily for Alessandra, everyone else who gave their word to Reed last night, kept it.

Logically, I know I should have expected Savage to break his promise to Reed. And yet, somehow, my heart stupidly held onto hope he'd finally do something kind and selfless, for once in his life. If only for Fish, who's a great and loyal friend to everyone. But I guess Savage is always gonna be Savage. A narcissist, through and through.

"Okay, guys," our director, Maddy, says. She looks at her watch. "With the remainder of our daylight, I'd like to shoot some close-ups and pickups. Shots of Laila and Georgina standing over the car, raising their bats and looking like badass bitches."

Georgina and I respond enthusiastically, of course. But as Maddy moves us into position, the unthinkable happens. A taxi pulls up a few feet away and Savage emerges, looking like a shit sandwich.

He drags his sorry ass to the stunned group, runs his hand through his dark hair, and says, "Am I too late to shoot my cameo?"

"No, not at all!" Maddy chirps. "We're *so* glad you made it!" She turns to Georgina and me. "Why don't you ladies take five while we shoot Savage inside for a couple minutes. This will be quick."

"That's okay," Savage says. "Finish what you're shooting here, while you've still got good light. I'm not in any rush."

"Oh, thank you," Maddy says. "Are you sure?"

"Absolutely." Savage walks over to stand with Fish and Reed, who are watching from a distance, while Maddy returns her attention to directing Georgina, Keane, and me.

Maddy says, "Laila, stand over there, holding the baseball bat over your head, like you're going to smash the car."

I comply with Maddy's request, and she looks at a nearby monitor.

"Great. Just move to your left a touch. Perfect. Now, give me your bitchiest face and stick out your chest."

I follow her directions and she hoots with laughter.

"You're so freaking gorgeous, Laila. And *so* photogenic. Okay, we've got what we need from you. Georgina, you're up. Same thing."

As Maddy directs Georgina, I can't help looking at Savage. And what I see there is molten lava. Which, frankly, pisses me off. He has the nerve to look at me with lust in his eyes, after spending the day in a marathon fuck session with that waitress?

I saunter over to Savage and stand next to him, shoulder to shoulder, watching Maddy finish up with Georgina.

"Hello, Adrian," I say.

"Hello, Fitzy."

"You look like shit. You didn't get much sleep last night, huh?"

He says nothing.

I shouldn't do it. I know it. But letting sleeping dogs lie has never been my strong suit. My jaw tight, I say, "I hope you signed the waitress' tits before you sent her on her merry way. That'd be an appropriate souvenir."

The slightest smirk curls Savage's sensuous lips. "I did, actually. Signed her ass and pussy, too."

"Lovely. So glad you two had fun."

"We sure did. How about you and Malik?"

"Oh, we had a blast. I can barely walk today."

"Lovely."

"It was. I'm so impressed you managed to get your ass down here, despite your marathon fuck session."

"What can I say? I'm a saint."

"That's the word I always think of when I think of you. Adrian Savage. He's a *saint*."

"Hey, fun fact. Did you know cheaters are the ones who are always the most paranoid about their girlfriends cheating on them?"

"Is that so? How interesting."

"It's a proven fact. Cheaters project what *they* do—aka *cheating*—onto their partner. And then, in some cases, attack innocent bystanders outside of restaurant bathrooms, usually because they're insecure about their tiny dicks."

"Well, that's not an issue for Malik."

"Glad to hear it."

"Me, too," I say, my eyes trained on the action in front of Maddy's camera. "In fact, I had the best sex of my life with Malik last night. Wooh! Hot, hot, hot."

"What does the 'best sex of your life' mean to you, Laila? Stamina? Emotional connection?"

"Both."

"Nice. I notice you didn't mention multiple orgasms. Squirting orgasms . . ."

"Oh, well, that, too. *Of course*. In fact, I've never had *two* squirting orgasms in a row the way I did last night. Woo! Man, oh man, Malik really got me going like a geyser."

His features contort with disdain. "You think squirting *twice* is 'coming like a geyser'? Ha! You poor thing." He pats my shoulder. "Thoughts and prayers."

Damn! I wanted my lie to sound believable, so I tried to pick a highly credible number. In truth, I haven't had multiple orgasms before, let alone a squirting one—or *two*—so I thought what I said would sound super impressive. But is having *two* orgasms, in rapid-fire succession, let alone squirting ones—actually unimpressive, or is Savage messing with me?

"We're ready for you, Savage," Maddy says, saving me from myself.

Savage smiles at her. "You only need me to sit at a table and pretend I'm watching Alessandra performing, right?"

"Yep. That's it. Easy peasy."

"Okay, good. If you'd said you need me to walk on-camera, or dance around or something, that'd be a tough one for me. I'm super exhausted from screwing a waitress all night and day and making her squirt, five times, in rapid succession."

"Oh," Maddy says. "Okay. Um. Yeah, no worries there. Just sit and nod your head a little."

"Cool." Savage opens the door to the coffeehouse, cool as a cucumber, and motions for Maddy to pass through. She enters the building, followed by her camera operators and crew. Then, Reed, Georgina, Fish, and Alessandra. Until finally, everyone has entered the building through the door held by Savage, except for me. Smiling politely at me, his dark eyes burning like hot coals, Savage says, "After you, my dear."

"I think I'll stay out here and get some fresh air," I say. "Maybe call my boyfriend and thank him for all the amazing sex last night."

"I'm sure he'll appreciate the call. Where is he, by the way? I would have expected him to come down here to cheer you on. Maybe even shoot a cameo himself. Why not?"

"Oh, he desperately wanted to come, but something came up this morning—some big basketball thing."

"A basketball 'thing'?"

"A meeting."

"A basketball *meeting*?"

"Mm-hmm. So, I told him to go to his thing to talk about basketball things and meet me back in our room tonight for another round of amazing sex."

"Cool. Well, here's hoping Malik watches a few instructional videos on YouTube before tonight, right?" He holds up crossed fingers. "A girl can hope." With that, he strides through the door, leaving me standing alone on the sidewalk, feeling even more homicidal than I did last night when I kicked that bastard Malik out of the SUV—and out of my life —for good.

FOURTEEN
LAILA

Atlanta, Georgia

The crowd cheers as I strike my final note of my final song. And when the music stops, the crowd breaks into a veritable roar. Their applause is mostly for me, I think. But I'm not stupid. I'm well aware they're also thrilled to be that much closer to Fugitive Summer finally taking the stage.

"Thank you, Atlanta!" I shout into my microphone, feeling practically drugged with euphoria. I can't believe I get to do this for a living! And that, in each new city, audiences have increasingly started singing along with *every* word to *every* song. Not just the big hit from my debut album. Not only the lead-off single from my sophomore one. And not just the catchy choruses. They're singing the verses *and* choruses of songs that haven't made a big splash on the charts, as of yet! When this tour began six weeks ago, I never would have dreamed that big.

I know the phrase "this is a dream come true" is frequently overused in this world. But that's the phrase that comes to mind whenever I'm performing. When I'm *offstage,* however? Not so much, thanks to the persistent tension between Savage and me, provoked by his constantly nightmarish behavior. I've said nothing. Held my tongue. But the tension between us could be cut with a knife. It's all worth it, however, because that forty-five minutes onstage every other day makes up for the aggravation he causes me by a long mile.

"Are you ready for Fugitive Summer?" I bellow to the crowd. And, as always, at the mention of the headliner, the crowd's cheering and applause morphs into a tsunami of excitement. Chuckling, I add, "Well, you're in luck, because they're coming out *really* soon—and, trust me, they're gonna blow you awaaaaaay!"

As the crowd continues to go wild, I exit the stage, blowing kisses and waving as I go. Once offstage, I do what I always do in moments like this: I share a group hug with my amazing backing band, accept a large bottle of water from my assistant, and then head down the hallway toward my latest assigned dressing room. Always the smallest one in the building, which is perfectly fine with me.

As usual, my post-show plan is this: I'll immediately remove my makeup and slip into something soft and comfortable. I'll enjoy a light snack and glass of white wine while listening to Fugitive Summer's set from my couch. Sometimes, depending on my mood, I might sneak into the wings to watch the headliner's show, taking care to stand where Savage can't see me. Wouldn't want to give him the satisfaction. But the truth is, no matter how horrible Savage has been offstage these past few weeks—ever since New York, he's turned into a freaking monster!—he's still one of the best performers in the business. To be honest, I not only feel enthralled watching him, every time, along with his fans, I also learn a lot about letting go onstage and leaving it all out there.

Once Fugitive Summer's set is over, I'll head to my hotel room, like I always do, in whatever city, and soak in my bathtub with a second glass of wine. Substitute "hot tub" for "bathtub," if there's one available to me. While soaking, I'll text with my sister or Mom, or Aloha, or read a romance novel, and then head to bed, where I'll watch a show of some sort. Probably pull out my vibrator, if I haven't already gotten myself off in the tub. And then, finally I'll close my eyes and drift off. All of it, to be rinsed and repeated in the next city. And you know what? I love the routine. In fact, I've come to cherish it. Because it keeps me sane to know what comes next in my little corner of the world, amidst Savage's ever-increasing chaos and animus.

Sometimes, I admit I want to break my routine to say yes to Kendrick's frequent invitations to hang out with Fugitive Summer after their show. I adore everyone in that band, other than Savage, and lots of staff and crew members, too. But there's no way I'm going to subject myself to partying with Savage these days. Not when I'm on the bitter cusp of exploding like a bomb and word-vomiting all over him about his horrible behavior throughout this tour, but especially since New York.

"Thanks, Katrina," I say, handing my assistant my empty water bottle. We reach my dressing room and open the door . . . and discover Savage inside the room. Sitting on my couch while flirting intimately with a groupie who's sitting on his lap. *Again.* Jesus! This is the *third* time in two weeks I've stumbled upon this exact vignette in *my* dressing room, immediately after my set! "Get out!" I shriek, the past weeks of aggravation boiling over into an uncontainable flood.

I've been biting my tongue for weeks. But this time, I

can't contain myself. I don't care if I'm embarrassing Mr. Rockstar in front of his new fuck buddy. I don't care if nearby staff and crew can overhear me shrieking like a madwoman. I don't care if Savage is the star of the headliner and I'm the peon opener. *I don't care about any of it!* He's turned into a monster these past few weeks—the biggest jerk I've ever met —nothing at all like the surprisingly cool dude I shared a bottle of whiskey with in Providence. And, truly, someone has to put this jackass in his place, once and for all. So, it might as well be me.

I shout, "The much bigger dressing room assigned to the *headliner* isn't big enough to contain your massive ego, so you needed to take over both yours *and* mine?"

Savage languidly twirls a lock of the woman's hair around his fingertip, his dark eyes boring holes into my face. "I took a wrong turn, Fitzy. Chill out. These hallways can be confusing."

God, I hate him. Literally growling with frustration, I bolt out of my dressing room, toward his. If Mr. Rockstar is going to hang out in my teeny-tiny dressing room with his latest groupie, then I'm going to hang out in his much larger one, with his band, all of whom I like a million times more than *him.* But before I've reached my destination, as I enter a large backstage area where lots of crew and staffers are busy getting ready for Fugitive Summer's entrance onto the stage, I feel Savage's body heat immediately behind me, sending tingles across my skin, against my will. I hear his footfalls and ragged breath. Sense the shift in the air that always happens in his presence.

He grasps my arm. "Laila. *Stop.*"

I whirl around and face him, breathing hard . . . and immediately lose it. I've been biting my tongue for several weeks now, ever since New York, when we tore into each other on the sidewalk in front of that restaurant—and I can't hold in my contempt for this rude, selfish man-child a second longer. In a torrent of angry words, I let loose on him, ripping him a new asshole for his selfishness, rudeness, and extreme unprofessionalism, especially over the past couple weeks. I rail against him for all the times he's been insanely late for soundchecks and the buses. And then, I scream at him even more passionately about the time, just last week, Savage kept a room full of VIP fans waiting a ridiculously long amount of time.

I wasn't there to see Savage's bad behavior at that VIP event, and it didn't affect me, personally. But I heard about it and it pissed me off! Apparently, when Savage finally arrived, after keeping those poor people waiting far too long for their demi-god, he only half-heartedly rushed through his duties in lightning speed. Totally unacceptable!

Wrapping up my diatribe, I shout, "Remember in Providence, you told me you feared becoming a rockstar cliché?" I take a step forward and shove my nose into his face, my breathing hot and heavy. "Well, guess what, *Adrian*? Transformation complete!"

Savage's dark eyes drift to my lips for the briefest moment. But then, he takes in the shocked faces of the crew and staffers who've witnessed my tirade. And, suddenly, he transforms into a raging lunatic, before my eyes.

Practically vibrating with rage, Savage grits his teeth and lets me have it for a full five minutes, basically telling me in every conceivable way I need to know my place, mind my business, and shut the fuck up. As the cherry on top, Savage also tells me I'm lucky to be on this tour at all—that, in fact, he didn't want me here, and told Reed as much, from the get-go.

"But since you *are* here, against my will," he spits out, "you should be kissing my goddamned ass, not ripping it a new asshole—and especially not in front of the entire crew."

He motions to the flabbergasted crowd of people standing around us, their mouths hanging open—a group that now includes not only staff and crew, but the members of Fugitive Summer, as well. "Know your place, Laila. Or, I assure you, you can and will be replaced." He smiles at whatever panic he's seeing on my face. "You think you're the one who makes every single one of these people's paychecks possible? You think the fans in this stadium paid to see *you*? Think again!"

He steps forward, closing the already small gap between us, and gets right into my face.

"Now, why don't you go to your dressing room and have your little glass of white wine and call your asshole boyfriend to tell him about me being a big, fat meanie to you tonight. Actually, I don't care what you do, as long as you stay the fuck out my way for the rest of the night, so I don't cut your ass from the tour, just to teach you a much-needed lesson in humility." He exhales, and his warm breath releases onto my face. "Now, if you'll excuse me, it's time for me to head onstage to entertain the thousands of people who came out tonight to watch me shake my ass like a motherfucking rock-star cliché."

Phoenix, Arizona

When Kendrick and I step outside the door of his hotel suite, the moonlit air feels unexpectedly warm for this late hour.

"Thanks for the birthday party, brother," I say, gripping Kendrick's sideways palm.

After releasing my hand, Kendrick looks around at the moonlit night and winces. "It's *still* hot as an oven out here, at this hour?"

"Welcome to Phoenix," I quip. As Kendrick knows, I spent my earliest years in this oven of a city, before moving to Chicago at age twelve to live with my grandma in her apartment complex, which was where I met the Cook brothers, whose family lived down the hall.

"You were ruthless in 'Birthday Truth or Dare' tonight," Kendrick says, laughing.

I shake my head. "You were way more ruthless on your

birthday. Surely, making the head of our label hate my guts is far worse than me making you *briefly* turn your balls into cucumber slices at the spa."

We laugh together, both of us reliving tonight's silliness. After Kai had passed out on the couch in Kendrick's suite, I dared my best friend to whip out his balls and rest them onto his brother's sleeping eyelids—you know, as if Kai were a customer at a spa and Kendrick's balls were a couple of cucumber slices. And thanks to the rules of our game, Kendrick couldn't refuse. In fact, the dude is such a good sport he even went so far as to remain in that compromised position for a full minute, albeit with his large hands covering his dong, and invited everyone at the party to snap close-up shots of his brother's ball-covered face.

It was priceless. Easily, the highlight of my birthday party. The lowlight, however? Laila not showing up, despite Kendrick extending an invitation to her. I don't blame her, of course. I knew the odds were low she'd come, given that she now hates me passionately. The thing is, as much as I've purposefully *tried* to make Laila hate me for weeks now, for reasons only a clinical psychologist would be able to explain to me, I realized tonight, rather starkly, while looking around at the people at my birthday party, I desperately wanted Laila to be there. I realized, in fact, that I'd very much like a do-over now, please. I'd very much like Laila to stop hating me now, please. The only problem? I have no idea how to dig myself out of this stupid hole I've been expertly digging for weeks. I wanted Laila to hate me with the force of a thousand suns? Well, mission accomplished.

Kendrick yawns. "I'm gonna head inside now, before Tracy falls asleep. Goodnight, brother."

He's talking about our tour manager. For the past week or so, Kendrick has been having a "tour fling" with her, which seems to imply he's finally given up on waiting for Laila to break up with Malik. Surely, it's no coincidence I'm only now regretting my strategy with Laila, after it seems crystal clear my best friend has *finally* taken himself out of the hunt.

To be honest, I would have bet any amount of money Laila would have ditched Malik's trashy ass by now. And yet, every single time I've walked past her in a hallway, or overheard her as she's stood nearby, she's *always* on her phone, talking with Malik. Giggling with him. Saying stuff like, "Oh, *Malik*! You're so bad, baby!"

It's the main reason I haven't swallowed my pride and extended an olive branch to Laila yet. Simply because I'm so shocked and appalled and downright pissed she's still giving Malik the time of day. What's wrong with her? But suddenly, now that I'm drunk again, for the first time since New York— only this time, thankfully, a happy kind of drunk—a birthday boy kind of drunk—I feel ready to swallow my pride and finally bury the hatchet with Laila. Now that Kendrick is sleeping with Tracy, and he's finally out of my way, I've decided to go for it, in earnest. I don't care if she's still with Malik. Mr. Basketball isn't here. *And I am.*

"Goodnight, brother," I reply to Kendrick, waving to him. "See you at the buses at *nine*."

Kendrick exhales. "*Eight*!"

"That was a joke."

Kendrick rolls his eyes. "You never know with you. Seriously, don't be late this time, Savage. Everyone is starting to get annoyed with you for being late so much. Not just Laila."

"Yeah, okay. I'll stop being an asshole. I was actually thinking of extending an olive branch to Laila."

"Yeah, that's a good idea. I was actually surprised, now that she's probably single, she didn't stop by the party. But—"

"Laila's *single*?" I blurt, my heart lurching into my mouth.

"Well, I'm *assuming*. I can't imagine she'd stay with Malik after that video of him leaked tonight."

I feel like I'm having a stroke. "*What* video?"

"You didn't see the video of Malik getting blown in a strip club? It's all over the internet! Everyone was passing it around at the party tonight."

Every molecule in my body feels like it's exploding, all at once. "*Nobody showed it to me!*"

"Hang on." Shaking his head, Kendrick reaches into his pocket. "I saw you looking at something with Kai on his phone, laughing your asses off. I assumed—"

"He was showing me Alessandra's funny music video that just released!"

"Okay, calm down." He quickly cues something up on his phone and hands it to me. And a second later I'm watching dark, grainy footage of what looks like Malik Wallace getting head from a woman kneeling between his legs who's wearing nothing but a thong.

My heart is crashing. "Has it been confirmed this is him?"

Kendrick nods. "There's other footage of him walking into the place, in those same clothes. And in that footage, you can clearly see his face." Kendrick takes his phone from me while I walk in tight circles, flailing my arms and breathing hard. After a moment of watching me act like a lunatic, Kendrick lets out a long exhale. "Stop, Savage. It's okay. You've got my blessing."

I stop moving and stare at him. But I don't speak.

"Go get her, man. She's all yours. I know how much you've been wanting her. I've known for a long time. So, go for it."

I can barely breathe. "I'm sorry," I say, a mixture of relief and guilt and excitement flooding me. "I've tried my best not to want her, KC. I've tried to keep my distance and push her away, as best I could, so you could take your shot with her. I swear, I've tried."

"I know you have, brother. Thank you."

I run my palm down my face. "I don't understand my obsession with her. She makes me *crazy*. I haven't even fucked anyone else since I laid eyes on her at Reed's party."

Kendrick's jaw practically drops onto the ground. "But I thought—"

"No."

"The waitress in New York?"

I shake my head. "No. Nobody."

Kendrick processes that for a long moment. "So, you thought making Laila hate your guts would make you want her less?"

"I guess so."

He narrows his eyes. "Or *maybe* you figured her out, even if it was subconsciously. Maybe, you realized making Laila hate your guts would only make her want you more."

"No."

"*Yes*. Don't you see? I've been nothing but nice to that woman since the second I met her. I've been her best friend. And where am I now? Irreversibly in her friend zone. While you've been nothing but an asshole to her from day one. And where are *you*? Firmly in her 'I want to fuck you to death!' zone."

My earlier mixed emotions streamline and converge into nothing but excitement. If that's what Kendrick sees, then it must be true. Because Kendrick Cook is fantastic at reading people, unlike me. I say, "I swear I wasn't trying to cockblock you."

"Not consciously." He exhales. "It doesn't matter. There was no other ending to the story for me. Even if you weren't here, she still wouldn't want me. I realize that now. Clearly, she likes flaming assholes who treat her like shit. Look how long she's hung in there with Malik! I can't compete with that, because I can never *be* that. But you can."

I think maybe he's insulting me. But I feel nothing but complimented. "You think?"

He laughs. "Yeah, I do."

In a flash flood, every drop of desire I've been holding back, denying, and ignoring for so long slams into me. "I'll go to her room now. Would you go inside and ask Tracy to text me Laila's room number?"

"No, Savage. Not now. It's after three and you're shit-faced drunk. Go to *your* room now, get some sleep, wake up and take a shower in the morning and get to the buses on time, and *then* take your shot with Laila in Vegas."

"But—"

"Savage, listen to me. I'm not sabotaging you. I'm *helping* you. You've been smoking like a chimney all night. You know how much Laila hates that. Get cleaned up and talk to her in Vegas, or you'll go there now and wake her up and get into another screaming match with her."

My shoulders slump. He's right, of course. Even if Laila liked me, which she doesn't, she'd shoo me away from her room for smelling like an ashtray. "Okay. I'll get some sleep and talk to her in Vegas. Thanks again for the birthday party." I twist my mouth. "For everything."

Kendrick winks. "Someone's gotta take care of your dumb ass."

"Glad it's you."

"Me, too." He smiles. "See you at the buses at nine."

I crinkle my forehead. "I thought you said eight."

"That was a test."

With a wink, Kendrick heads back into his suite, while I begin walking down a winding path toward my room on the far side of the hotel grounds. But when I reach a slatted fence enclosing the hotel's VIP pool area—an area that's been closed off to the general public for my band's private use during our stay—I suddenly decide a naked, moonlit swim would be the perfect way to cap off my twenty-sixth birthday.

After swiping my keycard and walking through the gate, I look around for an especially dark corner to undress in . . . and that's when I see the universe's birthday gift to me. *Laila Fitzgerald*. She's sitting in a hot tub in a far corner of the space with a large bottle of booze on the ledge, next to her head. Surely, she's drowning her sorrows about that humiliating video of Malik. Which thrills me to no end.

Laila's sandy hair is piled atop her head in a messy bun, making her chiseled cheekbones and plush lips all the more striking. Her alabaster skin, which always sort of glows, looks particularly supernatural in the moonlight.

Without hesitation, I begin walking toward her, whispering to myself as I go, "Happy birthday to me."

I come to a stop on the ledge of the hot tub and look down at Laila . . . and immediately discover that she's naked. *Hallelujah.* And that her body in that water is even more gorgeous than I've fantasized. Man, this birthday just keeps getting better and better.

"You're gorgeous," I whisper, and then press my lips together when I realize I've drunkenly blurted my thoughts aloud.

Laila smirks. "And you're drunk."

I bite back my smile. "A bit."

"Eyes up here, *Adrian.*"

I begrudgingly comply.

She cocks an eyebrow. "I presume you've risked softening your chiseled abs tonight with way too much alcohol, in celebration of your birthday?"

"That's right. Birthdays equal getting shitfaced. No exceptions."

"Happy birthday."

"Thanks. You were invited to the party."

"I was busy."

"Yeah, I bet. I saw the video. You've been drowning your sorrows tonight, I presume?" I gesture to the big bottle of booze on the ledge.

She takes a long swig from her bottle. "Fuck Malik. I don't want to talk about him."

"Fair enough." I bite my lip. Shift my weight. Stare at her tits. And, finally, address the elephant in the room. "So . . . you're single now?"

"I'm very, *very* single."

Hot damn. My eyes drift to her naked body again. And I swear I have to suck on my teeth, vigorously, not to physically drool down my chin at the sight of her.

"Eyes up here, Adrian," she says. And when I comply this time, she smiles and says, "So, are you finally ready to apologize for being an asshole to me?"

I pull a face. "Which time?"

She snorts. "Let's start with your diatribe in Atlanta and work our way from there."

"Nah. You deserved Atlanta. If anyone needs to apologize for being an asshole in Atlanta, it's *you.*"

"Me?"

"Laila, you read me the Riot Act in front of *everyone* on the tour—and, in case you didn't realize this, honey, you're the *opener.*"

She rolls her eyes. "Okay, I admit I *might* have been a little out of line to—"

"A little? Come on. Nobody's here. Admit you blew it. I had to say what I did. You were way out of line."

She twists her mouth. "I admit I shouldn't have said what I did in front of people. I should have pulled you aside and said it all in private. But I don't regret what I said. All of it was true. Really, all you had to say to me was, 'Hey, let's step outside to talk about this.' Or, better yet, 'No problem, Laila! I'll try to be more punctual and professional from now on, as a courtesy not only to you, but to every hardworking person on the tour, not to mention my fans!' And I would have said, 'I'm sorry I snapped in front of everyone. That was totally unprofessional of me.'"

"It was."

She throws up her hands. "Yes, but I picked a poorly timed fist fight with you, Savage. And in response, you pulled out a freaking Uzi!"

"Whatever, dude. We could go 'round and 'round about what happened in Atlanta, and who was the bigger asshole, until the end of time. It would be you, by the way. But what's the point?"

"I literally *hate* you."

I chuckle. "*Or*, we could stop arguing about this, and agree to disagree, and, instead, move on to you answering a *very* important question for me."

She tilts her head, clearly intrigued. "What's the question?"

I squat down, leveling my eyes with hers. "On the night your boyfriend cheated on you for the entire world to see, do you want to sit here, naked, in a hot tub, arguing with a guy who's got a big ol' dick and knows how to use it . . . *or*, do you want to agree to a temporary cease-fire with said guy, long enough to have the best revenge sex of your life?"

Her blue eyes gleaming, Laila bites back a wicked smile. She runs a fingertip across the rim of her bottle like she's teasing the tip of my cock. And every nerve ending in my body feels it. She says, "If I say yes, nobody can ever know."

I flash her a look like I'm deeply insulted. "You'd be *ashamed* for anyone to know you'd fucked The Great Adrian Savage?"

She replies with a look of her own that says, *Well, duh.* She says, "After the way you treated me in Atlanta, with everyone watching? Hell yes, I'd be ashamed for anyone to know I fucked you. Honestly, I'd be mortified."

"Says the girl who's been dating Malik Wallace for at least two months," I toss out. "But, whatever. *Fine.* Nobody will ever know."

"Promise me."

"I promise."

"It'd be revenge sex—a one-time thing that would never happen again," she declares. "Afterwards, it never happened."

"I get it, dude. No need to say it five different ways. Although I want to be able to tell *one* trusted person."

"Kendrick?" she asks.

I nod. "I tell him everything. Plus, I think it will help him let go of any lingering crush he might have on you."

She juts her lower lip. "Poor Kendrick. He's the sweetest person in the world."

"Don't feel sorry for him. He dodged a bullet. You're a psychopath."

To my surprise, she laughs. "True."

"Too bad for him, you're a psychopath who only likes assholes, eh?"

She doesn't correct me. She merely says, "I get to tell one trusted person, too."

"Naturally. Who?"

"Aloha. She'll scream at me. Tell me I'm a predictable idiot. She doesn't like you very much."

"Why not? I'm amazing."

"She thinks you're a player."

"Pfft. Tell her to get in line, sister. Any other conditions, terms, or stipulations, Fitzy?"

She ponders that for a moment. Or, at least, she pretends

to. "No. That's it. I'll probably hate myself in the morning, but I have to know."

"You have to know what?"

Her expression turns wicked. "If those famous shots of you in the shower were real or Photoshopped."

I waggle my eyebrows. "There's only one way to find out."

She pauses. "Do you have a condom?"

"I sure do."

"Okay, then." She pushes out her incredible tits, opens her thighs underneath the water, and purrs, "Then you'd better get your annoying ass in here, before I change my mind."

She doesn't need to ask me twice. With my dick as hard as a stone, I rise to standing and begin peeling off my clothes. When I get down to my briefs, and lodge my thumb underneath the waistband, the look of molten lust on Laila's face reflects my own desires back to me. Every cell in my body on fire, I slowly pull my underwear down, freeing my hard shaft and eliciting a sharp intake of breath from Laila.

"No Photoshop there," she purrs with appreciation. "Damn, boy."

I slip into the water across from her and she immediately rises and greets me. Without hesitation, she grips my dick under the water, while I take her stunning face in my hands, beyond excited to finally kiss the lips that have entranced me for so long . . .

But it's not meant to be.

Laila jerks back, saying, "You've been smoking." And when I nod, she adds, "We shouldn't kiss, anyway. That's way too intimate a thing for one-time-only revenge sex."

I'm disappointed, but such is life. I should have known.

I drop my hands to her bare shoulders and guide her to sitting, while she maintains her firm grip on my dick. My heart pounding, I smile and say, "*Kissing* that dirty little mouth of yours isn't what I've been fantasizing about doing to it, anyway."

She returns my smirk. "You admit you've been fantasizing about me?"

"You're not the only one who gets off on the idea of hate sex, Laila." With that, I reach down between her creamy thighs in the warm water, slide two fingers gently inside her and my thumb over her clit, and proceed to massage and finger her, methodically, without variation or mercy, while tracing her gorgeous lips with my free hand.

Soon, Laila's eyelids begin fluttering. A soft, husky groan rises up in her throat. As her eyes roll back, she takes my finger into her mouth and sucks on it, hard, voraciously, like it's giving her life—and a moment later, her body seizes with an insanely sensual orgasm that sends me to the very brink of release myself.

"Time for your penance," I choke out. My breathing ragged, I step up onto the bench, place my feet on either side of her seated frame, and shove my cock at her mouth, nonverbally commanding her to suck it. Thankfully, she follows instruction well, and takes my full length into her mouth without hesitation. Immediately, she begins sucking me off with enthusiasm, like she's auditioning for a managerial position at a brothel.

Muttering profanities, I grip Laila's sandy hair to steady myself. To keep myself from losing it and shattering into a million pieces. Is there anything hotter than getting blown by the same dirty little mouth that, only days ago, told me to fuck off? If so, I can't imagine it. Not in this lifetime, anyway.

But when my pleasure threatens to boil over, I decide it's time to move along. As much as I've fantasized about coming into Laila's mouth, many, many times, I've been dying to split her body in half with my cock, even more.

Shaking with adrenaline and arousal, I pull out of Laila's mouth and moan at the sultry sight of her. Her full lips are slightly swollen from her voracious effort. And the effect is insanely sexy. Her blue eyes are as ravenous and hungry as I've ever seen them. In short, she looks the hottest she ever has to me. And that's saying a lot.

"Come with me," I choke out, taking her hand. I guide her out of the hot tub and lead her to a nearby lounger in a cabana. After grabbing a condom from my pants on the ground and getting myself swiftly covered, I return to her in the dark shadows of the cabana, spread her smooth thighs as wide as they'll go—so wide, her pussy looks like a blooming flower on the cusp of losing its petals—and plunge myself inside her, growling feverishly as her body molds to mine.

I fuck her hard. So hard, I almost fuck her off the lounger. She digs her nails into my shoulders and keens like an animal as I move on top of her, and every sound she makes sends me higher and higher.

"Let me get on top now," she gasps out. "I come when I'm on top."

There's not a doubt in my mind she'd come like this, and any other way I might fuck her, as long as she's fucking me. But now isn't the time to argue. I've got only one shot to convince this woman to do this with me, again and again throughout the rest of the tour, so I'm going to let her have exactly what she wants.

We rearrange ourselves, until Laila is riding my cock while I'm massaging her clit and telling her how insanely gorgeous she is. How good she feels. And in no time at all, she whimpers from the depths of her abdomen, digs her nails into my chest, and comes so hard, the rippling sensation of her muscles gripping my dick snatches every drop of air from my lungs, while threatening to pull the cum from my balls.

Somehow, probably thanks to the booze in my system,

I'm able to hang on and keep going. I jolt to sitting and frantically begin devouring her breasts and nipples. I'm a hurricane of lust now. A crazed and rabid animal, and so is she. She pushes me flat onto my back again, and begins fucking me with a kind of fervor I've never experienced before. She's not holding back. And I can't get enough.

As she moves, I grope her ass. Grip her hips and move my body with hers. Sweat is pouring off me, mingling with the water still dripping off me from the hot tub. She's glistening, too, giving it her all.

Finally, when I'm sure enough time has passed and touching her clit will only feel good to her again, I start massaging her the way I've already surmised she likes the best. Little circles in a slow and methodical fashion. And soon, my sexy little freak has an orgasm that's so powerful, so forceful, so *hot*, it's like her body is physically *milking* the cum from my balls.

As I let go and surrender to bliss, stars momentarily blind me. Without a thought in my head, other than "I *want*," I sit up and grip Laila's stunning face in my palms, dying to kiss her. But, once again, same as before, she turns her head and denies me.

Quickly, I drop my palms and lie back, remembering the deal. Trembling, I rest my forearm over my eyes, my body and mind reeling in equal measure. That was the best sex of my life. By far. And that should be enough. I shouldn't want more. But I do. I want to kiss her. I want to taste her pussy, from every angle. And then I want to fuck her, again and again, in every position, in every new city.

But first things first. I'll make her come another ten times, right here in Phoenix.

"Come to my room now, Laila," I gasp out. "We're just getting started. Let me eat your pussy till it's time to board the buses."

She looks amused. "It's been a long day." She pats my cheek. "And the buses leave at eight. Thanks for that great revenge sex, though. I really needed that." With that, she slides off me and pads over to a chair, to a white fluffy robe draped across its back.

I sit up onto my forearms. "Let me make you come again and again, Laila. We're just getting started tonight, baby."

"No, we're done. I told you—one and done."

I scoff. "Come on, Laila. Haven't you heard, revenge sex is a dish best served . . . repeatedly and often, with a guy you can't stand?"

Laila chuckles. "I don't think that's the expression."

I'm encouraged by her smile. "You're *finally* single—and we're stuck together for the rest of the tour—*and you're turning me down*? Who else are you gonna fuck for the next month, if not me? Someone in the crew?"

"Maybe."

"Bullshit. You don't want anyone else and neither do I. We've both wanted this for a long time. So, let's do this." I sit up completely in the lounger as she finishes putting on her robe. "Laila, come on. We'll have smoking-hot hate sex in every position, in every city, for the rest of the tour. And when the tour is over, we will be, too."

Laila flashes the same dismissive look as before. "I told you, quite clearly, honey. This was a one-time thing that will never happen again. I was curious . . . and now I know." With that, she tightens the belt on her robe and begins striding away, tossing over her shoulder as she goes, "Don't be late for the buses, *Adrian*."

What the fuck? I just offered this woman a no-strings *month* of hate sex with me—with *me*!—a guy half the female population on planet earth would do *anything* to get with— and she's not taking me up on it? Despite the fact that we just had the hottest sex two people can possibly have?

"I'll text you my room number in Vegas!" I call to her. "Come to my room after tonight's show!"

"Not gonna happen!" she yells back.

"It's happening tonight!"

"One and done!"

"Tonight and every night for the rest of the tour!"

There's only silence now. No footfalls. No reply.

"Laila?"

But she's obviously gone.

Exhaling, I get up and grab my clothes off the ground. I dry myself off with my shirt and throw on my pants. And then, I grab Laila's bottle of whiskey, plop into a nearby chair, and stare at the starry night while drinking and replaying what just happened, over and over again, in my head. I knew it'd be hot with her, but *that* hot? Good lord. When we really got going, it was like she was a junkie, chasing a high. A hate sex high.

I freeze with the lip of the bottle against my mouth. *Now, that's a hit song.*

Hate Sex High.

My heart thumping, I grab my phone and record a flurry of voice memos. Some initial lyrics, a melody for the hook, an idea for the dirty, raunchy beat. Finally, when I get enough recorded to keep the song from slipping back into the ethers before I've arrived in my room to nail it down, I throw on my shirt and sprint out of the pool area, all the way to my suite on the far end of the hotel. Once inside the room, I rip off my damp clothes like a madman, grab my guitar, and start writing "Hate Sex High" in earnest, feeling like a man possessed.

When asked about my songwriting process in interviews, I often say it feels even better than sex, when it's going well. But after fucking Laila the Unicorn Freak, the Hate Sex Addict, the woman who just rocked my world like none other, I know my usual comment isn't entirely accurate. Now that

I've had hate sex with the one and only Laila, I know the more accurate statement is that songwriting, when it's going well, feels better than regular sex, and *almost* as good as hate sex with the hottest woman who's ever walked planet earth, Laila Fitzgerald.

SEVENTEEN

LAILA

Las Vegas, Nevada

As I speed-walk across the sprawling lobby toward the elevator bank on my way to Savage's suite on the twentieth floor of our Vegas hotel, I chastise myself for giving in to temptation. I shouldn't be heading to Savage's room. Not right now. And not at all. The plan, as of mere *hours* ago in Phoenix, was for me to resist Savage and his insanely delicious fingers and cock, that incredible body, those soulful, burning eyes and cut jawline, for the rest of the tour. On principle. To teach that rockstar cliché a lesson about the way he reamed me in Atlanta in front of everyone. To let him know his abundant charms have absolutely zero effect on me.

Ha.

I'm so mad at myself right now. And yet, powerless to change course. At least, if I was going to give in to temptation, which I swore to myself I wouldn't do, then self-respect *demands* I wait at *least* a full week to do it. *At a bare minimum*. Not mere hours. And yet, here I am, speed-walking like a middle-aged mom with a Walkman across this expansive lobby, on my way to Savage's room for Round Two, feeling like a hungry dog who's just heard the dinner bell.

Walking away from Savage on that lounger this morning, and not taking him up on his offer to head to his room, was one of the hardest things I've ever done in my life. But I did it! And I was so damned proud of myself! And now, here I am, not even waiting until after tonight's show to admit I'm hopeless.

I tried to resist Savage when I got his text a half hour ago, telling me his room number and begging me, literally, to let him eat me "from every angle" after tonight's show. Upon receiving that text, I put my phone down on the nightstand in my hotel room and muttered, "Nope. You have zero effect on me, Savage." But when I felt my resolve quickly crumbling like a beachside cliff, I stuffed my phone into my pocket and marched downstairs to the lobby, intending to spend the next few hours before soundcheck in the casino. What better way to distract myself?

But, unfortunately, I ran into our tour manager, Tracy, in the lobby, before making it to the casino. And that's when she mentioned Fugitive Summer had just finished an interview and that all the members of the band were heading to their respective rooms to chill for a bit before soundcheck. In that moment, I felt possessed by a demon. Incapable of waiting a second longer to let Savage make good on his offer to eat me from every angle. I knew, whether I liked it or not, I was a goner.

And now, here I am. Pounding on the call button at the elevator bank in the lobby like my very life depends on it. After only one time with Savage, I feel physically addicted to him. Like I don't care what pride I need to swallow to have him.

When one of the elevators opens, I lope over to it, lurch inside, and punch the button for the twentieth floor. But just before the doors close, two young women enter the small space, and immediately gasp.

"You're Laila Fitzgerald!" one of them says.

"I am. Hello."

"We love you!"

I thank them, and they ask for, and receive, a selfie.

"Are you going to the show tonight?" I ask, intending to offer them tickets if they say they're not already going.

But it's a moot point when they reply, "Hell yes, we're going! Fugitive Summer is our favorite. And you, too!" They look at each other and at the same time, scream, "*Savage*!" And then quickly burst into gleeful, giddy laughter at their silliness.

"He's definitely one of a kind," I say.

One of them says, "Everyone says he's your boyfriend?"

"No!" I bark, involuntarily, unable to keep the panic out of my voice. I clear my throat and try again, this time more calmly. "*No*."

But the damage is done. I've obviously come off as a lunatic. The woman who doth protest *way* too quickly and loudly. The girls pause, apparently sensing, accurately, that I'm off my rocker. "Sorry if we assumed," one of them says, slowly, like she's talking a jumper off a bridge. "We saw that video of you and Savage shouting at each other and—"

"That was a misunderstanding," I reply, my heart thumping. "But there's nothing going on between us, I assure you." They're referring to a video of Savage and me in New York, taken while we screamed at each other on the sidewalk in front of that restaurant. Thankfully, the street noise and other ambient sounds were too loud to capture our words with any clarity. But our body language was clear enough—fierce enough to instantly spark rampant rumors Savage and I were having a passionate lover's spat.

"Well, good, that just leaves him for *us,* then," one of the young women says, making her friend giggle.

The elevator stops on their floor, but one of them holds it open while asking me if I can get them backstage tonight. But now that I've revealed myself to be a total nut job, I'm too embarrassed to see them again.

"No, I'm sorry," I say. "I'm not allowed to do that."

"Oh well. It was worth a try. Say hi to Fugitive Summer for us, okay? Especially Savage!"

"I will!"

After the doors close between us, I begin pounding on the button for Savage's floor, despite it already being lit up. Now that I'm this close to Savage, I can feel his magnetic pull on me. Indeed, my mouth feels like it's physically watering at the thought of what I'm going to do to that man, the minute I have him alone. Hopefully, he'll be smart enough not to speak when I arrive. Or else, quite possibly, he'll talk himself right out of the best blowjob he's ever gotten.

As the elevator glides the rest of the way to the twentieth floor, the horrible thought occurs to me that Savage might not even be in his room, despite what Tracy said about the members of the band heading to their rooms. Savage gets easily distracted, after all. It's one of his defining characteristics. The thing is, if I don't go to his room now, and throw myself at his mercy, if I wait until *after* the show tonight, as his text mentioned, I'm quite certain I'll physically explode.

The elevator pings and stops moving and the doors glide open. As I walk into the hallway on the twentieth floor, I glance at Savage's text to remind myself of his room number, and quickly realize, based on the room numbers nearby, I've unwittingly used the least convenient elevator bank in this sprawling hotel to get here—one that put me all the way down on the farthest end of this long hallway from Savage's suite. As I begin making the trek down the hallway, I feel electrified with anticipation. I hate giving Savage the satisfaction of showing up at his room, especially this quickly, but I can't wait another—

I stop walking abruptly.

Savage has emerged from an elevator bank ahead of me in the hallway and is now walking toward his room at the far end of the hallway, with his back facing me. *And he's not alone.* Besides his two usual bodyguards, one walking ahead of him, and one behind, Savage is accompanied by an attractive brunette. Savage's left arm is draped casually over her slender shoulders while his right hand holds a large bottle of booze. Much to my dismay, the brunette is practically squealing with joy, the same way every one of those groupies sounded each and every time I walked in on Savage in my dressing room.

I try to catch my breath, but I feel like I'm hyperventilating. I'm instantly sick to my stomach. *Stupid, Laila.* A half hour ago, Savage sent me a text, begging me to come to his room tonight. And now, he's bringing some random woman to his room for a quickie before soundcheck?

My desperate brain decides to give the guy the benefit of the doubt. *You're misreading the situation,* I think, before speed-walking a few yards in order to get close enough to overhear Savage's conversation.

"I can't believe I'm here!" the woman is gushing, pressing herself into Savage's side.

Savage pulls her into him, making her squeal again. "You're my birthday present to myself."

My blood runs cold. When I was on top of Savage and fucking him passionately this morning, he looked at my body moving on top of his, grabbed my tits, and whispered,

"Happy birthday to me." And now he's saying basically those same words to this woman? I feel so gullible. So *played*.

"I feel a little tipsy," she declares. "How'd you convince me to have a drink this early? I never day-drink!"

"Hey, it's five o'clock somewhere," Savage says, laughing.

The woman squeezes Savage with enthusiasm. "Happy birthday, Adrian. Now, let me get my hands on that famous body!" She laughs. "*That's* your birthday present! I'm gonna make it extra good!"

"Knock yourself out, Sasha."

Okay, that's it. I've heard enough. Making an "eeww!" face, I turn around and start sprinting down the hallway, feeling physically ill. Where did he meet this one? At the interview he just finished? Was she the interviewer or maybe someone he spotted in the casino on his way to his room— and he simply couldn't resist inviting her back to his room for a quickie before soundcheck, the same way he so deftly invited that waitress to spend the night with him in New York?

I realize Savage never explicitly said his invitation to have sex with me for the rest of the tour would be an exclusive arrangement. But I don't think it's crazy that I assumed as much, given that he texted me his room number and *begged* me to come to him, mere *hours* after having sex with me. At the very least, I think it was fair for me to assume Savage wouldn't have sex with someone else before we possibly reconvened for Round Two in his room in only a few hours.

I pound the call button for the elevator, trembling with adrenaline. How did I let myself think I'd rocked Savage's world on that lounge chair, the way he'd rocked mine? After this morning's tryst with him, I couldn't even sleep, despite my drunk exhaustion. I was too wound up. Already enslaved by what he'd done to my body. And I assumed, like a fool, he was lying awake in his room, too, also reliving the deliciousness in his head.

Well, there's only one conclusion to draw now. The dude is a stone-cold sex addict. A megalomaniac narcissist who literally *needs* fawning validation every single minute of his life.

Rejection.

Humiliation.

Hate.

All of it is coursing through me, all at once.

But, mostly, *hate.*

An elevator going down finally opens and I step inside, physically shaking with rage.

You know what? I don't even care. Screw Savage. Screw Malik, too. And screw my cheating ex-boyfriend, Shawn, while I'm at it. I don't need a man. Especially not one who's going to make me forfeit my self-respect to be with him. *Never again.* Savage once told me to know my worth. Well, guess what? I'm going to follow his advice, from now on.

As the elevator descends, I tap out a text to the personal trainer assigned to the tour—a buff guy named Charlie. He's not on the tour for me, of course. He's a perk for the headliner. But Tracy, our tour manager, told me I'm welcome to use Charlie's services, whenever he's not otherwise engaged. Up until now, I've met with Charlie only here and there, out of respect for my place in the hierarchy. But now, screw it. I'm going to throw myself, and all these negative emotions, into a whole new obsession. A *positive* one. Namely, getting healthy, once and for all, in my mind, body, and spirit.

Me: Hey Charlie! By any chance, are you free to meet me in the hotel gym in fifteen for a session?

. . .

Luckily, Charlie replies immediately:

Charlie: I sure am. See you in 15.

The elevator doors open on my floor and I march toward my room to change into my workout clothes. Fuck Savage. And fuck every man like him. I'm officially done with bad boys, for good. Before now, the history of my romantic entanglements could be summarized as follows:

Laila: Is that a red flag? Nah. Couldn't be, despite its red color and uncanny "flag" shape.

Narrator: *And then she fucked him. Only to find out later, yes, it was, indeed, a red flag.*

Well, no more. Starting now, and for the foreseeable future, but especially for the remaining month of the tour, I'm sending myself to bad boy rehab. I'm going cold turkey, bitches! Thanks for the unsolicited advice about knowing my self-worth, Savage. I promise I'm not going to forget it, ever again.

EIGHTEEN
LAILA

Six weeks later
Los Angeles, California

"You clean up nice, yourself!" the woman onstage says brightly to her co-presenter. She's a longtime country star who won this same award last year, and he's a young buck with his first hit this year—an up-and-comer in tight jeans and a cowboy hat whose ass should be in a shadow box. And as the pair continues their scripted banter, aided by the teleprompter, I can't help craning my neck around a nearby production assistant, searching the backstage area in vain for any sign of my co-presenter, Adrian Savage —who, true to form, is ridiculously late. This time, cutting it so close, I feel like I'm going to have a heart attack.

It's the Video Music Awards and I'm standing in the wings, as instructed, right on time, awaiting my turn to present the next award with my assigned co-presenter. After the current duo finishes their thing, there will be a commercial break, thank God, which gives us a tiny margin of error. But then, whether Savage has arrived or not, I'll have to walk out there and present this damned award, one way or another. If he doesn't show up, I'll have to disregard all the scripted banter on the teleprompter, everything I practiced earlier today at the rehearsal Savage didn't attend, and I'll have to wing it. Which is something I hate doing, ever. But especially on live TV.

I haven't seen Savage since the tour ended two weeks ago, and barely saw him throughout the entire last month of the tour. I certainly didn't ask to be paired with him today. Apparently, the producers, like the rest of the world, saw that viral video of Savage and me screaming at each other in front of that restaurant and decided we'd bring in the ratings as co-presenters. It's fine, though. I got good at ignoring Savage for the final month of the tour, after seeing him for exactly who he is in Las Vegas. So, I can certainly summon my superpowers, once again, and ignore him while reading off a teleprompter.

I'm told Savage didn't make it to the quickie rehearsal earlier today, thanks to a flight delay out of Chicago. But now that he's not here, and the seconds are ticking down, I'm wondering if his supposed "travel delay" earlier was a flat-out lie. Is he standing me up, on purpose, to get back at me for ignoring him for the last month of the tour?

I look down at myself—at the dress I decided to wear tonight. If Savage doesn't show up and see this gorgeous work of art on me, I'll be so pissed. It's basically form-fitting netting with well-placed swirls that artfully, but barely, hide my most scandalous lady bits. I wouldn't have worn *such* a naughty dress for an awards show, typically. Even one as raucous as the Video Music Awards. But knowing I was going to see Savage for the first time since the tour ended spurred me on and made me want to remind him what he missed out on.

That nearby PA suddenly exhales with relief, the same way I've seen so many others do before her while awaiting Savage. And that's how I know Mr. Rockstar has arrived, approximately three minutes before we're set to walk onstage on live TV.

The air shifts and electrifies. And then, there he is. Rounding a corner.

Casually, he sidles up to me, like he's got all the time in the world. His eyes wide, he looks me up and down and says, "Damn, Fitzy. That's quite a dress. *Fuck*."

"Hello, Adrian," I say curtly, pretending not to notice the way his eyes are popping out of his head. His cologne and charisma, the intensity of his gaze . . . all of it is hitting me like a ton of bricks. But I ignore it all.

The superstar onstage says, "And the award goes to . . ." She opens the envelope and immediately stiffens at whatever she's seeing inside. She looks out at the crowd and smiles thinly. "*Hugh Delaney*."

Savage, the production assistant, and I simultaneously snicker, as the audience in the theatre collectively does the same. There's some scattered, half-hearted applause before the woman onstage finally chokes out, "I'm told Hugh can't make it tonight, so Taggert and I accept this award on his behalf!"

Savage leans into my ear, making my skin tingle at his proximity. I feel his warm breath as he says, "Yeah, no shit Hugh couldn't make it tonight. Ha."

I can't help snorting with him, totally contrary to my strategy of ignoring him. "Yeah, Hugh's a little busy tonight . . . *imploding spectacularly*."

It's an understatement. Four days ago, the world found out the fifty-three-year-old, iconic country star who's been the elder statesman on *Sing Your Heart Out* since the beginning, has been cheating on his world-famous actress-wife with their kids' Brazilian nanny—a twenty-year-old who claimed, once the sex tape of them leaked, she'd been "coerced" into having a long-running affair with Hugh.

In response to the shocking allegations, Hugh went on an epic bender, drove his Range Rover into a tree, and promptly got arrested for DUI. Right after that, Hugh's wife filed for divorce, while the nanny filed a civil lawsuit and sold her story to a gossip rag. The day after that, as in, two days ago, *Sing Your Heart Out* announced Hugh's termination, two weeks before shooting on the new season is set to start, saying he'd breached his contract's strict morality clause. And now, here we are, celebrating Hugh's win for Best Country Music Video.

The scandal has been catastrophic news for old Hugh, obviously, but fantastic news for whoever his last-minute replacement on the show will turn out to be. It's a long shot, but my agent, Daria, is already hard at work, trying to make Hugh's replacement *me.* I don't expect her efforts to bear fruit. I'm barely famous enough to have snagged a spot as a mentor this season. But my profile has expanded significantly since the success of my second album. Not to mention, since that video of me fighting with Savage in New York caused Google searches of my name to spike by one thousand percent. So, my agent figured it was worth a shot.

Daria's pitch to the show's producers has been: "You've already publicized Laila as a mentor this season and the response has been fantastic. So why not make a surprise announcement that you've expanded her role because you've realized she'll bring a fresh energy to the judges' table? Who better to replace Hugh at the last minute than his polar opposite—a young, enthusiastic woman?"

Yeah, we don't have high hopes that pitch will work.

Almost certainly, they'll replace Hugh with another big star, another man, who'll appeal to Hugh's same demographic. They've *always* had *one* woman and *two* men at the judges' table, since the beginning—and Aloha is still under contract for the next four years of the show.

The PA hands Savage the short script for our banter. "This is all cued up on the teleprompter," she assures him. "But you'll probably want to read this before walking out there, so you don't stumble on anything."

"I'll do that. Could you give us some space to rehearse in private?"

"Sure. Let me know if you need me. I'll come back and cue you, right before the announcer introduces you both."

As she walks away, Savage tosses the script onto a nearby speaker. "You're stubborn as shit," he says to me.

"Excuse me?"

"I kept my word and told no one. For a full month, I pretended nothing happened between us, whenever anyone was around. I kept my word to you and showed you I'm trustworthy. So why didn't you come to my room, even *once*? Why not answer a single one of my texts—either during the tour, or over the past two weeks? At the very least, you could have replied to *one* of my texts! But you just can't help yourself, huh? You're so used to being a bitch to me, it's now your default mode."

I grit my teeth. "Yeah, interesting to note I'm only a bitch with you. I'm actually really nice with everyone else. And if you must know, I never received any of your texts, except the ones you sent in Vegas, because I blocked your number."

Savage rubs his face, closes his eyes, and lets out a long and tortured exhale.

"If you actually got to know me," I say, "beyond the little sex kitten bitch nut job you think I am, you'd find out there's a whole lot more to me than all that."

He whisper-shouts, "How am I supposed to get to know you when you block my fucking number!"

"Look, there's no point to this. I told you it was a one-time thing. I said it would never happen again, so it shouldn't have surprised you in the least when it *didn't*."

He looks fit to be tied. "Yes, I know what your mouth said that night, Laila, but your body told me something *very* different."

I scoff. "Obviously, not. Or else I would have come to your room, wouldn't I?"

It's a dagger to his heart, obviously. "How did you resist me, though? That's the part I can't wrap my head around."

"Oh, jeez."

"No, seriously. Not because I'm 'Savage from Fugitive Summer.' Not like that. Because . . ." He shifts his weight, betraying his utter torment. "Laila, I've been losing sleep over this. How did you resist coming to my room, night after night, for a full month, after what happened between us in Phoenix? *How the hell was that even possible*?"

In this moment, I'm dying to tell Savage what I witnessed in Vegas—the sucker punch of him bringing a groupie to his room, the same way he'd brought those groupies into my dressing room. Although, in Las Vegas, unlike the times before, Savage couldn't have known I'd see him. And that fact laid to rest a certain theory of mine, once and for all. Before Vegas, I'd stupidly entertained the crazy, magical thought that *maybe* Savage had brought those groupies into my dressing room *only* to mess with me, but not to *actually* screw around with them. But when I saw him with that woman in Vegas, I knew I'd been deluding myself.

For so long now, I've wanted to tell Savage what I saw and how much it hurt me. I've wanted to scream at him, "How could you?" But, always, I decide, like I'm doing now, that small moment of vindication, that momentary "gotcha!"

wouldn't be worth admitting I practically sprinted to Savage's room mere minutes after receiving his text.

In the face of my silence, Savage leans in, looking like a madman on meth. "You started fucking Charlie right after me, didn't you?"

"What?"

"Don't deny it. It's the only thing that makes sense. I saw you two together, all the time, after Phoenix. Always laughing and eating meals together. Always looking so damned cozy together."

I bite my lip to keep from laughing out loud. Savage thinks I had a torrid love affair during the tour . . . with *Charlie*? A man who recently married the great love of his life . . . a former Marine named *Dave*? I know for a fact Savage had numerous sessions with Charlie during the tour. Did he not ask the man a single personal question, in all that time? Did he not try to get to know Charlie, the tiniest bit? That's so Savage, I hate him even more for it.

"Oh no," I whisper. "You figured me out. Did Charlie tell you? Shoot. I made him swear he wouldn't tell a soul about us." I lean forward. "Just like I made *you* promise the same thing after I fucked *you*."

Savage's nostrils flare. "Cut the bullshit, Laila. Did you fuck Charlie or not? I *need* to know."

"It's none of your business. But, yes."

"Are you messing with me or telling me the truth?"

"Wouldn't you like to know."

"I *deserve* to know, after everything you've put me through."

"After what I've put *you* through? Ha! Why do you even care who I've been with, when there's an endless supply of groupies, all of them *dying* to 'get their hands on you'?"

Savage's dark eyes are a scorching pyre of jealousy and fury. "Stop it. What happened the night of the hot tub was off the charts for both of us, and you know it. Let's press the restart button and give this a try. Laila, I can't get that night off my mind."

"Well, that's your misfortune, then. I've certainly been able to get it off mine, thanks, in part, to the masterful way Charlie fucked me, every single night of the tour after Phoenix . . . and *continues* doing to this day."

It's all a lie, of course, even besides the Charlie part. In truth, I've thought about that mind-blowing night with Savage in Phoenix on a running loop. Every single day since it happened. And even more so every night, when I'm all alone and lonely in bed. Hell, I've even started dreaming about Savage! But there's no way I'd admit that to him now. If he's feeling tortured and confused by my supposed immunity to his charms, then *good.* Serves him right.

Savage opens his mouth to reply, looking absolutely furious, just as the PA appears. "Here we go," she says brightly. She presses on her headphones, briefly, before nodding and holding up three fingers. 3-2-1.

An announcer bellows, "Please welcome Savage from Fugitive Summer . . . and Laila Fitzgerald!"

The audience applauds. The PA tells us to go. And Savage and I begin striding onstage, shoulder to shoulder, our eyes locked and our jaws clenched, with an energy I'd caption "homicidal lust" coursing between us.

I toss my hair behind my shoulder, like I'm getting ready to throw down in a wrestling ring, and belt out the last powerful note of my latest single—the third one off my sophomore album that's been taking off like a rocket. And when my song ends, Sylvia Lennox, the beloved host of this long-running daytime talk show, leaps up and applauds with her studio audience, before beckoning me to join her in a cozy sitting area.

As I walk toward my glamorous host, I wave and smile at the boisterous crowd, even though I feel like collapsing onto the floor in relief. I've felt extreme nerves during other high-stakes performances in my young career, especially lately, but nothing compares to *this*. I couldn't sleep last night, worrying I'd somehow screw this up. But, thank God, I think I just nailed it.

"That was *fantastic*!" Sylvia shouts above the din, before giving me a warm hug. "I *love* that song, Laila! So catchy!"

"Thank you so much, Sylvia."

We take our seats and make brief small talk about the album, and then about my weird hobby of making pottery on a wheel. Or, more accurately, *trying* to make pottery on a wheel. Until, finally, Sylvia crosses her legs, leans forward, and says "So, let's talk about your upcoming appearance on *Sing Your Heart Out*." She turns to her audience. "Have y'all heard Laila is going to be Aloha's mentor this season?" The audience claps, confirming, yes, they've heard the exciting news, before Sylvia returns to me. "Has shooting on the show started yet?"

"Not yet. Very soon."

"I've heard Aloha helped you get the job. True?"

"True." I tell the story, briefly, and sing Aloha's praises, and the audience claps.

"Who do you think will replace Hugh at the judges' table?" Sylvia asks. "It's a hot topic. They haven't made an announcement yet."

"I have no idea." Unfortunately, it's the truth. All I know is, it's not going to be me. I add, "I'm as excited as everyone else to find out who they pick."

Sylvia flashes me a suspicious side-eye. "Is it *you,* by any chance, Miss Laila, and you're being remarkably coy with me?"

I giggle. "No. And by the way, I'm perfectly happy being a mentor."

It's true, even though I'm slightly bummed the producers didn't bite. Apparently, the producers said they're not interested in a relative newbie like me as a judge. I'm way too green, they said. Plus, as predicted, they also claimed their "tried and true formula" is having two men and a woman at the judges' table. So, that was that.

Daria thinks there's still a slim possibility she could convince them to reconsider their position, if I do exceptionally well today on *Sylvia.* Or, if not, she said a particularly buzz-worthy interview today will almost certainly open *other* doors for me. So, either way, she encouraged me, strongly, to say or do *something* to make this interview go viral. So, that's what I plan to do.

"Well, if you ask me," Sylvia says, "they should give you Hugh's spot. I think it's high time they had *two* women at the judges' table. Don't you?"

The audience claps energetically.

I chuckle. "Did my mother pay you to say that, Sylvia?" Everyone giggles and claps again. "In all honesty," I say on an exhale, "I'm thrilled to be on the show, in any capacity. Growing up, my mom, sister, and I had two shows we watched religiously. Yours and *Sing Your Heart Out*. So, I'm a lucky girl to have two of my biggest dreams come true."

"Aw, you're so sweet, Laila. Isn't she sweet?" The audience confirms my sweetness. "I hope you don't mind me saying your darling personality kind of surprises me."

I feign offense, making Sylvia chuckle.

"It's a compliment," Sylvia insists. "Your songs are so fierce and sassy, and you're such a confident performer, I assumed that's how you'd be offstage, too. Who would have thought the woman who belts out those sassy songs like a ferocious little tiger is actually a sweet little pussycat?"

I chuckle. "Well, I'm not *always* a sweet little pussycat. My tiger's teeth and claws come out, when appropriate. But, yes, I admit I'm a softie, in real life. It's the push and pull of being a strong woman, don't you think? My mom always taught my sister and me that nobody is better than us, and we're no better than anyone else. So, we try to live up to that, as best we can."

Sylvia claps with the audience. "Words of wisdom! Don't you just love this strong and talented woman? I adore her!"

The audience claps their agreement, and I sigh with relief. So far, so good. I don't think I've said anything to make this clip go viral yet, however, unless maybe my mother's mantra resonates with the internet?

Sylvia shifts her position in her armchair. "Speaking of your tiger's teeth and claws . . . let's talk about some of the lyrics on the album. More specifically, some of the *inspirations* for the lyrics." She flashes me a side-eye. "Girl, *someone* did you dirty."

I join her in chuckling. "I should say, in my defense, I try to get all my murderous impulses out in my songwriting. My mother would be so disappointed if I went to prison for murder."

Sylvia laughs. "How much are your songs inspired by real people and events?"

"Quite a bit. That's how I write. Autobiographically."

"That's what I thought." She cocks an eyebrow. "Care to name names?"

What the hell is she doing? Sylvia has to know I *never* confirm my romantic entanglements, including the inspirations for my songs. In fact, it's become a "thing" for my fans to decode my lyrics, with the help of internet sleuthing, to try to discern which songs are about which potential exes.

As if reading my mind, Sylvia adds, "I know you don't usually confirm who or what inspired your songs . . ."

I nod. "I prefer to let the songs speak for themselves."

"You don't even confirm your *relationships.*"

"Correct."

"No making it 'Instagram official' for Laila, huh? Even when there are paparazzi photos basically doing it for you."

I shrug. "The world can think what it wants. I like keeping my private life private, as best I can. Otherwise, I worry I'll start to feel like I'm *performing* in my relationship, rather than being genuinely present in it."

"That makes sense. I do think that could be a double-edged sword, however. Since you've never confirmed or denied anything, rumors become perceived fact, until the whole world is certain they know the full list of your exes, when that might not be the case."

"Oh, I can confirm that *isn't* the case." I chuckle. "If the internet is to be believed, my list of exes is so long, I'd have a revolving door in my condo."

"Ooooh," Sylvia says, wiggling her fingertips. "I like this line of conversation."

Uh oh.

Sylvia leans forward. "Tell us someone you've been linked to, *falsely.* I respect your privacy, darling, but telling us someone you *haven't* dated couldn't *possibly* violate it."

Clever woman.

I normally wouldn't play this game. But Daria *did* tell me to make this interview go viral. And what better way to do that than giving Sylvia an "exclusive scoop" about my love life?

"Okay, Sylvia," I say. "I'll give you a little something-something. But only because it's you."

She squeals. "How exciting!"

I lean forward, like I'm Deep Throat in a parking garage, about to spill a state secret. "Colin Berretta. The drummer for 22 Goats? All the rumors about us having a torrid fling are *false*. We're nothing but friends."

Shoot. The look on Sylvia's face tells me Colin's name wasn't the one she was hoping for. In fact, if this conversation were a game of basketball, I'm pretty sure I just airballed a free throw. It surprises me, to be honest, considering Colin's high profile since his Calvin Klein underwear campaign. He's a hot commodity lately. So why isn't his name doing the trick?

"What a pity," Sylvia says, apparently trying to salvage my airball. "Colin is gorgeous. Have you seen his Calvin Klein ads?"

"I have. And, yes, he's a gorgeous man. But we're just friends."

"Friends can become more."

"Not in this case. He's a really nice guy. And that's a big problem for me, Sylvia."

She laughs, along with the audience, and I know I'm onto something here.

I nod solemnly. "Unfortunately, I've got a fatal weakness for bad boys, Sylvia." I lean forward. "I'm that friend you want to slap silly for her horrible choices in men."

The audience bursts into laughter and applause, and Sylvia visibly perks up.

"Oh, we've all been there, sweetie, especially in our twenties." Sylvia turns to her audience. "Haven't we *all* had a 'bad boy' phase, against our better judgment?"

Everyone claps and hoots, confirming that, yes, we've *all* had a bad boy phase.

Sylvia winks. "It's okay, sugar. Take it from me, this is the perfect time in your life to get burned by the deliciously toxic flame of a scorching-hot bad boy."

"Or two or three," I mutter, again making Sylvia laugh.

She pats my arm. "It's okay. How else will you learn to recognize Mr. Right when he finally comes along and treats you *right*?"

"That's a lovely spin on an unhealthy addiction. Thank you."

"It's not a spin," Sylvia insists. "The only way to rid yourself of the bad boy addiction is to overdose, go to rehab, and vow to yourself to never relapse."

"I'm actually in the rehab phase now. At least, I'm trying to be."

"Is that so?" She snickers, signaling she's not convinced. "We all saw that photo of you sitting courtside at a Lakers-Knicks game earlier this year . . ."

I shake my head. "No comment."

"Mm-hmm. And what about the video we've all seen of you arguing with a certain bad boy rockstar? Someone with whom the entire world is certain you've had a torrid love affair . . .?"

And there it is. How did I not see this coming? Shoot. The last thing I want to do is give Savage the satisfaction of hearing me say his name on national TV. Especially on a show as popular as *Sylvia.* But I can already see where this is headed, and that my fate is sealed. Sylvia is a salivating dog before me. And there's no way she's going to release this bone without me giving her something spicy.

"Aw, come on, Sylvia," I say in a last-ditch effort to stave off the inevitable. "Have mercy on me."

Sylvia giggles. "What fun would that be, when you and Savage have so much chemistry?" She addresses a guy in a headset behind a camera. "Tom, can we put up a photo of Savage, please? Any ol' photo of him will do."

Poof.

In a flash, a photo of Mr. Pouty Pants magically appears behind us on a large screen. And, no, it's not just "any" photo. It's from a smoking-hot photo shoot he recently did for the cover of *Gentleman's World* magazine—a cover that caused quite a stir when it came out a few days ago. In the shot, Savage is particularly drool-inducing. His jaw looks like it was forged in steel. His dark eyes look particularly pene-trating and soulful. And, of course, his famously chiseled abs are on full display, peeking out of an unbuttoned shirt.

"Isn't he *gorgeous*?" Sylvia coos, her eyes trained on the screen behind us. She turns to the audience. "For anyone who's been living under a rock, this is Savage of the rock band, Fugitive Summer." She fans herself. "How is someone *so* talented, also *so* gorgeous? Those abs could grate cheese! That jawline could sharpen my knives! And those *lips*." She touches my forearm again. "Please, Laila, tell me you've at least had the pleasure of kissing those lips, if only for a chaste little peck!"

Well, that's a lucky break. The way Sylvia has worded her question, I don't even have to lie. "I'm sorry to disappoint you," I begin. "But, no, I swear on my life my lips have never touched Savage's. Not even for a chaste little peck." I mean, yeah, my lips have been wrapped around his thick, juicy cock. In fact, I've sucked that man's dick like I was sucking an orange through a watering hose. But that wasn't the question, now was it?

Sylvia grips her chest dramatically, like I've shot her with an arrow. "Noooo!"

I nod. "It's sad but true. All those rumors about Savage and me having a secret romance are categorically . . . *false.*" It's yet another true statement, if you ask me. Nobody in their right mind would characterize one drunken, meaningless tryst as an actual "romance."

"Well, I'm heartbroken," Sylvia declares. "Is there any hope of you two getting together in the future?"

"No."

"No?"

"No."

"Well, that seems awfully final."

"Because it is."

"Again, you surprise me. If I were you, I'd take a big ol' bite of that apple, if given half the chance." She arches an eyebrow. "Weren't you two on tour together pretty recently— for several months?"

Cheese on a cracker. The woman is relentless. "Yes, we were—for three months. But, to be honest, our personalities didn't really mesh."

Sylvia's face ignites. "Oooooh. Now, we're really getting some exclusive dirt!"

I shrug. "Not really. You've all seen the video. It certainly wasn't a secret during the tour that we didn't get along. If Savage were here, I'm sure he'd say I was as infuriating to him as he was to me."

Sylvia's face is positively on fire now. "*Infuriating*? My, my. Such a *passionate* word."

"*Annoying*," I correct, quickly, feeling my cheeks redden. "I'm just saying we got under each other's skin."

"*Under each other's skin.* Oh, Laila. Freud would have a field day with you."

Fuck! How did I lose my grip on this tiger's tail so quickly?

Sylvia smirks. "Speaking of that video . . . Hey, Tom, can we put that up now? Thanks."

And there it is. The famous video of Savage and me that's been making the rounds—the one where we're screaming at each other in front of that restaurant in New York.

"You've seen this, right?" Sylvia asks.

"I have."

"It's impossible to hear what you two are saying, unfortunately. Can you fill us in?"

"I don't remember. It wasn't anything important. We constantly annoyed each other, so . . ."

"*Constantly*? Does that mean you two had more fights than this one during the tour?"

Crap. Does she have a spy who's already told her about our knock-down, drag-out screaming match backstage in Atlanta? Or is she simply fishing? "No, that argument was the only one," I say, trying to sound casual. "Adrian and I mostly stayed out of each other's way during the tour."

"Adrian? You're on a first-name basis with him, huh? I don't think I realized that's his first name. What a sexy name."

"I . . . I used to call him that to annoy him, while he called me Fitzy to annoy me. See? There were no fireworks between us. More like grade-school teasing, combined with total and complete *indifference.*"

"*Huh,*" Sylvia says, conveying an ocean of disbelief with that one syllable. She addresses the guy with the headset again. "Can we bring up the meme now? Thanks."

Holy hell. The meme, too? I feel like I'm being water-boarded.

Poof.

Like magic, the meme that's been flooding social media this past week, ever since the Video Music Awards, appears on the screen behind us. It's a photo of Savage and me, taken as we walked onstage together, our eyes locked in fiery anger. In the shot, Savage is smoldering at me like a volcano about to blow, while I'm glaring at him like I'm plotting his slow and painful dismemberment, starting with the piecemeal removal of his cock and balls. And, of course, since this is a meme, there's a caption across the top and bottom that reads: "I hate you so much . . . *I want to fuck you to death.*" Although for Sylvia's daytime audience, the f-bomb in the caption has been blurred out.

"Have you seen this one?" Sylvia asks innocently.

"I have."

Sylvia addresses her audience. "Have y'all seen this one?"

The audience applauds, confirming they've seen it, too.

"I don't know, Laila," Sylvia says. "Looking at this photo, I can see why those pesky rumors about you and Savage simply won't die. I mean, look at the chemistry between you two! Those are some serious sparks!"

The audience expresses its agreement, while I find myself wondering how the heck I managed to walk straight into this landmine. Did Daria set this up with Sylvia, to make sure this clip went viral? I bet she did.

"Those aren't *sparks*," I say. "They're *daggers*. Right before Savage and I walked onstage, we had a little disagreement. Surprise, surprise. So, what you're seeing there isn't me wanting to jump his bones, as the meme would have you believe. It's me wanting to murder him."

Sylvia smirks. "I think you're missing the whole point of the meme, darling. The point is that—and this is something I think we can all relate to—a woman can *simultaneously* want to murder a man *and* jump his bones. It's called hate sex, honey. And from my experience, it can be awfully fun."

The audience roars with laughter. Oh, Sylvia. She's a gem.

Sylvia continues, "I'd think that'd be especially true when you're having hate sex with a specimen who looks like *that*." She motions to the screen behind us while I gape like a fish on a line, fruitlessly racking my brain for a witty retort. Finally, before I've managed to find adequate words, Sylvia looks directly into one of the cameras and says, "Big thanks to the lovely and talented Laila Fitzgerald for joining us today! Buy her album and watch her on *Sing Your Heart Out* this season! When we come back, we'll be joined by Chef Claude, who's going to teach us how to make the perfect French *croissant*!"

The audience applauds. The red lights on the various cameras turn off. A producer announces, "We're clear." And Sylvia throws her head back and lets loose with a belly laugh.

When she straightens up, she grips my forearm. "That was solid gold, Laila. Absolute *perfection*!"

I exhale what feels like my entire lung capacity. "It was?"

"It was brilliant." She mimes a chef's kiss. "I don't know if you just lied to my face about Savage, little girl. Or if you're silly enough *not* to have taken a big ol' bite of that apple during your tour. But, God help you, if you were stupid enough to resist him when you had the chance, then take some advice from a woman twice your age." She leans forward. "Fuck that man, Laila. Call him now and tell him to meet you in a hotel, and fuck . . . that . . . man." She guffaws at my flabbergasted expression. "Honey, when you get to be my age, you'll realize the only regrets in life are the things you *didn't* do. The mistakes you *didn't* make." She smirks. "Trust me, honey, having hate sex with a man who looks like that delicious specimen is one mistake you'll *never* regret."

The air is electric. The stage, flooded with lights. The packed audience in this massive arena is singing along with me to "Hate Sex High" . . . which makes no sense, now that I think about it, since the album with that song on it is currently being mixed and mastered. Did someone at the label leak the rough cut of the album?

A warm breeze wafts over my body, caressing every inch of my skin . . . including my dick and balls. And when I look down, perplexed, I realize I've been prancing around onstage . . . completely in the nude.

I look behind me, at the gigantic Jumbotron projecting my every movement, and, yup, there's my naked dick, blasting out into the arena, as big as a barn. My eyes drift to Kendrick behind me at the drum kit and he guffaws at my stupidity, while not missing a beat in the song.

I turn around again, toward the audience, and discover everyone is holding up their phones, trained on me. Or, rather, trained, with sniper-like precision, on my dick. Which means, here we go again—my dong is once again about to become an internet star.

I suddenly hear Eli's voice, screaming my name. Shit. My manager already knows about this latest fuck-up? Panicking, I look toward the wing of the stage, assuming that's where I'll find Eli. But the person I behold in the wings is a whole lot hotter than Eli. *It's Little Miss Laila.*

Well, well, well. I knew she'd finally come crawling back to me, eventually, begging me for another ride on my pony. She's standing in the wings, wearing that eye-popping dress from the awards show—the one that left only the tiniest sliver of flesh to the imagination. Not that I need my imagination to fill in the gaps when it comes to Laila's gorgeous body, since I've already seen every glorious inch of it on the best night of my life. Every inch, that is, except her glorious pussy, up close and personal.

What did Kendrick say last week while showing me Laila's interview on *Sylvia*? He said, "I think you've got a fish on your line, brother." And now, *hallelujah*, it turns out Kendrick was *right*.

Laila's blue eyes burning with sexual desire, she begins banging her fist against a nearby wall, commanding me to stop gawking at her and get my ass over to her in the wings.

"Patience," I coo, enjoying her little tantrum. After everything Laila has put me through, I must admit I'm enjoying her obvious desperation. Taking my sweet time, I stroll languidly toward her, like I've got all the time in the world, like I haven't been dying for this moment to arrive for half my life. And when I finally come to a stop mere inches from Laila, when the tip of my naked cock brushes against the sheer fabric on her belly, I physically spasm with pent-up arousal and anticipation.

I lick my lips, poised to say, "I knew you wouldn't be able to resist me forever."

But she shuts me up by gripping my cock, the same way she did the night of the hot tub.

"Don't speak," she cautions. "And don't kiss me, either. Just fuck me. Fuck me, hard, like you did in Phoenix."

Exhaling a stilted breath, I wordlessly unzip her dress and peel it off her, until it's in a crumpled heap at her feet. With my cock dripping, I pick her up by her glorious ass, push her back against the wall, press my aching tip against her wet entrance, and—

"Savage!"

No.

It's my manager, Eli, again.

"Savage!" he shouts. "Open up. It's an emergency!"

No, no, no!

All of a sudden, Laila disappears from my arms in a puff of sensuous smoke. There's another banging sound. And then Eli's voice rips me from my dream and into stark consciousness. I open my eyes and discover I'm not backstage in an arena, on the cusp of finally fucking Laila again. I'm in a hotel room. Naked and alone in bed, in the late morning light. Also, damn, I'm nursing one hell of a hangover.

Groaning, I rub my pained forehead—and as I do, Eli's yelling and banging on the door persists and becomes even louder. I glance at my phone on the nightstand and curse at the time: 10:18. That's way too early for anyone to wake me when I'm not on tour, especially the morning after Kai's birthday party. Whatever brought Eli here, it'd better be damned important.

At the thought, goosebumps erupt on my skin. And not the good kind.

Mimi.

Quickly, I swipe into my texts, making sure I don't have something from Sasha. And, thank God, I don't. Exhaling with relief, I throw on a pair of underwear and shuffle to the door. And the minute I see my manager's facial expression, I know whatever "emergency" he's come to tell me about this morning, he's not here to tell me the worst possible news. The news I've been dreading since Mimi took a turn for the worse. Which means, whatever it is, I really don't give a fuck.

Scratching my belly, I lean against the doorjamb and yawn so wide, I'm sure Eli can glimpse the inside-bottoms of my ball sacs through my mouth. "Whatever this 'emergency' is," I drawl, "it'd better be damned important. I was in the middle of an amazing dream."

Eli motions to the hard-on bulging from behind my briefs. "So I've gathered. Put that thing away before you poke some-one's eye out." He barges past me into the room and scowls at my briefs again. "Jesus, Savage. Seriously. Think about drowning puppies or something." He strides toward the bath-room. "Are you alone in here, Player?"

"Yeah."

Ignoring my reply, he peeks into the bathroom to see for himself.

"Why ask me, then?" I mutter, flopping into an armchair. I'm not surprised Eli wants independent corroboration of my answer. As Eli has said many times, he doesn't consider me a "reliable narrator" on my best day, let alone after a night of hard partying with my best friends.

When he returns to me from the bathroom, he looks furious with me.

"What's wrong with you?" he yells. "You signed the contract on Thursday morning and turned around and breached it on Friday *night*?"

"I didn't *breach* it," I assure him. "All I did last night was—"

"I know exactly what you did! And so do the producers! Savage, you know how paranoid they are about avoiding scandals with their judges this season, big or small, thanks to The Hugh Debacle. They told you, repeatedly, in writing and verbally, they want you to be a Boy Scout for the entire season."

"And I will be. Shooting begins on Monday. Don't worry. I didn't do anything bad. It was all in good fun."

"I know everything you did!" he shouts. "And you wanna know how? Because you stupidly threw Kai's birthday party in the pool area of a busy hotel—where *any* guest of the party, and any guest of the hotel, or any *employee* of the hotel, could see your antics—and by that I mean your naked swan dive into the swimming pool!—and snap as many photos and videos of you in action as they pleased. *Which is exactly what a whole lot of them did*!"

I chuckle. "It's fine. It's nothing the world hasn't already seen. I've told you about 'Birthday Truth or Dare,' right? It's harmless fun."

"Not harmless!" he shouts, practically pulling out his dark hair with frustration. "You signed a multi-million-dollar contract that included a strict morality clause. And a day and a half later, a screen shot of your dick is, yet *again,* trending on Twitter!"

I put my palms together in prayer. "At number one?"

"Fucking hell, Savage!" he shouts, his dark eyes bugging out. "This isn't funny! The producers called me an hour ago, wanting to terminate your contract."

Well, that gets my attention. "Because of a little full-frontal nudity?"

"That, and the fact that they don't trust you as far as they can throw you. You made promises that you've totally disre-garded. It's a family show! And Hugh has sullied their brand. They need to know they can trust you—that they can *control* you. What was one of the most important rules they impressed upon you at the meeting? *No more going viral for all the wrong reasons*!"

My pulse is racing now. "Shit. I didn't think they'd care if

I added a couple more shots to my internet dick pic collection. It's part of my branding by now, don't you think? Might even help the show, I'd think."

He shakes his head, looking like he wants to slap me. "I hate you right now. You made a promise—a four-million-dollar promise—and now they think you've broken it. It's as simple as that."

I take a deep breath and rub my forehead. "Okay. I get where they're coming from, I guess. How about we give them a call and I apologize? I'll tell them I'm sorry and it won't happen again."

"Oh, we're way past that now, fuckwit. You have no idea how much shucking and jiving I had to do this morning to keep them from *immediately* announcing your termination." He takes a deep breath. "Thankfully, I think I've got them sold on an idea to make lemonade out of last night's lemons. They've given me until five today to deliver on my idea, or else you're toast."

My chest suddenly feels tight. "Whatever you have to do, you need to fix this for me, Eli."

"I'm trying, Savage. But you're gonna need to work with me."

"I will. I *promise*."

"Don't you dare use that word with me. It's meaningless."

"No, it's not. Yes, I was stupid last night. But I totally get it now. I'll do whatever it takes."

"I don't believe you."

"Well, you should." I sigh. "I didn't want to tell you this yet, but . . . I signed a contract to buy that house yesterday."

Eli looks flabbergasted. "The house for Mimi?"

I nod.

"Savage, *no*. I told you *no*!"

"I know. But I had to do it. Who knows when or if it'll

ever come on the market again? I wanted Mimi to have it. You know we're running out of time."

Eli looks sympathetic. "Please, tell me you haven't told Mimi about the house yet, so you can back out, if I can't fix things with the show."

"I've told her. She cried tears of joy."

Eli flops into a chair. "*Savage.*"

"I had to get it for her. You know the story of that house."

"How much did you agree to pay? Please, tell me you at least got a smoking good deal?"

I pause. It seemed like a no-brainer at the time when I knocked on the door of that house last week and made them an offer they couldn't refuse. The house wasn't even on the market, actually. And they insisted it wasn't for sale, at any price. So, I offered to pay them a king's ransom to change their mind. I figured, *Why not?* The tour was massively successful, which means I can afford to burn my entire salary, and then some, from *Sing Your Heart Out* on a gift for Mimi. But now, I'm thinking maybe it was a wee bit extravagant to blow every penny of my salary, and more, on that one purchase. "Okay, actually, I told you a little white lie," I admit. "The house wasn't actually on the market . . ."

"Oh, God. No. How much, Savage?"

I grimace. "Five million."

"No!"

"I had to offer that much, or else—"

"Savage, no!"

"It's okay. For what it's worth, the house is going to be in my name, so, one day . . ." I trail off, not wanting to think of the ending to that sentence—the obvious implication that Mimi won't be around to enjoy her fancy new house on a hill forever.

"Your salary from the show won't cover that," Eli says, like I don't know basic math. "Not to mention, you won't even get paid, all at once, by the show—assuming I can fix this for you. Plus, even if you do wind up staying on the show, *if* I can save your stupid ass today, then half your salary will go to taxes and commissions."

"*Half?*" I blurt. "Well, shit."

Eli looks genuinely distraught on my behalf. He fidgets in his armchair for a moment. "Savage, even if I can get the show to keep you on, that was the most irresponsible purchase, ever. You already bought Sasha a house last year—and you don't even have one for yourself!"

My stomach flip-flops. "Look, I'm not gonna apologize. I had to do this for Mimi. She's the first person in the world who ever truly believed in me, even when I didn't believe in myself. The first person who told me I actually mattered." I swallow hard, keeping my emotions at bay. "There's no way to know how much time she has left, Eli. But things aren't looking good. So, whatever time she's got, I want her to get to lie in a huge bed fit for a queen in the master bedroom of *that* particular house, while watching me sit at the judges' table—in Hugh Delaney's fucking chair—on her all-time favorite show."

Eli runs his palm down his face. "Aw, Savage. You're such a fucking . . . *softie.*"

I press my lips together. That's not how I thought Eli was going to end that sentence. I was expecting him to say idiot. Or maybe asshole. And I can't deny his word choice has moved me.

"I'm sorry I messed up last night," I murmur. "I considered last night a last hurrah before I turn into a pumpkin, you know? I truly didn't think they'd care if I added to my dick pic collection."

"You were already a pumpkin. That's my whole point. The contract was effective the minute you signed it. And the infuriating part is that I told you that."

"The good news is that, besides that *one* naked swan dive, I truly was a Boy Scout last night. A popular Instagram model practically *begged* me to take her upstairs to my room, but I said no." I gasp. "Hey, let's call the producers and tell them about *that*!"

"They already know, dumbass. *Everyone* already knows because that highly popular Instagrammer posted a video about her interaction with you this morning, which is now making the rounds on the internet, right alongside screenshots and videos of your gigantic dong, mid-flight."

I furrow my brow at my manager. "What do you mean the Instagrammer made a video about her interaction with me last night? There was nothing to say because I turned her down."

"That's exactly what she said," Eli replies. "It's the supposed *reason* you turned her down that's making her video take off. And thank God it is, because that video is the only reason I've got a snowball's chance in hell of fixing this mess for you."

I blink in confusion. "What'd the Instagrammer say in her video?"

"Tell me your version of your conversation with her, first. Word for word, if you can."

I release a puff of scornful air. "I can't remember what I said to her, word for word. I was drunk. Plus, the party was noisy, so I couldn't hear everything she said."

Eli rolls his eyes. "Okay, I'll get you started. She approached you at the party and said she's a huge fan. Sound about right?"

"Yeah. But that's what always happens. And then, she

suggested we head upstairs to my hotel room for sex. Or to fuck. Something like that. And, like I said, I turned her down."

"But what reason did you give for turning her down?"

I pause to recollect. "Honestly, I wasn't interested in her. But I didn't want to hurt her feelings. So, I think I said something like, 'I can't because of the morality clause in my contract with the show.' Now, show me her video. I'm freaking out."

Eli hands me his phone, all cued up. "Fair warning, this is going to piss you off. But keep in mind this video is your saving grace."

My stomach churning, I look down at the screen in my palm, and there she is. The Instagrammer from Kai's birthday party last night. Long, sandy hair, blue eyes, full lips. She's gorgeous, obviously. But not my type. Apparently, besides being gorgeous, she's also a greedy little bitch who didn't hesitate to spew lies about me for her fifteen minutes of fame. So, good on me for sensing her character and immediately turning her down.

With a deep sigh of resignation, I press play on the video and the frozen woman on my screen instantly springs to life. "Hey, guys!" she says brightly. "You won't believe what happened!" And off she goes, telling the story of last night's "star-studded" birthday party. First off, she admits she basically sneaked in, thanks to a friend of a friend with a connection. Next, she talks about the famous people she saw. And, finally, she gets to the part I've been waiting for—the part about me. "He's even hotter in person, guys," she gushes. "He's *godlike* in person."

"I like her," I declare, making Eli chuckle.

"And when I told him I'm a model," she says, "Savage goes, 'Well, I'm not surprised about that. You're *stunning.* Actually, you know who you remind of . . .?'" She pauses for effect, her blue eyes dancing, before finishing with, "'*Laila.*'"

"Oh, Jesus," I mumble.

"Pause it," Eli commands. And when I comply, he asks, "Did you say that?"

"I . . . I don't know," I stammer. "Would it be bad if I did?"

"There's no good or bad answer here. Only the truth."

I shrug. "I guess it's possible. Like I said, I was drunk. And she definitely looks a bit like Laila."

"She's her doppelganger."

"No way. Laila is way hotter." Eli furrows his brow with surprise, so I quickly bark out, "Can I press play again, please?"

"Sure."

My heart pounding, I cue the video. And once again, the woman springs to life.

"So, after some flirting," she says, "I decided to make my move. I suggested we head to Savage's room upstairs—"

"See?" I mutter.

"So he could make my fantasies come true. And guess what Savage said to me in reply to that? You won't believe it. Brace yourselves. He said, 'Sorry, I can't . . . because of . . . *Laila.*'"

"Bullshit!" I blurt.

The woman clutches her heart, just above her ample breasts. "I was like, 'I knew it!' And Savage just laughed and winked."

"I did not. She's a *liar.*"

The Instagrammer continues, "And then, *I* said, 'You're the sweetest boyfriend, *ever.*'"

"Fuck!"

"And he goes, 'I'm not being *sweet.* I made a *promise* to her, and I'm going to keep it.'"

"What the fuck?" I yell. I pause the video and practically hurl the phone at Eli. "I said none of that! Zippo. Zero! Either she's lying, or she misheard me. I think she said something like, 'Thanks for being so sweet about this.' And I said, 'I'm not being sweet. I made a promise.' But I was talking about my contract! The morality clause! I didn't say I couldn't fuck her because of *Laila.* Why would I say that? I'd never say that! Laila never even crosses my mind!"

Eli chuckles. "Calm down, Player. I know she's full of shit. And so do the producers. If you ask me, the most logical explanation is that you said she *looks* like *Laila,* which she does, and then, when you said the next thing, she made the mental leap that you'd said the word 'Laila' *again.* My bet? You told her you needed to 'lay low' because of your contract."

Oh, thank God. I feel like he's just thrown me a lifeline. "Yes!" I shout. "That's exactly what I said! *Lay low*! Not *Laila*! That's obviously what I said!"

"You use that phrase a lot."

"I do! I totally do!" I exhale with relief. "I remember everything now. I said I had to 'lay low' because of the show. And when she said thanks for being sweet, I said, 'I'm not being sweet, I made a promise to the show.' *Boom.*" Oh, God, I'm so relieved. I sit quietly for a beat, rubbing my forehead, feeling like I've dodged a bullet. Until, suddenly, a horrifying thought strikes me—one that makes my blood turn cold. "Oh, fuck. Laila can't see this video, Eli! Hand me my phone. I've got to post a rebuttal video, explaining what I *really* said, so Laila doesn't see this bullshit and think—"

"Like hell you will. That video, and the fact that the whole world believes every word of it, is the only thing keeping your job on life support right now."

"How?"

Eli gestures to the phone in my hand. "Watch the rest."

With a loud groan, I press play again, and this time, the woman says, "So, guys, I can confidently report the exclusive scoop that Savage and Laila Fitzgerald are, indeed, secretly together, despite their denials."

"I've never denied anything," I mutter.

She continues, "Am I disappointed about Savage being off the market? Absolutely. But, at least, I'm thrilled to know he's so happy and devoted to his girlfriend." She leans into the camera. "Now, don't you dare break our Savage's heart, Laila. Or I'm coming for you, bitch." She snarls comically and the video ends.

I hand Eli his phone, my heart thudding in my ears. "I don't see how this isn't a horrific disaster for me. The thought of Laila seeing that and thinking I actually said any of that stuff makes me want to throw myself off a bridge."

Eli laughs. "Forget Laila's reaction. That's a casualty of war. All that matters is what the world thinks. And thanks to that, the producers have given me until five today to pull a rabbit out of my hat."

"What rabbit? Stop speaking in code and tell me what's going on."

Eli grins. "A rabbit called *Laila*. If we can convince her to be *your* team's mentor this season, rather than Aloha's—and for *three* episodes, rather than one, and if—"

"Kendrick's going to be my mentor this season!"

"Not if we can get Laila."

"She won't do it. She hates me. Even for a three-episode stint, she'd never agree to it."

"You didn't let me finish. There's something else she'd have to do besides being your mentor for three episodes." He smiles. "She'd also have to pretend to be your girlfriend."

My jaw hangs open. My manager has rendered me speechless.

Eli smiles. "Just like the Instagrammer said."

"That's . . . the stupidest thing I've ever heard."

"Maybe so," Eli says with a shrug. "But it's the only way for you to stay on the show. The producers don't believe the Instagrammer's version of the story, any more than I do. But guess who *does* believe her? Your fans and Laila's. You should see the comments online. People are losing their minds. They're obsessed. And that's got the producers' attention. After the debacle with Hugh, they're desperate to lock in some huge ratings this season. And they think this storyline— a romance between you and Laila, unfolding before the audience's eyes for three whole weeks—will be a ratings bonanza."

My mind is racing. "Did they tell Laila about this idea yet?"

Eli nods. "They called her this morning. I'm told her answer was, 'Hell to the fucking no.'"

I throw up my hands in exasperation. "Then why are we even talking about this?"

"Because it's your only option, Savage! Because I have to believe Laila's agent is smart enough to tell Laila that her knee-jerk reaction, if, indeed, that's truly what it was, was stupid. I have to believe Daria, Laila's very smart agent, has only conveyed her client's alleged knee-jerk reaction, if that's what it was, as a negotiation tactic. Daria is one of the best in the business. She knows this is a massive opportunity for Laila—the kind of exposure that will make her a household name. I have full faith Daria will eventually help us talk some sense into Laila."

"Good luck with that. Nobody can talk sense into Laila Fitzgerald."

"Well, we have to do it. And by five o'clock today."

"So, you're saying you think Laila's agent only said Laila flatly refused, to get her more money?"

"*Exactly*. She's playing hardball."

"Okay, then. Cool. Call the producers and tell them to sweeten the pot. What does that have to do with me?"

Eli shakes his head. "I already tried. They were adamant they won't negotiate against themselves. It's *our* job to get Laila to agree to the deal—or, at least, to come to the table to negotiate more money—by five o'clock today. The producers didn't say this, but I have to believe, if Laila says she's *open* to being your mentor and fake girlfriend for the right *price,* they won't let this ratings magnet slip through their fingers. They know this would be a win-win-win."

"The problem still remains, Eli. I can't convince Laila Fitzgerald to do a damned thing. Trust me on that."

"Well, you've got four million reasons to try. If you want to keep your job—and the fat salary that comes with it—then you'd better do or say whatever it takes to make her say yes."

I scoff. "If I knew how to make Laila say yes, trust me, I would have done it a long time ago. Plus, this isn't going to work, regardless. Now that Laila knows I *need* her to keep my job, she'll say no, just to spite me."

"Do you think I'm stupid?" He leans back in his armchair. "Laila doesn't know you need her. I made sure the producers won't tell her that."

I flap my lips together. "*Fine.* I'll do my best. But I'll need to call Laila from your phone, because the little psychopath blocked my number during the tour."

Eli scoffs. "You're not gonna *call* Laila, dumbass. You're gonna do this in person."

"What?"

He stands. "Come on. Get showered and dressed, Player, while I call room service for some coffee and breakfast for you. And make sure you put on some cologne and make yourself look extra irresistible. Your future fake girlfriend and her agent are expecting us at noon."

"Look, I get that you think Savage is an arrogant jerk," my agent, Daria, says, although she doesn't know the half of it. "But I think you should put your emotions aside and think about this as a business decision, Laila. I really think this could be a game changer for you."

I'm sitting across from Daria in her Beverly Hills office. I'm in jeans and a T-shirt. She's dressed like the goddess she is in a Gucci pantsuit and large gold hoops. And, honestly, I don't know why I'm here, seeing as how we've already talked about this on the phone and I've told her the offer is a non-starter. If it were anyone else, I would have refused to race down here to talk about the producers' crazy offer, yet again, only this time in person. But I suppose, at the end of the day, I respect my agent's opinion far too much to ignore an "urgent" request from her.

"I'm sorry," I say. "Like I said on the phone, I couldn't pull off a fake romance, even if I wanted to. My dislike of Savage runs too deep. After one episode, let alone three, the whole world would know I'm a liar."

"Aw, I have faith in your performance skills," Daria coaxes. "All you'd have to do is focus on nothing but Savage's physical beauty, and ignore everything else about him, and, *voila,* you'd convince yourself he's the great love of your life." She leans forward across her sleek desk. "In other words, I'm telling you to think like a man."

We both giggle at the joke.

Daria leans back in her high-back chair again, steepling her fingers. "Do you think you'd be able to fall in 'fake love' with Savage for the right price?"

I shake my head. "You know they reserve the real money in their budget for the judges. They'd never offer me anything even close to what I'd need to feel tempted."

Daria lifts an eyebrow. "Ah, so you admit there *is* a number, at least, theoretically, that could make you say yes."

"Hypothetically, sure. But whatever that number is—and, honestly, I don't know what it would be—the show would never offer it to me, so it's a moot point."

Daria looks like the gears in her head are turning. "I'm not so sure about that. When I spoke to the executive producer, Nadine, this morning, she played it cool, but I could tell she was *dying* to make this happen. Thanks to that video of you and Savage arguing on the sidewalk in New York, and your interview on *Sylvia,* and, the meme from the awards show, and now, this Instagrammer's viral video, I don't think it's an understatement to say you and Savage are a power-house. A shoo-in to grab massive ratings. Surely, Nadine knows that."

None of this is new information. Daria said all of this, essentially, during our conversation on the phone.

When I shrug and say nothing, simply because I don't believe for a minute the show would pay me what it would take, Daria puts her elbows onto her desk and smiles.

"What do you make of that Instagram video?" she asks.

"Do you think she was telling the truth about what Savage said?"

I snort. "Heck no. If a beautiful woman suggested going upstairs, I guarantee I didn't even cross Savage's mind. Obviously, that Instagrammer came up with a story she knew would make her video go viral."

Daria looks unconvinced. "Well, for God's sake, don't let on you don't believe the video when you see Savage. Let him think you believe every single word."

"I don't plan to see him. Even when I'm on-set in a few weeks, I'm going to avoid him like the plague."

Daria smirks. "Actually, you'll be seeing Savage sooner than you think." She looks at her watch. "He was supposed to be here five minutes ago, actually."

"Daria!"

She shrugs. "His agent called and begged me for a meeting and I felt it would be in your best interests to hear him out."

I cross my arms over my chest. "I don't want to see him."

"Come on. At the very least, won't it be fun to torture him by pretending you believe every word that woman said? That has to be his worst nightmare."

I twist my mouth. She's got a point. "Still," I say, "the fun in that wouldn't outweigh the discomfort I'd feel at seeing him."

"Why do you hate him so much?" Daria narrows her eyes. "You two really did get together, didn't you? You fell for him, and he cheated on you?"

"Oh, God, no. Daria, listen. I sincerely appreciate you looking out for me and fighting so hard for my career, but there's no point in having this meeting with Savage and his agent. The show won't offer me enough to tempt me. And you said yourself three episodes as a mentor won't make that much more of an impact than one."

"You're misconstruing what I said."

"Regardless, it's not like they're offering me a seat at the judges' table with a paycheck to match. So, let's just—"

"Well, now we're getting somewhere," Daria interrupts. "Are you saying, if I *could* get you that—a seat at the judges' table with a paycheck to match—you'd say yes?"

My lips part in surprise that she's even saying that out loud. "They already said they don't want me as a judge. Hence, the reason they hired Savage to replace Hugh, rather than me."

"True, but that happened before today—before that woman's video went off like an atomic bomb on the internet." She leans back and swivels in her chair. "I could be wrong, but I've got a hunch the landscape dramatically shifted underneath Savage's feet this morning. Don't you think it's a bit weird his agent called me, asking for this meeting? He made it sound like Savage was willing to do *you* a favor by saying yes to this . . . but would Savage *really* do a favor for you?"

"Absolutely not." I pause. "So . . . what, then?"

"I'd bet money Savage's job is on the line this morning, thanks to his shenanigans last night. My hunch is that Savage's head is on the chopping block, and thanks to that woman's video, and everything that's come before, the producers have made *you* a condition of Savage's continued employment."

My mouth hangs open as my eyes widen with glee.

"Now you understand why I begged you to come down here for this meeting. If I'm right about Savage's job depending on *you*, and if I'm right about the show practically drooling over this idea, then I think I can leverage both sides against the other to get you an offer you simply can't refuse."

I clutch my heart, feeling like it's beating a mile a minute. "Okay, this might be a stupid question, but if you're right about Savage's job being on the line, then why wouldn't I say *no* to being his fake girlfriend, thereby getting Savage shit-canned, and then swoop in and take his job?"

Daria shakes her head. "I'm sorry, honey. If they fire Savage, I'm sure they'll replace him with some other heart-throb. On your own, your platform simply isn't big enough yet. But with Savage, you're in the cat's seat. So let's agree to help Savage keep his seat at the judges' table . . . as long as he agrees to help you get a seat right next to his."

I gasp. "At the judges' table? Not as his mentor?"

"Correct. For the entire season. With a salary to match."

I'm reeling. Losing my mind. "You really think that's possible?"

"It's a long shot, so don't get too excited. But it's worth a try. My gut tells me Savage is desperate, and the producers are frothing at the mouth. So, let's see if we can exploit all of it to your advantage."

I look out the floor-to-ceiling window of Daria's office at the glamorous hustle-bustle of Beverly Hills for a moment, trying to collect myself. And when I finally return to my agent, I can't hide it. I'm excited. "Okay," I say on an exhale. "Let's give it a try."

As Daria whoops, a buzzing noise rises up from the intercom on her desk, followed by a male voice announcing, "Ms. Brown, Eli McKenzie and his client are here to see you."

A demonic smirk lifts one half of Daria's mouth. "Keep a poker face at all times. If I say something blatantly false, nod your head subtly and roll with it."

"Got it."

Daria presses a button on the intercom with her long fingernail and says sweetly, "Thank you, Hunter. Please, escort my guests to my office." She winks at me. "We're ready for them."

TWENTY-THREE
SAVAGE

The office door opens and a striking Black woman I vaguely recognize is standing before Eli and me. She says hello to Eli, whom she clearly already knows, and introduces herself to me as Daria Brown, before leading us into her elegant office.

We follow Daria into the spacious room and find Laila sitting in a corner, her body language in her armchair like she owns the place.

When Eli and I reach Laila, she doesn't stand. Eli greets Laila with a handshake, but I don't bother extending my hand. She won't take it, anyway.

"Hello, Fitzy," I say, as I take a seat next to Eli on a small couch.

"Hello, Adrian," she replies stiffly.

"You're looking well," I say, leaning back and spreading my legs slightly. It's an understatement. Every time I see this woman, she hits me like a ton of bricks. I add, "As always."

"Thank you. So are you." She smirks. "As *always*."

I don't know how Laila does it. Her words were complimentary, like mine, but her tone somehow transformed them into a dig. But that's Laila for you. A master at throwing shade that gives you whiplash.

"Sorry we're a bit late," Eli says, eliciting a barely audible scoff from Laila—one that conveys she's not the least bit surprised. Eli pauses, briefly, at Laila's interruption, before adding, "A couple paparazzi were waiting for Savage as we left his hotel. So, we took the long way around, to be on the safe side."

Laila's blue eyes are fixed on mine now, so I flash her a look regarding Eli's explanation that says, *See? This time, it wasn't my fault.*

In reply, Laila shoots me a look that says, *I don't believe it for a second.*

And in reply to that, I roll my eyes and look away.

Daria, the agent, says, "It was the right call to play it safe. If we're successful in putting together a deal, we wouldn't want anyone knowing about this backdoor meeting."

"Exactly my thoughts," Eli says.

"There's no need to apologize for being late," Laila says sweetly. But when she shifts her gaze back to me, her expression turns snarky. "I was on tour with Savage for three months, remember? I never expected him to be on time for this meeting, in the first place."

Eli chuckles at Laila's dig, while I exhale and shake my head.

"Well, this is gonna be fun," I mutter.

Daria clears her throat. "Why don't we get down to business, fellas." She leans back in her armchair and crosses her legs. "You gentlemen requested this meeting, so go ahead and make your pitch to Laila as to why she should do this huge favor for Savage."

"Oh, it wouldn't be a favor for *Savage*," Eli insists. "Like I said on the phone, this would be Savage doing a huge favor for *Laila.* He knows how much this would help her career, and—"

"Cut the bullshit," Daria snaps, jerking forward. "Nadine told me everything, on the down low, so let's skip ahead to the part where you try to convince Laila to save Savage's ass from getting shit-canned."

I can't believe my ears. Eli swore Laila would never know I need her to save my job! My jaw hanging open and my eyes bugging out, I look at Eli, as if to say, *Can you believe Nadine ratted me out?* And, instantly, I know I've screwed up when Laila's agent across from me blurts, "I knew it!" while pointing at my face.

"Goddammit, Savage," Eli says, shooting me a murderous glare. "I told you to maintain a poker face at all times."

I look down. Shit. He totally did.

Laila chuckles. But I'm too pissed to look up at her. Fuck.

Daria says, "It's time to put your cards on the table, Eli. Savage messed up last night and, now, his ass is in a sling. The question is: what is Savage willing to do for Laila to save himself?"

Eli leans back. "Savage doesn't need to do a goddamned thing for Laila. This opportunity is way too big for her to pass up. Savage could walk away from this show and still have a monster career that's ten times bigger than Laila's. I'm sorry, Laila, but it's true. This opportunity would be a game-changer for you. You need to be smart."

"Don't address my client directly, please," Daria says. "Especially not to condescendingly tell her to 'be smart.' I represent her in this negotiation, and I'll tell her what I think is 'smart.' And then she'll use her big ol' brain to make the final decision."

Eli bristles. "I apologize, Laila. No disrespect intended."

"It's fine."

Eli returns to Daria. "I'll say this to you, then. You're

doing your client a *huge* disservice, if you're letting her think, even for a minute, she should turn this opportunity down."

Daria sniffs. "I disagree. The per-episode fee for mentors is an insult, especially when they want Laila to take on the added duty of fawning all over your client like he's the great love of her life."

"Fair enough," Eli says. "Then do your job. Rather than sitting here busting my balls about the money, call the producers and demand a sweeter deal."

Daria looks fit to be tied. "Oh, is that how negotiations work, Eli? Thanks for mansplaining it to me." She narrows her eyes. "Believe me, I know exactly what I'm doing. Before I'd even *think* about calling the producers to 'demand a sweeter deal' for my client, we'll first need to reach an understanding between ourselves about our joint demands."

Eli pulls a face. "Our joint demands? We have none. Whatever 'demands' you might have, they're between Laila and the producers."

"Jesus, Eli. Either you're full of shit, or genuinely terrible at this. I'll assume it's the latter, and break it down for you. If you want to lure *my* client to the negotiating table with the producers, then *your* client will need to promise to present a united front with her, during those negotiations, on all her key demands."

Eli sighs and drapes his arm over the back of the love seat. "Which are?"

"Thank you for asking." Daria smiles. "Laila would consider taking part in the proposed fake romance, *if* she's doing so as a full-fledged *judge* for the entire season."

"Ha!" Eli blurts, as I sit forward gaping like a fish.

Daria calmly says, "We want a seat at the judges' table for Laila, and we want Savage to help her get it, or this whole deal will be dead and Savage can kiss his job goodbye."

I look at Laila, trying to gauge if she's onboard with this

attempted extortion, but her face is impassive. A perfect poker face, unlike mine.

"It's impossible," Eli says.

"Nothing's *impossible*," Daria insists. "They hired *Savage* as a judge, in the first place, despite his reputation for being a womanizing man-child who can't keep his donkey dick off Twitter." She smiles at me. "No offense, Mr. Savage."

I can't help returning her smile. "None taken. I actually thought you were complimenting me."

Daria bursts out laughing. "And there's that famous charm. By the way, I thoroughly enjoyed Twitter this morning. That was a top-notch swan dive."

"Why, thank you. I was simply doing my part to spread joy in an otherwise bleak world."

"You're a saint."

"Would you tell Laila that, please? She seems to think I'm the devil." I glance at Laila and smile when I discover her poker face has been replaced by a grin. A reluctant one, but it's there. I explain to Laila, "It was Kai's birthday last night. He dared me, so I had no choice."

"Ah. Birthday Truth or Dare," Laila says, having heard stories about our long-running game from Kendrick. She adds, "Well, then, screw the morality clause in your contract. You had no choice but to strip down and take that naked flying leap."

"See? I knew you'd get it. Why can't the producers?"

Her reluctant grin widens, and for the first time in a long time, we share an easy smile. One that feels genuine and not laced with arsenic. And I can't help thinking that's probably a good sign for my chances here.

Daria says, "The producers know The Savage and Laila Show would bring in record ratings. And that's all they care about, really. *Ratings*. So, let's work together to convince them that's exactly what they'd get."

Eli chuckles. "I admire your tenacity. But you're aiming too high. They haven't budgeted for a fourth judge and the season starts shooting in two days. Please, Daria, let's talk more realistically and find a middle ground we can—"

"There's no middle ground," Daria says flatly. "Laila needs to be offered a full-fledged judgeship this season, with a salary to match, or she'll stick with her current contract and appear for one episode as *Aloha's* mentor. Agree to present a united front with us on a phone call, or this meeting is over."

I flash Laila a look that says, *Damn, maybe I need another agent.* And she flashes me a return look that says, *Right? She kind of scares me a little bit.*

I smile.

So does Laila.

Again.

And, suddenly, I feel tingles skating across my skin.

"For the record," Eli says, "I think you're trying to climb Mount Everest in stilettos. But we're willing to stand united with you, while you try. Right, Savage?"

I nod. "Honestly, I think Laila would make a great judge. I'm all for it."

In truth, I'm deeply skeptical Daria can make this happen for Laila, but why not let her try? It'd be no skin off my nose, if Laila became a judge. In fact, I'd kind of like having her around. First off, to amuse and distract me while I try to stave off the inevitable hives that will surely come from my presence on such a stupid show. But, more importantly, the more weeks Laila appears on the show, the more time that will give me to try to get her into my bed—to finally convince that stubborn woman to let me eat her pussy while she eats her words. The ones that have been torturing me for two months. *This will never happen again.* If Daria's pitch isn't successful, I'm sure she'll cave and negotiate some middle ground for

Laila—which, in the end, will keep me on the show, either way.

"Thank you, Adrian," Laila says, looking genuinely touched. And I feel a sudden jolt of optimism that maybe Laila could find her way to falling out of hate with me, at the end of all this.

I wink. "Sure thing, Fitzy. I truly meant that. I think you'd be great." Laila beams a huge smile at me and I feel myself blush. My heart racing, I look at Daria. "All right, then. Let's make the call and convince the producers to make Laila's little girl dreams come true."

"I can't emphasize this enough," Nadine, the executive producer of *Sing Your Heart Out,* says to our foursome—Daria, me, Savage, and his agent—on speaker phone. "*If* we were to bring Laila on as a fourth judge this season, we'd require Savage and Laila to really sell the romance, both on and off camera, for the *entire* season—plus, a one-month grace period after the finale airs, so nobody thinks the romance was a set-up."

We've been talking to Nadine and some other producers on her end of the call for the past twenty minutes. And much to my shock, Nadine and her people *still* haven't hung up the call and/or told us to pound sand. On the contrary, without committing to anything, Nadine and her team keep artfully testing the waters, lobbing out different concerns and hypothetical non-negotiables they'd require "if" they were to agree to Daria's "unthinkable" proposal. And through it all, true to his word, Savage has maintained a united front with me, casually saying "not a problem" to literally everything the producers have demanded.

Which, by the way, included the shocking demand that

Savage and I would cohabitate this season in a location supplied by the show. When I freaked out, Nadine explained it would make the relationship more believable. Plus, it would make it easier for us to post daily on social media, like a real couple, which would be another requirement. And, finally, Nadine assured us the chosen place would be large enough for Savage and me to cohabitate without murdering each other, and full of enough amenities we'd feel like we're on vacation. And what did Savage say to that particular bit of craziness? To my surprise, all he said was, "Just as long as our place has a hot tub. Laila and I would *definitely* need a hot tub."

Savage was equally unfazed when the producers made it clear they'd require him to quit drinking for the duration of the season, *if* they were to agree to Daria's proposal. All Savage said that time was his usual, "Not a problem."

Currently, Nadine is saying, "We'd also expect Laila to help keep Savage in line. You know, make sure he gets to the set on time and keeps his dick off Twitter."

Everyone on the call, and in Daria's office, laughs, while Savage pushes back for the first time.

"I don't need a babysitter," he says.

"Shut the fuck up," Eli says.

And Savage presses his lips together and looks out the window.

"So, is everything doable, then?" Nadine asks on speaker phone.

"Savage?" Eli says.

"Fine," Savage replies.

"Laila?" Nadine asks.

"Fine for me, too," I say. I look at Savage. "But if I'm going to babysit you, you'd better not give me any trouble."

Savage flashes me a look that says, *Hey, I make no promises.* And without meaning to do it, I smile in reply.

Nadine says, "We're a bit concerned about the relationship being outed as fake. The last thing we'd want is for a flurry of your recent hookups to come out of the woodwork and create a 'cheating scandal' for us. How far back can we safely say this relationship started?"

Savage and I look at each other, neither of us wanting to speak first. On my end, I haven't been with anyone since Savage. And before him, I hadn't been with anyone since my ex-boyfriend, Shawn. So, I'm a clean slate for the past six months. But I certainly don't want to tell Savage that, especially not after our tiff backstage at the Video Music Awards, when I demonically fanned the flames of Savage's ridiculous jealousy about Charlie.

"What if we were to say you two have been living together for the past . . . month?" Nadine ventures. "Would that work?"

Everyone in the room, including me, looks at Savage, since we all know his reputation with women. Indeed, from what I saw first-hand on tour, I can't imagine Savage hasn't been with a virtual army of women over the past month.

Nadine continues, "In theory, we could track down a *few* people and ask them to sign an NDA to make this work. But if we're talking about too many people, then the risks of a leak are probably too high."

Again, the room stares at Savage, prompting him to blurt, "Why is everyone looking at *me*? Laila's the one who jumps from relationship to relationship, from basketball player to fitness trainer, without pausing to catch her breath."

I glower at him. "Hello, pot. Meet kettle."

"Actually, I've been a monk this past month. Since we got back from the tour, I've been keeping crazy hours in the studio, recording our new album."

"Well, that's a lucky break," Nadine says. "Talk about dancing through raindrops! Laila? How about you?"

I can't find my voice. Savage hasn't been with *anyone* since we got back from touring a full month ago? I shouldn't do it. But I have to know. I ask, "You mean everyone you've been with this past month has already signed an NDA, so you're all set?"

"No, I mean I haven't been with anyone. I've practically been living in the studio, except for when I flew home to Chicago for a short visit. I've barely had time to work out this past month, let alone screw around."

I make a face that says, *Color me shocked.*

"Laila?" Nadine repeats. "Can you make that timeline work on your end?"

Crap. I've *so* enjoyed letting Savage think I had a torrid fling with Charlie the Personal Trainer during the tour—and that, maybe, said fling has continued since then, right up until last night. But, oh well. I've got no choice. On the bright side, Nadine only asked about this past month. If I had to admit the full truth, that I haven't had sex with anyone, other than Savage, over the past six months, I'm certain I'd die of humiliation.

I clear my throat. "I'm all clear for the past month, too. I've been really busy myself."

Savage's face is lit up like the Fourth of July. "You've been busy doing *what*?" he asks. Surely, he knows I haven't been hard at work on my next album. Not this soon, when my current album is still spitting out singles. Luckily, though, I've got a fairly credible answer at the ready. One rooted in truth, even if it's not entirely true.

"I've been working a ton on a couple of side projects," I reply. "A collaboration with 22 Goats and a duet with Alessandra Tennison—the one from the video shoot? Her single is doing so well, she got a full-album deal."

"Good for her," Savage says, apparently believing my every word.

I sigh with relief. The projects I've mentioned are real. But while I've laid down vocals for both tracks this past month, the time commitment for both projects combined amounted to only two sessions in the vocal booth. Hardly enough time to claim I've been "working a ton" this past month. In reality, I've been decompressing from the tour. Hanging out with my family, binge-watching shows, working out, and making weird butter dishes, bowls, and vases on my pottery wheel for friends and family who'll never use them. But there's no way I'm letting Savage know I've been a lazy bum this past month, with ample time, but zero interest, in dating.

"So, have we heard all your terms, Nadine?" Daria asks.

"Yes," Nadine confirms. "Are Savage and Laila prepared to agree to all of them?"

Looks are exchanged on our end of the call. Nonverbal confirmations given.

Daria announces, "Yes. Savage and Laila agree to everything."

A cheer erupts on Nadine's end of the call.

"Wonderful!" Nadine says. "We'll email the contracts to you within the hour and—"

"*Whoa*," Daria interjects, holding up her palm, despite Nadine not being here to witness the hand gesture. "Let's not get ahead of ourselves. We still need to deal with the small matter of Laila's *salary* before—"

"Laila's *salary*?" Nadine booms, sounding genuinely flabbergasted.

"Of course. Now that Savage and Laila have agreed to *your* terms, the next item on the agenda is negotiating—"

"Fucking hell, it is!" Nadine shouts, going from zero to sixty in a heartbeat. "This whole conversation, we've been assuming Savage and Laila had already worked out Laila's additional compensation on *their* end!"

"What?" Eli shouts. "Of course, not!"

Nadine counters, "*Of course*! We assumed you called us to offer *two* judges for the price of *one*!"

Well, that's it. Eli loses his mind, going off on a diatribe that makes Daria sit back in her chair, calmly steeple her fingers, and smile. And that's how I know this isn't a glitch. This isn't a sign that everything is falling apart. That, in fact, as far as my brilliant and conniving agent is concerned, everything is going exactly according to plan.

Savage leans into me. "Sorry it didn't work out for you, Fitzy. Honestly, I was pulling for you."

"Thanks for trying," I say. And it's all I can do not to smile wickedly as I say it. I don't know what Daria is up to, exactly. But whatever it is, I'm here for it.

After much shouting on the phone call, Nadine says to Eli, "I told you, quite clearly this morning, we don't have another cent in the budget to add to Laila's salary. We offered her a deal where she'd be Savage's mentor for *three* episodes, and that's all the money we've got at our disposal. Any compensation Laila requires in order to be promoted to a full-fledged judge this season—which, by the way, would give her the kind of publicity money simply can't buy—would need to come out of *Savage's* pocket, not ours."

Well, that gets Savage's attention. He jolts to standing and barks, "There's no way I'm paying Laila a dime of my salary. I was willing to support her crazy idea, as a *favor* to her, as long as it didn't affect *me,* but—"

I jump up, matching Savage's angry body language. "As a favor to *me,* my ass. You did it to save yourself! If anyone is doing a favor here, it's *me* doing one for *you*!"

"Bullshit," he grits out. "You know you've got me

between a rock and a hard place, and you're shamelessly exploiting me."

"*Exploiting* you?" I retort. "*You're* the one who breached his morality clause, not me. *You're* the one who needs a fake girlfriend to 'redeem' your stupid fuckboy ass this season. You'd already be fired right now, if it weren't for me and the world's bizarre obsession with us being a couple."

Savage scoffs. "Gee, Laila. I wonder how the world got obsessed with that idea? Could it be you purposely fanned the flames of that rumor on *Sylvia,* for your own benefit?"

"I did not!" I shout. "I tried to put the fire *out* on *Sylvia*! I literally denied we're a couple!"

His tone dripping with sarcasm, Savage says, "Yeah, and you did it *sooo* convincingly." He rolls his eyes. "Ninety percent of all human communication is *nonverbal*, Laila. And guess what *your* nonverbal communication screamed on *Sylvia*? 'Hell, yes, we're totally fucking!'"

I gasp like this is news to me, even though countless friends texted me after that interview to razz me about that very thing. But good friends can tease me about that—not assholes I hate! Assholes who texted me their room number, begging me to show up so they could finally taste me, so they could "eat me from every angle," and then, minutes later, brought yet another groupie to their room.

"People were already obsessed with us being a couple before my interview," I insist. "That's why Sylvia brought up your name. And you should be grateful she did, because that interview going viral is what convinced Nadine to hire you as Hugh's replacement in the first place. Right, Nadine?"

"No comment."

"So let me get this straight," Savage says. "You shamelessly used me as click-bait on *Sylvia* to further your own career, and you want me to *thank* you for doing it?"

"Oh, you mean, kinda like how you used *my* name as click-bait last night, with that Instagrammer?"

Savage pulls a face like I've just barfed straight into his mouth. "I didn't even mention your name to that Insta-grammer last night! I said I needed to 'lay low' because of the *show.*"

"Sure, Jan," I say, invoking a famous meme from *The Brady Bunch.*

Savage says, "If you think a single word of what that Instagrammer said was true, then you're either crazy or projecting, or both."

"Projecting *what*?"

"*Your* obsession with *me* onto *me*!"

I roll my entire head, not only my eyes. "Oh, please. I haven't given you a moment's thought since the tour ended."

"Sure, Jan," he says, throwing my comment back to me.

"Was last night some kind of a staged set-up?" I ask.

Savage's features contort with disdain. "You're asking if I conspired with a random Instagrammer I'd just met at a party to post a crazy story about you and me . . . for publicity?"

It sounds even crazier when he says it back to me. But I persist. "Maybe. You had to know she's got a *huge* following."

"I didn't, actually."

"And you also had to know she *constantly* posts about her infatuation with *you*. She's practically president of your fan club! So, I don't think it's crazy to assume you knew she'd post about her interaction with you, however insignificant—see exhibits one through a million on Twitter—and you decided to give her something to post about. Something you knew would go viral."

Savage shakes his head. "You know you sound like a deranged lunatic right now, right?"

He's right. I do. I'm a stone-cold nutter. But I don't care.

I'm a runaway train. "It's not any crazier than believing you told her you had to 'lay low' and she heard 'Laila.'" Come on, Savage. We both know you said my name. And you *knew,* with all the publicity we've had lately—we're a freaking meme, dude!—that mentioning my name would be like throwing a lit match onto a puddle of gasoline!"

"I didn't say your name, for the love of fuck!" he roars, absolutely beside himself with frustration. "Thanks to your stupid interview on *Sylvia,* she *assumed* we must be fucking —just like everyone else assumes it! Do you have any idea how many friends texted me after seeing that interview? They were like, 'Dude, if you two aren't already having sex, then buy yourself a huge box of condoms, pronto, because Laila's gonna show up on your doorstep any day now, demanding to fuck you for a solid week straight!'?"

I gasp loudly.

"Don't even bother fake gasping with me, Laila Fitzgerald," Savage says. "I spent three months on the road with you. I know nothing fazes you."

He's right. That gasp was totally fake. And, unfortunately, a little over the top. But I don't care. I gasp again and say, "Nobody sent you a text about me after *Sylvia.* You're a liar."

"*Everybody* did," he replies.

"And by 'everybody,' you mean Kendrick and Kai?"

"Kendrick and Kai and lots more. C-Bomb . . ."

"And . . .?"

"Lots of people."

"Bullshit."

"Swear to God.

"Prove it."

"I can." He pulls out his phone and starts swiping angrily. "I saved *all* their texts, in case I'd ever have the opportunity to rub them in your smug little face."

I snort. "Ha! That was a trap, Einstein, and you walked

right into it. If your goal is to convince me you're *not* totally obsessed with me, then admitting you saved a bunch of texts about us being secret fuck buddies isn't helping your cause."

"I didn't *save* the texts," Savage insists. "I never *deleted* them, because I didn't get around to it."

"Wow, shocker. Yet another thing I can't stand about you. All your unread texts! Look at your inbox right now and tell me how many you have. I bet it's more than a thousand."

He looks down and makes a face that tells me I've guessed right. "They're not *all* unread. Just because I haven't clicked on them doesn't mean I haven't seen them in the preview pane or—"

"Hey, guys," Nadine interjects on speaker phone, and we both freeze. She continues, "This is highly entertaining. Truly, it is. But I've gotta stop you now." As Savage and I exchange a look I'd call, *Well, that's embarrassing,* Nadine chuckles and says, "Damn, I wish I had a big bowl of popcorn right now. Or maybe a vibrator."

Everyone on Nadine's end of the call explodes with laughter, as Savage and I return to our seats and exchange angry looks that say, *This is all your fault!*

"You two really would be ratings gold," Nadine says wistfully. "Great job, guys. If this 'fight' was your clever way of coaxing us to throw some more money into the pot for Laila, consider your tactic a success. We really don't have another dime in the budget to offer, but in an effort to close the deal, we're willing to offer Laila a performance slot in the finale."

Whoa.

That's the brass ring. The kind of publicity that catapults any song straight into the Top Ten, if not to Number One.

I look at Daria and she winks, yet again confirming everything is going exactly according to plan.

Eli interjects, "Savage would require a performance slot, as well."

Nadine exhales with annoyance. "Hold, please." She places the call on hold for an eternal moment, during which Savage and I exchange dirty looks to the beat of the elevator version of "Fuck You" by CeeLo Green. Finally, Nadine returns to the call and declares, "Okay. We'll give Savage and Laila a *shared* performance slot in the finale. They can do a mash-up of their respective singles, or anything else they come up with. But we only have *one* performance slot to offer the happy couple, collectively. So they'll have to learn to *share*."

Savage and I look at each other, conciliation slowly passing between us. It's not ideal, granted. But we could make it work. We might both have been posturing like peacocks with splayed tails for the past few minutes, but there's no denying a performance slot in the finale, even a shared one, is too big a perk to pass up.

"I could make that work," Savage murmurs.

I nod and look away, letting him know I agree, but only *barely.*

"Laila is on board, too," Daria says. "Unhappy about it but on board."

"Wonderful," Nadine says. "So, can I *finally* send over the contracts, then?"

"Not quite yet," Daria replies. "We have a deal, as far as *you're* concerned. But we still need to reach an agreement on our end about Laila's compensation."

"Jesus Christ, Daria," Eli snaps. "Savage isn't going to pay Laila a dime out of his pocket!"

Daria shrugs nonchalantly. "Then I'm sorry to say the deal is dead." She smiles ruefully at the phone on her desk. "Thank you for your time, everyone. We're sorry we couldn't make this work, but Laila is still thrilled to be Aloha's mentor for one episode this season."

"Eli!" Nadine barks. "Don't be a fool! Negotiate with

Laila about her compensation. For the love of all things holy, Savage is the one who screwed everything up here—so, if someone has to lose an ass cheek to make this work, it's going to be *him*!"

Savage and his agent exchange a look, and I know, in my bones, Savage realizes the truth of what Nadine said. It's a surprising development, to say the least, to witness Savage being so willing to make this work. Especially given what I know he thinks of this show. He said himself, in Philadelphia, he thinks it's cringey-ass. So, why did he say yes to being Hugh's replacement in the first place? And why is he fighting so hard to keep his job now? All I can think is the show must have offered Savage an arm, a leg, and two huge butt cheeks to do the show—some amount of money that made Savage willing to endure the "hives" he's sure to contract every time he steps on-set.

I look at Daria and it's instantly clear she's thinking what I'm thinking. *How much money did the show offer Savage to get him to say yes?*

"Hey, Nadine," Daria says, leaning over the phone on her desk. "What's Savage's salary this season?"

"Don't answer that," Savage's agent barks. "That's none of her business."

"I can't divulge that," Nadine confirms.

Daria places her palms on her desk, on either side of her phone. "I know what Aloha is making this season. Ten mill." She looks up at Savage, apparently trying to gauge his reaction. "I'm guessing, all things considered, Savage's deal would be *significantly* less than that. Maybe . . . a third of that?"

"Say nothing, Nadine," Eli shouts.

"I can't confirm or deny," Nadine replies. But something in her tone feels a whole lot like she's screaming, "Confirm, confirm, confirm!" Daria turns her dark, sultry eyes on Eli.

"Come on, Mr. McKenzie," she coos. "Let's get this deal done. Both of our clients stand to make a shit-ton of money from endorsements and increased music sales after the season."

The adults in the room begin sparring, and while they do that, Savage sidles up to me at the proverbial kiddie table, his body language cocky and decidedly sexual. He takes an empty armchair next to me.

"Hey, Fitzy," he says, like we're back in Providence, sharing a bottle of booze outside the twins' birthday party in the moonlight.

"You can't charm me into taking less money," I say flatly.

Savage bites his lower lip, well aware he looks irresistible when he does that. "I'm not trying to charm you into doing anything. I'm merely pointing out that, if we do this, we'll be stuck together in a kickass house—with a hot tub—for three months." He licks his lips in a way I've seen him do many, many times. Like he's thinking about performing oral sex. "I'm saying all the orgasms I could give you during our fake romance should be factored into your calculations. I'd think they'd be worth *something*."

I roll my eyes, even as every inch of my skin erupts in lustful goosebumps. "Not gonna happen. I told you that was a one-time thing that will never happen again."

Savage straightens up, all hint of seduction gone. "I'm not paying you a dime, Laila. Everything Daria's already negotiated for you is well beyond anything you dreamed was possible when you woke up this morning. So, stop being greedy."

I clench my jaw. "I'm not being greedy. This is business, and I'm letting my agent get me the best deal possible, which is exactly what your agent initially did for *you,* and what he's also doing now. Don't think, even for a minute, your donkey dick is some kind of dangling carrot for me."

"Sure, bunny. You're not any more believable now than you were on *Sylvia*."

"If anyone is being greedy, it's you. You're the one who messed up, not me. So, you should be the one to have to sacrifice to fix your mess."

Sexual heat washes over him. He leans forward sharply, sending his sexy cologne into my nostrils. "You wanna see me being greedy, sweetheart? Then let me eat your pussy. I'll show you a kind of greed that'll take your breath away."

I inhale sharply, taken aback by the hungry look in his eyes.

"Laila!" Daria barks from across the room. "Stop talking to him right now!"

I lean back sharply, feeling like a kid who's been caught saying a curse word. "He wasn't convincing me of anything," I blurt. But even I can hear the lie in my tone.

"Oh, jeez," Daria mutters, throwing up her hands. "Seriously? The world is full of big dicks, Laila. He's got nothing to offer that can't be found elsewhere." She leans into the speaker phone. "Nadine, we're gonna have to call you back. Savage is trying to charm the pants off my client, literally."

Nadine replies she'll give our side fifteen minutes to reach a deal. "We're running out of time here, folks," she says sternly. "If you don't call us back within fifteen minutes, saying you've reached a deal on your end, we're going to cut bait and move forward with our Plan B—someone else we've already lined up to replace Savage, if needed."

Well, that gets everyone's attention, especially Savage's.

Daria ends the call and rests half her bottom on the edge of her desk. "Okay, gentlemen. You heard Nadine. She's already got someone else lined up. So, the question Savage needs to ask himself is this: 'Do I want one hundred percent of *nothing* . . . or *fifty* percent of *something*?'"

"He'll give her *ten* percent," Eli says.

And Daria replies by launching into a long speech about why I'm not going to take anything less than half Savage's salary, whatever it is. "This would have to be an equal partnership in all ways," Daria says. "Because Savage needs Laila as much as she needs him."

Eli protests. Daria gives as good as she gets. And through it all, I bite my lip to prevent myself from caving. Honestly, if left to my own devices, I'd take the offered ten percent and be done with this. At this point, if push came to shove, I'd do the damned show for free, for nothing but the exposure and that invaluable performance slot in the finale.

"Laaaailaaaaa," Savage coos softly, like he's camped between my legs and has just raised his head. "Sweetheart, call off your pit bull. Let's do this. Ten percent."

"Mr. Savage," Daria says, "Laila hired me precisely *because* I'm a pit bull. Fifty-fifty, or she walks. Tick tock." Daria glares at me, her dark eyes commanding me to keep my mouth shut. But I can't help myself. The pressure is getting to me. Maybe I am being greedy here, like Savage said.

"Savage, I have family members I want to help out with—"

"No, Laila!" Daria commands, putting up her index finger. "You don't need to justify getting yourself paid. Men negotiate *massive* paydays for themselves in every industry, and *nobody* ever holds it against them or wonders if they have family members to support."

I look at Savage, suddenly remembering our conversation in that green room in Philadelphia, when I admitted I'd been hired as a mentor on *Sing Your Heart Out*. "Actually, that's an excellent point, Daria. In the past, I've made the mistake of mixing business and emotion and not realizing what I'm worth. A really savvy businessman once told me not to do either. So, this time, I think I'll follow his brilliant advice."

Savage narrows his eyes and practically snarls.

"So, what's it gonna be, gentlemen?" Daria says. "We've got four minutes before Nadine hires Savage's replacement. We want fifty percent of Savage's take, whatever that is. Final offer."

Eli throws a Hail Mary. He says Savage has four bandmates, and a shitty deal with River Records, which means he nets far less from his music royalties than we probably think.

"Cry me a river," Daria replies. "Fifty percent. Yes or no?"

The guys huddle up. And as they do, I clutch my sides and rock in place, feeling like I'm going to explode from anxiety. But, finally, Eli and Savage break free of their conversation and confirm we've got a deal.

"Hallelujah!" Daria shouts, springing out of her chair. She shakes Eli's hand, and then Savage's, before wrapping me in a warm hug. And when I nuzzle my face into my agent's neck, a dam breaks inside me. As I cry into Daria's neck, she whispers into my ear, "This is gonna change your life forever."

After thanking her profusely, I disengage from Daria, expecting to find Savage awaiting me, the same way his agent is doing. But to my surprise, as I shake Eli's hand, Savage is sulking in a corner of Daria's office, gazing out the window.

"I'll call Nadine and tell her the good news!" Daria chirps, ignoring the thick anger wafting off the rockstar in the corner. She picks up her phone, but pauses. "Real quick. Now that we've shaken on it, what's Laila's fifty percent worth?"

Eli addresses his sulking client. "You wanna tell her?"

Savage turns his burning eyes from the window to me, leveling me with a glower that takes my breath away. "Congratulations, Miss Fitzgerald," he says, his jaw tight. "You just extorted me for two . . . *million* . . . bucks."

With jackets draped over our heads, Laila and I are guided into the backseat of an SUV in Daria's underground parking garage—the chariot sent by the show's producers to whisk us off, discreetly, to whatever overnight "hideaway" they've arranged until our permanent digs can been finalized. I hear the click of the back door as I settle into the backseat next to Laila's body heat. Then, the sound of the car's front doors opening and closing, followed by the voice of one of our two handlers—a bodyguard and driver sent by the producers—announcing, "All clear. You can uncover your heads now."

I remove the jacket from my head to find Laila, her sandy hair mussed and her face aglow, sitting next to me in the large SUV. Without delay, the driver starts the engine, prompting Daria and Eli to wave goodbye to us through the windshield like proud parents, and off we go, under cover of dark tinted windows, out the garage and into the midday sun on Wilshire Boulevard.

"This is wild," Laila says, sounding giddy. "I feel like 'the package' in a spy thriller!" She touches her ear, like she's talking into an earpiece. "The Package . . . is on . . . *its way.*"

She giggles, but I'm still too pissed about the money to join her. I was more than happy to help Laila secure a seat at the judges' table, if doing so didn't impact *me* and my bottom line. But I never would have lifted a finger to help her if I'd thought, even for a minute, it would pave the way for her to fleece me out of half my salary. I need every dime of that salary, and then some, to comfortably pay for my grandmother's house. I'm sure I can make the deal work somehow, probably with a loan. But a loan wasn't part of my plan when I decided to buy that house.

The giddy expression on Laila's face evaporates when she sees my sour one. "Oh, come on," she says, shoving my shoulder. "You're *still* grouchy about the money? Let it go!"

"Yes, I'm *still* grouchy. It's been less than an hour since we signed our contracts, through which you extorted me for two million bucks."

"Extorted," she mutters, rolling her eyes. "You made a willing and informed decision, based on expert guidance from your agent. Now, get up, dust off your knees, and get over it."

"*Get over it*? Laila, I'm rightfully going to be pissed about two *million* bucks until the day I die."

She holds up her water bottle, like she's toasting me. "Well, here's hoping that day comes sooner, rather than later, for both our sakes."

"I never even wanted to do the stupid show!" I blurt. "When they first offered it to me, I said *no*. They offered me two mill, and then three, before I finally, begrudgingly, said yes for four. I never would have done it for two mill!"

"Well, lesson learned," she says. "Maybe next time you won't take a two-million-dollar naked swan dive into a swimming pool where anyone could see you, huh?"

"It was a *dare*."

"No," she says. "It was Drunk Savage's way of self-sabotaging—of getting himself out of a contract he wishes he'd never signed in the first place."

I open and close my mouth. Is she right about that? It rings true. I've definitely had a problem with self-sabotage throughout my life. Case in point, the way I pushed Laila away, so vigorously, during the tour. I lean toward her. "Tell the truth, Laila. Now that the contracts are signed and your agent isn't here to get you all fired up about the gender pay gap, you *know* you let Daria commit highway robbery on your behalf today, right?"

She scoffs. "Absolutely not. Am I elated about the way things worked out? Hell yes, I am! *Whoop*! This is one of the best days of my life." She narrows her eyes. "But I don't feel sorry for you. You're already making more money in a year than most people make in a lifetime. Way more than me, I'm sure, despite what your agent said about you having four bandmates and a shitty deal at the label."

"I'm not nearly as flush as you probably think. I've made some big purchases recently."

"Oh, *waah, waah*. You're blessed to be doing the thing you love most as your actual job, for some amount of money that would make anyone else feel like they won the lottery. So, suck it up. Your agent advised you to give me half your already-inflated 'salary' so you wouldn't get fired, due to your own screw-up. If you want to be mad at someone, be mad at yourself for being a self-sabotaging idiot."

Well, damn. I look out the window, so she won't see me smile. I don't like getting bitch-slapped by most people in this world. But when Laila does it, I can't deny that it turns me on.

Laila continues speaking to the back of my head. "Now, if

you don't mind, I need you to stop complaining about the money, so I can try to get into character, which I can't do when you're acting like a whiny little bitch."

I return my gaze to hers. "Get into character?"

She nods. "Somehow, against all odds, I need to convince myself I'm not in deep *hate* with you, but in deep and abiding *love*." At that last word, she sticks out her tongue, like a cat getting rid of a fur ball. And, once again, I look out the window to hide my grin. A lot of things suck about this situation. But being stuck with Laila for the next three months ain't one of them.

For the millionth time, I find myself wondering how she resisted coming to my room in Vegas and beyond. I would have bet *anything* she'd have caved at some point. In fact, I was so positive she'd relent and come to me in Vegas, I stayed up all night after that show, alone in my bed, waiting for her. Thinking every sound outside my door was her. I must have opened my hotel room door or peeked out my peephole ten times that night. Each time, feeling more and more deflated when she wasn't there.

"So, that's it?" Laila says, filling the silence. "You're going to look out your window and sulk and not speak to me?"

I take a deep breath and return my gaze to hers. "I'm not *not* speaking to you. I'm processing everything that's happened. It's been a crazy day and I've still got a hangover."

"Speaking of which, you think you'll be able to handle not drinking for the next three months?"

"Starting tomorrow, mind you. And yes, I'll be fine."

"I'll do it with you, if you'd like."

"They didn't require that of you."

"True, but what self-respecting fake girlfriend would make her fake boyfriend resist temptation for three months, all by himself?"

"Thanks. I'd appreciate that."

"Sure thing," she says. "You want to get shitfaced with me tonight, as a last hurrah?"

"I'm down."

"Fair warning: I'll probably be a lightweight tonight," she says. "I haven't been drunk for a while. I've been on a health kick lately. Eating clean."

"Yeah, you look *really* good."

"Thanks. So do you."

Heat passes between us. Or, at least, I feel it. And, again, I find myself wondering how the hell she resisted me for a full month—after *knowing,* for a fact, we're a five-alarm fire together. Was Charlie *that* amazing in bed?

My phone buzzes in my lap and I look down to find a text from Kendrick, asking me what happened at today's meeting with Laila. I motion to my phone. "Kendrick is wondering what happened at the meeting today. Do you think it'd be a breach of my contract to tell him the truth about the situation? You know, about you and me?" As Laila knows, the producers were adamant that the truth about our fake relationship is "top secret." To be divulged only on a "need to know" basis.

Laila purses her lips and shifts her position on the car seat. "I think it's fine. The producers said not to tell anyone not directly related to the show, remember? But Kendrick *is* directly related to the show, since he's going to be your mentor this season. Even if you didn't trust him like a brother, I'm sure his contract contains a confidentiality clause, the same as ours."

"Excellent point, counselor."

"But don't worry, if I'm technically wrong and you aren't allowed to tell him, I promise on our fake love not to rat you out to the producers for spilling the beans."

Warmth pools in my chest at the adorable look on her

face. "Thanks. If you want to text your mom and sister and tell them the situation, I also promise on our fake love not to rat you out. I know how close you are with them."

Laila's eyebrows shoot up in surprise. "How do you know that?"

My chest tightens. "You talked about them during the tour."

"Not to you. I'm sure I never told you anything about my mom and sister."

I feel my cheeks turning red. "You told Ruby or Kendrick when I was sitting nearby, I think . . ."

She looks floored but says nothing.

My cheeks burning hot, I say, "You mentioned your mom a couple times during your hideously exploitative *Sylvia* interview. You know, the one where you used me as clickbait? So, maybe that's what I'm remembering."

Laila rolls her eyes.

"So, are you going to tell your family or not?" I ask, desperate to deflect.

"No. I think I'll keep things to myself for a while. My sister is trustworthy, but give my mom some wine and a few of her best friends, and she'd likely babble the whole damned story, without meaning to do it."

I chuckle. "Yeah, it's probably best to keep things tight as a drum for now, and stick with only telling people directly involved with the show."

"Agreed. Better safe than sorry."

"So, are you gonna tell Aloha, then?" I ask.

"Yeah. She's going to laugh her ass off." Chuckling, she grabs her phone while I grab mine.

"Tell Aloha I say hi," I say.

"The same to Kendrick. Oh, hey . . ." She pushes on my thigh, and her touch sends a blast of arousal streaking through me. "Ask Kendrick to send me the scoop on babysitting

Adrian Savage, since keeping you from self-destructing is apparently my actual *job* now."

"I can already tell you what he's going to say: 'You're fucked. There's no owner's manual. Every day with every one of Savage's many personalities is a new adventure.'"

She snorts. "More like a *nude* adventure."

I can't help laughing. "Are you complaining about that? Because if so, you're the only one."

"Oh, God. I've got to endure three months of this?" With that, she looks down and starts tapping away. I watch her for a moment, admiring her profile. And, finally, grab my phone and tap out a reply to Kendrick.

Me: Crisis averted. The meeting was IN-FUCKING-SANE, but, in the end, I'm still a judge, by the skin of my teeth, and you're still my team's mentor. But in a shocking twist, Laila is now the show's first-ever fourth judge and my live-in fake girlfriend for the entire season.

Kendrick: WHAAAAT?!?!?!

Me: It's reality TV, baby! LOL. They think a "romance storyline" will bring in record ratings. They're getting us a cool pad with lots of amenities so we can do tons of behind the scenes social media stuff. You know, like a real couple.

Kendrick: I'm shook. I got a text from the producers a few minutes ago, telling me to pack an overnight bag, clear my schedule for the rest of today and tomorrow, and stay tuned for further info. What's that about?

Me: They're pulling together a last minute promo shoot with the full cast this afternoon. They want to have every-thing ready to go right after tomorrow's press conference.

Kendrick: Where are you right now?

Me: In a car with Laila, being driven to some secret hideout for tonight.

Kendrick: I'm surprised you agreed to go along with this. But I'm SHOCKED she agreed.

Me: It took half my salary to get her to do it. And by that, I mean I'm literally paying her half my salary out of my own pocket.

Kendrick: WHAT?!?!?!?! WHY?!?!?!?!

Me: Long story. I'll tell you in person. Trust me, I'm not happy about it. But, in the end, it'll be worth it.

Kendrick: Yeah, regardless, you're still getting paid a shit-ton of EASY money, dude. And the show will sell a lot of records for us.

Me: Exactly.

Kendrick: Yo! I just got a text from the show. They're sending a car for me in an hour.

Me: Then I guess I'll be seeing you soon.

Kendrick: Be nice to Laila in the meantime.

Me: Now, why would I do that, when she likes assholes so much?

Kendrick: LOL. Okay, Player. You do you.

And then, hopefully, Laila, I think. But, of course, I don't say that to Kendrick. He's been cool about me getting with her in Phoenix, but there's no need for me to rub salt in my best friend's wound.

"Did Kendrick have any good babysitting tips for me?" Laila asks, when I put my phone in my lap.

"I forgot to ask him. But, like I said, there's no point. His reply would be, basically, 'You're fucked.'"

"You never know. Ask him, anyway. I've never babysat a full-grown man-child before, and I need all the help I can get."

I tap out the message and read Kendrick's immediate reply. "Kendrick says, 'Babysitting Savage is all about giving him positive reinforcement when he's a good boy, redirecting or gently scolding when he's a bad boy (but only if you catch him in the act). And, most importantly, always give him lots of chew toys so he doesn't destroy your couch or slippers because he's got a major oral fixation.'"

Laila giggles. "Tell him thanks. That's actually very helpful."

Damn. The look she just shot me was pure fire.

She motions to my phone. "Aren't you gonna tell him thanks?"

My eyes drift to her lips, briefly. "Uh. Yeah." I tap out the message and then plop my phone onto the car seat between us. I ask, "So, you want to start hashing out the backstory of our 'romance' before tomorrow's press conference?" It's what the producers told us to do, so our answers sound credible and consistent.

"There's no time like the present," she says. "What's the story of how we first got together, my darling? Let's start there."

"Hmm," I say. But before I've said more, our SUV hangs a right onto a quiet residential street, and, suddenly, I know exactly where we are—and where we're headed. I gesture toward the distinctive iron gate coming into view at the end of the long street—the one I recognize as the gate in front of Reed Rivers' hilltop mansion. "Looks like we're staying at Reed's tonight."

"Oh, wow . . ." she says, peering through the windshield. "That's his gate?"

"It sure is," I mumble. "Shit."

"You don't like Reed?"

"I like him fine," I lie. But, really, me not liking Reed isn't the problem. The truth is, I was looking forward to spending the evening alone with Laila. She already mentioned she's down to get shitfaced with me. And the last time we were both shitfaced, I practically fucked her off a lounge chair. But it's fine. Whether we're alone or staying at Reed's tonight, the plan is the same. It's now my mission from God to eat this woman while making her eat those fateful words that have plagued me since the night of the hot tub: *This will never happen again.*

TWENTY-SIX
SAVAGE

After our SUV passes through Reed's iron gate and comes to a stop in his large, circular driveway, there's a flurry of activity already in progress in front of the large house. Several vans and cars are parked there, and an army of workers are coming in and out. One of our bodyguards advises Laila and me to stay put in the back-seat for a moment while he "inspects" the area for paparazzi, and when he's satisfied we're all clear, he swiftly escorts us from the SUV into Reed's house, as Laila giggles and makes another crack about the imaginary "spy thriller" we're star-ring in.

Upon entering the mansion, we're greeted by the executive producer of *Sing Your Heart Out*, Nadine Collins, who explains the workers are busy creating a studio in Reed's game room, where Laila and I, and the entire cast—all four judges and their assigned mentors—will shoot some promo videos and photos to be released after tomorrow's press conference—which, Nadine explains, will also take place at Reed's house, to minimize the potential for leaks.

"I've sent production assistants to collect some personal

items for your stay tonight, as well as at the permanent location," Nadine says. "We should have the new place lined up by tomorrow night."

We thank her and she asks if we have any questions.

"Have you been able to confirm my mentor yet?" Laila asks. As was discussed today during one of our phone calls with the producers, now that Laila has been unexpectedly promoted to judge, both Laila and Aloha will need mentors, both of which will be selected by the producers with an eye toward maximizing ratings.

"We've got several mentor candidates we're in talks with," Nadine replies. "I've got a scheduled call to finalize our decision in . . . " She looks at her watch. "Damn. I'm late for my call. Reed is out back having a get-together with some friends. He said for you to come outside and join him." She calls to an elegant older woman who looks to be Latina, and when she arrives, the woman introduces herself as Reed's longtime housekeeper, Amalia. Nadine tasks Amalia with escorting us outside and getting us fed before scurrying off for her call like a chicken with her head cut off.

"Would you prefer to see your rooms before joining Reed outside?" Amalia asks. "Or *room*, if that's what you prefer?"

"We'll definitely need separate rooms," Laila replies. "Is there food outside?"

"Yes, lots of it."

"Then I'd prefer to go outside now and see our rooms later, please. If that's okay. I'm starving."

"Of course, dear. As you wish. I'll be here all night."

We follow the elegant housekeeper toward a set of double doors. And I can't help feeling an illogical pang of disappointment Laila said we'll need separate rooms.

Outside, we find Reed partying with a small group of friends. We're introduced to the only people we haven't met before—a couple Reed introduces as Henn and Hannah. From there, we greet the rest, all of whom we know. When Laila greets everyone, she gives them hugs like they're her lifelong besties, while I dispense a series of simple hellos. I'm especially standoffish with the wife of Dax Morgan, the lead singer of 22 Goats. Dax's wife, Violet, is also Reed's little sister. The one I flirted with a few years ago at a party, long before Violet had met Dax, without me realizing her connection to Reed. I don't know if Dax knows the story, but I wouldn't put it past Reed to tell him, and I feel a bit awkward about it.

Besides Dax and Violet, I'm relieved to see Fish, the bass player of 22 Goats, and his cute girlfriend, Alessandra, the artist from the music video in New York, are also here. Those two are as nice as humans come from the factory. So, at least, until Kendrick gets here, I won't feel like the entire party hates me.

As conversation continues, I hang back and watch my fake girlfriend flit around Reed's patio like the social butterfly she is, easily engaging with everyone, the same way she did during our tour. Staff, crew, musicians. It didn't matter during our tour. There was nobody Laila Fitzgerald couldn't charm and easily befriend. Unlike me. I mean, I can charm people. That's easy. But genuinely befriending them comes a whole lot harder for me.

As Laila and I are talking to Fish and Alessandra, Reed pointedly brings his date over to say hello to Laila and me. And, once again, like in New York, his date is none other than Georgina. The sultry reporter for *Rock 'n' Roll*. How Reed still hasn't gotten bored with her and moved along to the next yet, or, conversely, hasn't royally messed things up with her, I have no idea. But, plainly, by the couple's body language, they're still going strong.

As Laila hugs Georgina in greeting, Reed trains his steely

gaze on me. "You remember my fiancée, Georgina, don't you, Savage?"

Reflexively, my eyes dart to Georgina's left hand. And, I'll be damned, she's wearing a glittering golf ball on her ring finger.

Laila expresses effusive congratulations to her friend—apparently the women bonded quite a bit during the music video shoot—while I say, "Yeah, of course, I remember Georgina. Congratulations, Reed. You're a lucky man."

"Yes, I am," Reed replies. And there's no doubt in my mind he means it. Also, that he's still holding a grudge from months ago, when I had the audacity to hit on Georgina when she appeared to be a single reporter at a party. It's so on-brand for Reed to be holding a grudge for something so stupid, I can't help chuckling to myself.

"What's funny?" Reed asks.

"Nothing. I'm so happy for you, I'm bursting with joy."

Reed glares at me like he wants to punch the smile off my face. So, I smile even more broadly at him. Why does Reed always have to make it so damned hard to like him? For the love of fuck, I didn't know Violet was his little sister when I hit on her a thousand years ago! And I didn't know Georgina was destined to become his future wife when I hit on *her*! Which, by the way, I only did for Kendrick's birthday amusement, in the first place.

Feeling thoroughly annoyed, not to mention kind of peopled out, I wander away from the group to fill a plate at a nearby food table. Once I've got my meal in hand, I wander to a quiet corner and gratefully take a load off.

After a while, Laila appears, holding her own plate and a glass of wine. "Is this seat taken, fake boyfriend?" she asks.

"I was saving it especially for you, fake girlfriend."

She sits. "Crazy day, huh?"

"It definitely took an unexpected turn."

"Are you still mad about the money?"

"Nah. I'm over it. It's only money. I can always make more."

"Now, that's the spirit." She peers at me. "You still look grumpy."

I shrug. "That's just my face."

She laughs. "I'm the same way. Unless I'm smiling, everyone thinks I'm pissed or angry. The irony is, when I'm smiling, it's far more likely I'm plotting murder. So never judge my emotions by my face."

"I think you've plotted my murder a time or two."

"Or a thousand."

"At least."

We eat in silence for a bit, until Laila says, "You don't like parties very much, huh?"

I pick up a chicken wing. "I like parties, as long as I'm not required to speak to anyone I don't know."

"Yeah, I picked up on that during the tour. You never once came to a single game night with the crew and staff."

"They had game nights?"

"Every Thursday night. It was fun."

"Nobody ever invited me."

"Would you have come, if they did?"

"No. But it would have been nice to be invited."

We're silent again for a while, eating and drinking. Looking at the spectacular view.

After a while, I say, "I don't think it's weird to prefer hanging out with my best friends, rather than strangers. Doesn't everyone prefer that?"

"Yes and no. Sometimes, it's nice to meet new people. Get to know them. Hear their stories."

I shudder and she laughs.

"You really hate to mingle, don't you?"

"I *hate* it. We have to do it so much in our line of work, so when I'm not 'on,' I'd much rather be totally 'off.'"

"I get that."

"But it's not the way you're wired."

"Not really. I love being alone to recharge, for sure. But I also love being around people, too." She takes a long sip of her wine, and I watch the movement of her lips as the fluid passes them, suddenly feeling overwhelmed with the desire to taste them. I remember them wrapped around my cock. The way they were swollen and red when I pulled myself out of her mouth.

"What about Fish?" she asks, pulling me from my reverie.

"What about him?"

"He's a friend of yours, right?"

"He's a friend of everyone's. He's like Kendrick. Why?"

"I was surprised you seemed kind of standoffish around him, earlier."

"I wasn't being standoffish. I was just . . . standing."

"It seemed like you were upset."

"Laila, that's just my face."

Laila laughs. "Okay."

"Honestly, I'd probably hang out with Fish a lot more, if he wasn't always hanging out with his bandmates."

She furrows her brow. "You don't like Dax and Colin? How is that possible?"

"I like them. They don't like *me.*"

Laila scoffs. "That's impossible. Dax and Colin like everyone."

"C-Bomb is a good buddy of mine." I don't need to say anything further. Everyone at River Records, and probably in the world, knows the 22 Goats' smash hit, "Judas," penned by Dax, is about Dax's beef with the drummer of Red Card Riot.

Laila nods, apparently buying my explanation. I don't think it's the whole truth, though. But there's no way I'm going to mention I once hit on Dax's wife and also had a fling with Colin's ex-girlfriend to the woman I'm hell-bent on sleeping with.

"So, should we talk about our backstory now?" she asks.

Reflexively, my eyes drift to her mouth again. "Yeah."

"If we go by Nadine's suggested timeline," she says, "we got together around the end of the tour."

"Mm-hmm." My eyes are on her tits now. I haven't spent this much time in Laila's presence in a long time. I'd forgotten how intoxicating her simple presence is to me.

She takes a bite of food before saying, "The only bummer about that timeline is that it makes me out to be a bald-faced liar on *Sylvia*. Two weeks ago, I swore on national TV there was no truth to the rumors about us. And now, suddenly, it turns out we're in love and *living* together? So embarrassing.*"*

"It serves you right," I say. "You *were* a bald-faced liar on *Sylvia.*"

"No, I wasn't."

"Laila, I made you come three times, and during your last orgasm, you saw God. So, saying there was *no* truth to the rumors was, to put it mildly, not a true statement."

She pushes a lock of her sandy hair off her face. "Having meaningless sex with you *once* doesn't equate to me having an actual *relationship* with you—which is what Sylvia asked me about."

"You implied we'd never so much as kissed," I say. "Which was a lie."

She drops a chicken wing onto her plate in protest. "Sylvia specifically asked me if I'd ever had the pleasure of kissing your lips, and I *truthfully* said no."

When she mentions my lips, my eyes flicker to hers, ever so briefly, and when my gaze returns to her ice-blue eyes, she's smirking.

"So, what are you suggesting we do?" I say. "If you're suggesting we should say we got together *after* your interview on *Sylvia,* just so you can avoid looking like a liar, then no dice. I'd need way more time than that to fall in love with you. More than a month, actually. But I'm willing to say that to avoid the mess of our relationship overlapping with the tour."

"You'd need longer than a whole month to know you want me?"

"No. I'd need half a second to know that. I'm saying I'd need longer than a month to know I *loved* you. To want to live with you. Or, so I'd imagine. I've never fallen in love or lived with anyone before. But I think a month would be lightning quick for me to do either."

"Well, it's not like we *met* only a month ago. We've known each other for a long time now. Oh! I know! We could say you were secretly in love with me throughout the tour. That'd give you plenty of time to develop feelings of love, wouldn't it?"

For some reason, my breathing has become a bit difficult. "I'm not gonna be the simp who sat around, pining for you, while you fucked Malik, and then Charlie, during the tour. Fuck that."

She pauses. Opens and closes her mouth. And finally says, "It was only an idea."

"Yeah, and a terrible one. I'm not gonna be your puppy, Laila, even in a fake romance. You're gonna have to suck it up and admit you lied on *Sylvia.* We'll say we wanted our privacy and people will understand."

"Fine. But in exchange for me being outed as a liar, then you have to admit you were the one who caught feelings first. *You're* the one who pursued *me.*"

"Well, of course, I pursued you. Look at you."

She giggles. "How did you finally make your move?"

I pause to consider. "When the tour was over, I realized I missed seeing your face every day. Your bitchy, evil little face."

She laughs again.

"So, I called you—from Kendrick's phone, of course, since you'd blocked my number—and I asked you to come over to my hotel room for pizza and fucking, minus the pizza."

She snorts. "Wow, how romantic."

"How would you prefer I did it?"

She twists her sultry lips. "You invited me to your house for dinner. But not *pizza*. Wine and dine me, dude!"

"I'd have to come to your place if that's the story. I've been living in a hotel since we got back from the tour."

She gasps. "Why?"

"Because I don't own a place."

"You mean you rent?"

"I mean I don't have a permanent residence. There's no point. I'm on the road so much."

"Ugh. I'd hate that. I love my condo."

I shrug.

"Okay, so you called me and apologized profusely. So, I suggested—"

"Apologized for what?"

"You know for what. Let's not go down this road again."

I pause. "Okay, fine. I apologized. But only after you did, for reaming me in front of everyone on the tour."

"Hell no! You apologized first."

"That's not believable," I say. "Anyone who knows me knows I *never* apologize first."

"Well, neither do I."

We stare at each other for a long moment, at an impasse.

She exhales with frustration. "Why would you call me after the tour to take your shot and *not* apologize first? That makes no sense. The way it went down is you called me and apologized for being a dick during the tour, and then *I* apologized, too, and invited you to my condo for pizza. And you said, 'Pizza? Hell no! Let me cook for you, baby.' And then, you came to my house and made me an amazing meal that melted my panties and made me invite you to stay the night. And you never left. Which makes perfect sense, since you don't have anywhere else to live."

I purse my lips for a beat. "I can live with that."

"Fabulous. So can I. What did you make me for dinner when you came to my place?"

I flash her a flirtatious smile. "Do you like seafood?"

"I *love* it."

"Then I made you my specialty. My grandma's recipe for *cioppino*."

"Oooh. That's sounds fancy. What's that?"

"Italian fish stew in a spicy tomato broth. Growing up, my grandma made it for me on my birthday every year. It was a big deal because money was tight and the ingredients are expensive."

"Is your grandma Italian?"

I nod. "Her parents came here from Sicily."

Her eyes darken with heat. "I should have known you've got Italian blood in you. Italian men are always the most gorgeous—and *passionate*."

My body jolts with arousal at her sexual tone. "My family's name in Italy was *Salvaggio*, but my great-grandparents changed it to Savage after coming here to sound more American."

"Ha! This whole time I thought Savage was a stage name."

I wink. "Nope. I was born Savage, baby."

She giggles.

"So, it's settled," I say. "I made you my specialty. And the look on your face while you ate it was so hot, I didn't let you finish your meal. Midway through, I pulled you out of your chair, laid your back on the table, and ate your pussy like I'd been dying to do since the tour." I smile wickedly. "I ate your sweet pussy, *greedily*, like it was a goddamned bowl of *cioppino.*"

A long, involuntary exhale escapes her. "Okay. I can get behind that."

"After that," I say, "I dragged you off the table, bent you over it, and fucked you from behind while fingering your clit, until you came so hard, you squirted all over my cock and balls."

Her chest heaves. "Whoa. That sounds . . . good."

I'm on the cusp of leaning in and kissing her, but before I do, a commotion on the other side of the patio draws our attention. A big group has entered Reed's patio—this season's cast of *Sing Your Heart Out*: our fellow judges, Aloha and legendary rocker, Jon Stapleton. Kendrick and another mentor, the one assigned to Jon. And last but not least, there's the drummer of 22 Goats, Colin Beretta. The guy who hates me for having a short fling with his ex when they were on a break. Damn. When I saw Dax and Fish here, and not Colin, I thought I'd magically dodged a bullet tonight and wouldn't have to feel the discomfort of Colin shooting me death glares. I guess not. Is Colin here to party with his two bandmates . . . or is he a cast member?

"Look, it's Colin!" Laila chirps, getting up excitedly. "I wonder if he's here to hang out, or if he's a mentor this season." She gasps. "If he's a mentor, I wonder if he's assigned to Aloha . . . or *me*?"

I bristle at the hopeful way she says *me*. But I shrug and say nothing.

"Come on, Savage!" she says brightly. "Let's go say hi to everyone." She squeals. "This is gonna be so much *fun*!" And off she goes, traipsing across Reed's patio like a happy gazelle.

"Fuck," I mutter, shuffling behind her, suddenly consumed by a sense of dread.

Laila swore on *Sylvia* that she and Colin have never hooked up, right before swearing the same about me. And I can't help thinking, If she lied about *me* in that interview, did she lie about Colin, too? Which then leads logically to my very next thought: Did the clever producers of *Sing Your Heart Out* hire Colin to be Laila's mentor this season, specifically hoping his presence would stir up a little trouble in paradise for the happy couple? My gut tells me the answer to that one is almost certainly going to be . . . *yes*.

The promo shoot is done. We got a whole bunch of stuff—video spots and still photos—with the four judges and each of their assigned mentors. Also, with each judge/mentor pair. As it turns out, my hunch about Colin was spot-on. He's Laila's mentor this season, fuck my life, while Fish is Aloha's. And now, we're back out on Reed's patio, having a legit party with the entire cast and their dates, some producers and crew, and some of Reed's friends. We're all letting it rip in recognition that tomorrow the grind will officially begin. Kicking off with tomorrow's press conference, followed the next day, on Monday, by our first official day of shooting.

At present, I'm sitting on one end of the patio with Kendrick, who's been talking me off the ledge about Laila and Colin, while Laila is sitting in a group by a large fire feature on the other end of the patio—a group that naturally includes Colin, since he's close friends with all *Laila's* closest friends. *And I'm slowly losing my mind.*

"Did you see the way Colin flirted with Laila during the entire photo shoot?" I say to Kendrick. It's a running theme.

I've been obsessing about Laila's chemistry with Colin for the past hour. Ever since they looked at each other during their judge/mentor photo shoot like they wanted to rip each other's clothes off.

"He wasn't *flirting* with her," Kendrick says, his annoyance with me plainly escalating. "He and Laila did what the photographer asked him to do. The guy said, 'Smile at each other.' And that's what they did. It was the same thing *we* did in our photo shoot. Were you flirting with *me,* big boy?" He walks his fingertips up my arm, like a cartoon character would do when flirting, making me laugh, despite my foul mood.

I wink at him flirtatiously. "Maybe a little bit."

Kendrick chuckles and drops his flirty flingers.

"Seriously, KC. I'm not imagining this. They have insane amounts of chemistry."

"So what? All that proves is he's not blind and neither is she. You've seen his underwear campaign, right? He's a good looking dude."

I take a sip of my drink. "That's my point. He's a good-looking dude and she mentioned him on *Sylvia,* right before mentioning me. So, I can't help thinking this must be a set-up. Did the show hire Colin to set the stage for a love triangle plot twist midway through the season? Are they gonna pay him a little bonus if he breaks up the happy couple? Because I'm not doing that shit, Kendrick. Laila's supposed to be *my* faithful girlfriend who's totally in love with *me.* I'm not gonna look like the fool who turned down that Instagrammer, so she could drool over Colin Beretta on national TV."

"Calm down, Tiger. She's not gonna do that to you."

"She's already doing it to me, right this very second! Not to mention, she did it to me, repeatedly, during the tour!"

He looks at me like I'm crazy. "Laila didn't do *anything* to *you* during the tour. Malik was her *boyfriend* during the tour, Savage. *You* weren't. Have you forgotten what a prick you were to her?"

I exhale and guzzle my drink. He's right, of course. But I can't help the way I feel, even if it's irrational. Throughout the tour, I felt the same way I do right now. Jealous. Like Malik, and then Charlie, were horning in on *my* woman. I realize I acted like a prick to her, unfortunately, but only because . . . I'm a flaming idiot. Why'd I do that again? Shit. I run my hand through my hair. "I can't keep watching her do this to me, Kendrick. Every time I turn around, I've got to compete for her attention. It's driving me fucking insane."

"You're your own worst enemy. Get out of your own way, man. Stop lashing out and *chill.*"

I take another sip of my drink. "The thing I'm worried about is Colin setting his sights on Laila, not because he genuinely likes her, but to get back at *me* for having that fling with his ex."

Kendrick pulls a face that says, *Quite possibly.* But what he says is, "Laila's not stupid. And she's totally into you."

"First off, Laila *is* stupid—she dated Malik Wallace for how long? Also, she's emphatically *not* into me. She thinks I'm Satan's spawn."

"Yeah, and lucky you, her celebrity crush is Satan."

I can't help chuckling at that, despite how tightly wound I'm feeling in this moment.

Kendrick says, "Whatever you do tonight, do *not* let Laila know you're jealous of Colin. Trust me on that, Savage. You let her know she's got that power over you, then she'll use it against you."

"I'm not stupid," I say.

"Oh, yes, you are."

"Yeah, but not that kind of stupid."

"Oh, yes, you are."

"Hey, boys," a woman says. And when we look up, it's

that British pop star, Penelope something, who's going to be Jon's mentor this season. She holds up an unlit cigarette and smiles flirtatiously at me. "A little birdie told me you might have a light?"

"Sorry, no," I reply. "My girlfriend hates cigarettes, so I quit."

Kendrick looks at me funny, probably thinking, *I saw you smoking like a chimney last night at my brother's birthday party.*

I add, "I quit tonight, actually. For Laila."

Penelope flashes a snarky look. "She's your *girlfriend,* eh?"

"Mm-hmm. Yep."

Penelope snickers, leans forward, and whispers, "The cameras aren't rolling yet, love. That same little birdie told me your 'relationship' is starting *tomorrow.*" With a wink, she throws her unlit cigarette into a nearby bush. "I don't smoke, anyway. I was looking for a reason to come over here." She giggles, but I don't join her. She's blocking my view of Laila and Colin, which is causing me distress. If Colin is hitting on Laila, and I can't see it and sprint over there to stop it, I'll make this British chick rue the day.

Penelope makes a few more attempts at small talk, mostly directed at me, as I crane my neck to spy on Laila. Finally, Kendrick throws himself on his sword and enters into a full-blown conversation with her. Which is Kendrick for you, in a nutshell. The guy's the best friend in the world.

Gratefully, I get up, muttering something about the bathroom, and then start walking toward Laila and Colin, who've drifted away from the group and are talking one-on-one. But on my way to my destination, I get stopped by Aloha, who's tickled pink by today's unexpected events. She's with her husband, Zander, a cool dude I've met a couple times. We chat for a moment while my gaze continually drifts over

Zander's extremely broad shoulder at Laila and Colin. But when I notice Laila's body language seems particularly flirty, particularly animated, I disengage from my conversation and barrel over to my fake girlfriend.

When I get close enough to overhear Laila and Colin's conversation, Laila is in the middle of saying, "No, I swear! Savage told her he had to 'lay low.' He didn't say *Laila*. But the producers ran with it. It's all about ratings, baby."

"Hilarious," Colin says.

"*Laila*," I bark out, lurching forward and invading their personal space. "I need to speak with you, my *love*. Right now."

"Is something wrong?"

"Yes, something is very, very wrong." I pull her up, avoiding Colin's glare, and yank her across the patio and into Reed's house, down a hallway, and through a random door, which empties into a laundry room.

"What the hell?" Laila blurts, as I whirl around from shutting the door.

"What do you think you're doing?" I demand, my heart racing.

"What? When?"

"Your conversation with Colin!" I shout. "I heard every word, Laila."

She wrinkles her forehead, apparently not understanding. "Every word about *what*?"

"You told him the truth about our 'relationship'!"

"So?"

"You're not supposed to tell *anyone*! It's top secret!"

She's flabbergasted. "But Colin's my mentor. He's part of the show! We agreed on the way over here we could tell anyone from the show, remember?"

"No, that's not at all what we agreed. Not *anyone*. We agreed I could tell *Kendrick* because he's my best friend and is *also* on the show. And you could tell Aloha for the same reason. We didn't decide we could run around telling every single person in the entire cast and crew!"

"But Colin is my friend and assigned *mentor*. I trust him. Besides, he signed a contract today that surely contained a confidentiality—"

"We're not telling anyone but Kendrick and Aloha!" I shout, sounding like a maniac, even to myself. "That's what we agreed. As far as Colin or anyone else needs to know, we're an actual couple, Laila. You're *my* girlfriend. You're in love with me. Head over heels and totally addicted." Suddenly, I stop short, as the upside of what Laila said to Colin suddenly hits me like a ton of bricks. "Wait. You admit I didn't say *Laila* to that Instagrammer? You've been fucking with me this whole time, pretending you believed I said your name?"

"No. Of course not. I'm one hundred percent positive you said my name to her. I just told Colin your stupid fake story because he was needling me about the whole thing and I wanted to be nice and save you from embarrassment."

"Bullshit."

"It's true."

"Well, if it's true, which I don't believe, then you didn't do it to be *nice* to me. You did it because you want Colin to think you're available."

"Absolutely not."

I throw up my hands. "You can't do that, Laila! I just got finished telling that Penelope chick you're my girlfriend! And that's how I expect you to play this, too—to remain in character at all times, with everyone, including Colin."

"You don't get to decide that."

"I sure as hell do. I paid two million bucks to get to decide that and anything else having to do with this ridiculous arrangement."

Uh oh. She's no longer amused. She's downright pissed now. "And '*anything* else'?" she parrots. "What am I—a mail order bride? A blowup doll?" She scoffs. "News flash, Savage. You paid two million bucks to save your own ass. *Not to purchase me.*"

"You know what I meant."

"Yeah, I do," she says. "And that's the problem. Regardless, even if I were going to agree that you're my lord and master and omnipotent in all ways, we still can't put the genie back in the bottle regarding Colin. He knows we're not really a couple, and that's that, unless you want me to run out there and scream, 'Just kidding! I'm actually desperately in love with Savage!'"

"Sounds like a plan to me. Go on now, baby. Chop chop."

She rolls her eyes.

"At a bare minimum," I say, "I demand you to stop flirting your ass off with Colin."

She gasps. "I wasn't flirting with Colin!"

"Well, he was sure as hell flirting with *you.*"

"We're *friends.*"

"Have you ever fucked him?"

"No, not that it's any of your business."

"Kissed him?"

She shakes her head. "*We're friends.*"

I narrow my eyes. "*Friends* don't smile at each other like that, Laila. And they don't lean in like that." I scoff. "Oh, don't look at me like that. I know what I saw."

"You're insane."

"Not everyone here is associated with the show. The photographer is still here. Same with the caterer. And what about Reed's friends and housekeeper? What's to keep any of them from hearing the news about our 'relationship' at tomorrow's press conference and then realizing, 'Huh. That's weird. I saw Laila flirting with some other guy all night long.

Hey, I think I got some video of her flirting with him in the background. Why don't I post that now on Twitter!'"

"You belong in an insane asylum."

"No, I'd be insane if I didn't learn from my past experiences. I'm once bitten, twice shy." I take a few steps to my right, lean against the washing machine, and sigh. "You've never experienced my level of fame before, Laila. I'm not saying that to be a jerk. I'm trying to explain you can never be too careful. You *never* know who might leap at the chance to get their fifteen minutes, on your back. I'm saying we can't take *any* chances. I don't want this job to get fucked up, because you forgot this isn't actually a romcom we're starring in together, it's a spy thriller."

Well, she can't help grinning at that, no matter how annoyed she's felt up to this point. Her shoulders visibly soften. Her eyes sparkle. "I understand. I'll be much more careful, going forward."

"Thank you."

"And don't worry. If Colin seemed to be flirting with me a tiny bit, I promise it was harmless. He and his girlfriend recently broke up, and this is the first time we've both been single at the same time, so I think—"

I throw up my hands again. "*You're not single, Laila!*"

She jolts at my sudden shift in tone.

I can't help myself. I shout, "*You're in a relationship with me.* What have we been talking about this whole time? Jesus Christ, Laila!" When she looks at me like I'm crazy again, I see myself through her eyes and realize I might really and truly be devolving into madness. Quickly, I add, "That's what you need to be thinking. That's what I mean. Like you said in the car, we need to stay in character. Like, you know, method actors."

"When we're in front of the *cameras*."

"No, at all times, or nobody will buy our performance.

Haven't you heard about method actors who won't let anyone call them by their real name on-set? Ever seen *Fast Times at Ridgemont High*?"

"No."

"Oh. Well, we gotta watch that one together. Sean Penn played this stoner surfer dude. And he stayed in character throughout the entire shoot of the movie, both on and off camera. Wouldn't let anyone call him by his real name. Only the character's name—Spicoli. Because that's the kind of commitment it takes to make a performance truly *believable.*"

She pauses for a very long moment. "Which actor is Sean Penn? What else has he been in?"

"Sean Penn's illustrious career doesn't matter! All I'm saying is that from this point on, unless you're *sure* we're alone, behind closed doors, and nobody else is around, then we need to agree we're always going to remain in character."

She twists her mouth adorably, no longer looking pissed. But she says nothing.

And, suddenly, thanks to the way she's contorting her sensuous lips, I'm flooded with the urge to kiss her. I clear my throat. "I know you're pissed when I bring up the money, Laila, but have mercy on me. I'm paying you two *million* bucks. The least you can do is deliver an Academy-award-worthy performance."

She licks her lips, drawing my gaze to her mouth again. And when my eyes return to hers, I feel a shift between us. Heat crackling in the gap between our bodies.

"Okay," she says softly, her gaze drifting to my lips. "I promise I'll do my very best."

My chest is tight. My skin hot. "Thank you. That's all we can both do."

"Better safe than sorry," she says, her gaze drifting, yet again, to my lips.

I step forward, deciding this is it. The moment, at last. I'm going to kiss Laila and then bend her over that washing machine and fuck the living hell out of her. But when I step forward again, she steps back. So, I freeze. She takes a deep breath, clears her throat, and says, "I'm really glad we talked. Thanks for setting me straight." And then, after licking her lips and taking a shuddering breath, she turns on her heel and literally sprints out of the small room.

After my conversation with Laila in the laundry room, she played a few rounds of Beer Pong with her friends, while I sat at the fire feature, watching her while pretending to listen to Jon Stapleton, my co-judge, give me advice about being on the show. But when Laila left her post at Beer Pong to play Team Jenga—during which she was paired with Alessandra, thankfully, while Fish was paired with Colin—I excused myself from Jon, grabbed a bottle of whiskey from behind Reed's bar, and slithered my shitfaced ass into a dark corner to watch her.

The good news? As promised in the laundry room, Laila's been noticeably ignoring Colin's flirtations during their entire game. The bad news? Based on Colin's body language, it seems clear he's the sort of sick fuck, like me, who gets off when a hot woman ignores him.

A large whoop rises up from the game as Aloha's husband, Zander, makes a move for his two-person team— Aloha and himself. And in response, everyone but Zander and his popstar wife throws back another shot, at which point

Colin leans into Laila and says something that makes her throw her head back and laugh.

It's worst-case scenario, actually, because I can tell Laila wasn't *trying* to flirt with Colin. She didn't laugh to mess with me. He *genuinely* made her involuntarily guffaw. I've got to think that's a very bad sign for me.

My inebriated blood flash-boiling, I jerk to standing, every fiber of my body telling me to march over there and mark my territory. To kiss her in front of Colin. And then throw Colin into the fire.

"No, Savage," a voice says sharply. And when I look, it's my boy, Kendrick, standing before me and physically blocking my movement with his muscular body. "Sit down, brother," he says. "Don't do it."

The devil on my shoulder is whispering, "Do it." But, somehow, I manage to reply casually to my friend, "Don't do *what*?"

"Whatever you drunkenly decided to do to Colin." He points at my chair. "Sit back down and listen to me for a minute."

Reluctantly, I sit. Kendrick rarely orders me around. So, when he does, I listen. "I wasn't gonna do anything bad," I murmur. "I was just . . ." I trail off. There's no point. Kendrick's staring at me like he can read my mind. Which he probably can. He's known me for almost half my life now. He, better than anyone, knows how my mind works.

Kendrick takes the chair next to me and leans his fore-arms on his knees. "It's time for you to put that bottle down, walk inside the house, and go to bed."

"I'm not ready for bed yet."

"Nothing good will come of you sitting here, alone in a dark corner, drinking whiskey from a bottle, watching Laila get hit on by Colin."

"Aha! So, you admit he's been hitting on her! I told you so."

Kendrick leans back. "I think he's doing it to piss you off, more than anything else. So, don't give him the satisfaction. Play it cool, brother."

I take another long sip of whiskey and mutter, "Tonight was supposed to be a fun last hurrah before I'm not allowed to drink anymore. I thought Laila and I would party together. I never intended to sit here, alone, marinating in whiskey and jealousy."

"Then get up and join the party. You always do this, Savage."

"I don't want to join the party. I want to sit here, alone."

"Then, that's your problem."

"But when I pulled Laila into the laundry room, she said she'd stay in character, from now on. And yet, she's been playing games with her friends, and Colin, ever since."

Kendrick blinks slowly. *"When you pulled Laila into the laundry room . . .?"*

I immediately realize my mistake. "To talk to her . . . about the importance of keeping up the charade at all times. So the truth doesn't get out."

He's onto me. "You told her you're jealous of Colin."

"Of course not. I simply told her she can't flirt with Colin, or anyone else, because someone could see that and post about it."

"You dragged Laila into a laundry room and chewed her out about Colin, didn't you? And now you're sitting here, drinking from a bottle in a dark corner, watching her with him like a stalker. Like Reed behind that bush, however many months ago. Does that summarize the situation accurately?"

I pause, weighing my options. And quickly decide lying to Kendrick isn't in my DNA. I speak on an exhale, "Yeah.

That's pretty much it. I've become Reed fucking Rivers, standing behind a bush."

Kendrick leans back and rubs his face. "When will you learn?" He takes a second to collect himself before letting out a long exhale and sitting forward again. "Okay, buddy. Listen to me. I know this chick better than you do. Do you want her?"

I groan. "So much."

"Then, it's simple. You have to remember she's exactly like *you*. I love you both, okay, so this is said with love. But you're both the same kind of sick fuck. You both always want what you can't have. The truth is, if you knew Laila like I do, I don't even think you'd even want her. Not the *real* her. She's actually super nice. A sweetheart."

"*Yeccch.*"

"Exactly. You'd hate her, if you knew her."

"She sounds awful."

"She is. Awfully sweet and cool and funny and surprisingly goofy. None of which you know about her, I'm sure, because you're always on the outside, looking in. Provoking her. Savage, I'm not trying to piss you off here. I'm saying I think you want her because you can't have her. Because she's the one woman who doesn't fall at your feet. So maybe recognize that's what's happening and try to get some perspective here."

I say nothing.

Concede nothing.

But, instead, take a long pull from my bottle and watch the Jenga game for a long moment, where Laila is just now throwing back yet another shot with her partner, Fish. After a moment, the tower collapses, and it's clear the current game has ended. In short order, the game gets rebuilt and the teams reshuffled . . . and this time, Laila gets assigned to her new partner, *Colin*, through no fault of her own.

"Oh, hell no," I mutter, standing. "I don't care *why* I want her. The end result is that I *do*."

Kendrick rises and grabs my shoulder. "*Sit down*. I'm not finished talking to you."

"No, Kendrick. I need to pull her away and—"

"*No*. That's the last thing you should do. Not when you're drunk and jealous and the press conference is tomorrow. *No*." He points at the chair. "Sit down."

I pause, breathing hard. But sit.

With a sigh, Kendrick resumes his seat. "If you want to sit her down and tell her how obsessed you've been since the tour, then do it. But not tonight. Not now. Do it after you get to know her a bit and figure out if she's who you really want. Because, I swear to God, if you give her that speech and then turn around and dump her, I'll fucking kill you for hurting her."

I swallow hard.

"Plus, I doubt your speech would move the needle with her right now, anyway. Because she doesn't know you any better than you know her. Not really. She still thinks you're this asshole fuckboy who doesn't give a shit about anyone else. Because that's all you've ever shown her because you're scared to death to show her anything else."

Again, I say nothing. I can't remember the last time Kendrick bitch-slapped me like this. It's blowing me away.

He exhales a big breath. "You really want her?"

I nod.

"Then don't let her know how much you want her. Not yet. And, for fuck's sake, don't let her know her attempts at pushing your buttons are working. I know her *way* better than you do. Like I said, she's the sweetest girl you'll ever meet. But when it comes to men she actually wants to sleep with—a group that *clearly* doesn't include me—she craves a challenge, the same way you do. You can get any woman you want. Well, Laila can get *any* man she wants. And she knows it. She's you, in female form." He sighs. "It's actually crazy how much you two are similar. So, think, dumbass. If she's exactly like you, then what will make her want you?"

I pause. "Me not wanting her."

He touches his nose. "I once overheard Laila talking to Ruby about her exes. And, dude, I'm telling you, she gets off on bringing a player to his knees. But guess what happens when she gets him there? Can you guess, Savage?"

"She . . . loses interest?"

He touches his nose again. "She gets bored and moves on. It's all about the thrill of the chase for her. Sound familiar?"

"So, what's your point? Laila and I are gonna be living together for the next three months. You want me to *ignore* her, while living under the same roof with her?"

"No, but you need to keep your cards close to your vest for a bit. Keep her guessing. For instance, she doesn't need to know you're jealous of Colin. Why give her that? Play it cool. Let her chase you a bit. Let her get frustrated that her usual tactics aren't working. And in the meantime, get to know her over the next few months. Figure out if the attraction you think you've been feeling has more to do with *Laila*, as she really is, or conquering some fantasy girl who doesn't fall at your feet."

I take a long chug from my bottle but say nothing.

"Now, go to bed. The longer you stay down here, watching her and drinking from that bottle, the higher the chance some kind of shit will hit the fan. And you don't want that. Nadine is still here. She's inside, talking to Reed. Do you want her to hear some drunken screaming match between you and Laila, after you go over there and pick a fight with Colin? Because if you stay down here, that's where this is headed."

He's right. As usual. I look across the patio, where Laila

is happily doing yet another round of shots with her friends. "Thanks, brother."

"I've got your back, Savage. I'll always have your back."

"I know. I have yours, too. For what it's worth."

"I know you do."

"Will you make sure Laila gets to her room tonight—*alone*?"

"I will. Now, go on. Walk into the house without so much as a glance at her. I promise, it'll drive her crazy."

I resist the urge to look at Laila. "Okay. Goodnight." I stand. "Thanks again."

"Don't you dare go knocking on Laila's door tonight, looking for a booty call."

I scoff. "I'm not stupid."

"Yes, you are."

"True. But I don't know which room is hers."

He laughs. "Goodnight."

"Goodnight, brother." With that, I fist-bump Kendrick and do as I'm told: I head toward the house, without even a passing glance at my fake girlfriend.

TWENTY-NINE
SAVAGE

When I enter Reed's house, I glimpse his housekeeper, Amalia, slipping into the kitchen, so I follow her in there, like a drunk driver following tail lights. When I enter the kitchen, I find her dressed in a sleek robe and slippers, quietly filling a kettle with water.

"Oh, hello there," she says when she notices me filling the doorway.

"Hi. Amalia, right?"

"That's right, Mr. Savage. I'm making myself tea. Would you like a cup?"

"Sure. Thanks."

I take a seat at the large kitchen table and watch her putter for a long moment. As she approaches with two steaming mugs, I say, "You remind me of my grandma. She loves tea."

Amalia takes a seat after placing a steaming mug in front of me. "Are you close with your grandma?"

I nod. "She's the one who raised me."

"And look at you now. She did a fine job." She blows on her steaming tea. "Is your grandmother still alive?"

I nod. "She's really sick, though."

"I'm sorry to hear that. I hope she recovers."

"The chances are low. But she's a fighter. We still have hope."

Amalia puts a hand on mine. "I'll pray for her. What's your grandmother's name?"

"Maria. But I've always called her Mimi, rather than grandma."

"I'll keep Mimi in my prayers, Mr. Savage."

"Thank you. Call me Adrian."

She smiles warmly. "Are you able to see your grandmother very often?"

"As much as I can. She lives in Chicago. I visit about once a month, whenever I'm not on tour. But I FaceTime her almost every day. I sing to her or tell her a story. She likes seeing my face. The medicine she takes gives her weird nightmares."

She touches her chest. "Oh, bless her heart."

I bring my mug to my lips, but the tea is too hot to drink. "I offered to take the year off to hang out with Mimi while she's in treatment," I say, "but she was adamant she didn't want that. She insisted on getting to watch me 'being a rockstar.' She loves that I've been touring the world. Performing for huge audiences. She collects every interview and magazine cover."

"She must be so very proud of you."

"It's all because of her. She bought me my first guitar when I was twelve. Our first Christmas together. She thought making music would help calm me down. Help me work out my anger issues. I was a handful back then."

"All the more reason for her to be proud of you now."

"Honestly, she'd trade all my success with the band to watch me settle down, get married, and give her a great-grandkid." I chuckle. "I told her, 'Sorry, Mimi, that's not gonna happen. At least, not any time soon. A kid can't raise a kid.'"

"How old are you?"

"Twenty-six. But, see, when you're in a band, that's like being eighteen or nineteen."

"Like dog years, only in reverse?"

"Exactly. Dog years make a dog older than their chronological age, and 'musician years' make a guy younger, in terms of emotional maturity. Especially if he's the lead singer or guitarist. Double points if he's both, like me."

She chuckles. "Why is that, you think?"

I shrug. "Lead singers, at least the ones like me, always get the most attention. Everyone tells us we're gods among men, so we start believing the hype. In my case, it's especially hardcore because my face and body are a big part of our branding. We shamelessly sell me as much as we sell the music."

"That sounds exhausting to me."

"It's fine. I was born with this face, so might as well make money off it. And I'd work out, anyway, because I like being fit. I'm sure I'd drink more and eat more crap if I didn't feel like my looks were a big part of the job. I'm actually glad I have good reason to stay healthy and take care of myself." I lean in. "I've got some self-destructive tendencies, Amalia."

"Oh, dear. Well, I'm glad you know that."

I blow on my tea. "Honestly, I'm always one tick shy of becoming a train wreck."

"Why is that, Adrian?"

"I don't know."

"If things are happy, you don't trust them?"

"I think that's a fair statement."

"If things are happy, you start testing them? Poking at them, trying to test your theory they're not as happy as you think. And then, by poking at them, you ruin them?"

I waggle my finger at her. "Hey now. Get outta my head, woman."

She laughs.

"That's probably why I don't even have a permanent place to live. I feel like I can't sit still. Whenever I'm not touring, I live in a hotel or in my best friend's spare room."

"Oh, dear. I'd go crazy if I didn't have a place to call home. I love staying in hotels for vacation, but in my real life, I need security and consistency."

"I don't care where I live. When I was little, I slept in a closet, literally. And when I moved in with Mimi, we lived in her tiny, shitty apartment in Chicago. The place was the size of a shoebox! Want to hear something amazing? When I moved in with Mimi, she didn't even know I existed before then. My 'father,' her son, hadn't even told her about me because he was too ashamed he'd gotten some random chick, my mother, knocked up. But Mimi took me in, anyway, even though she barely had two nickels to rub together and certainly wasn't planning on raising a wild little asshole at that point in her life."

"Ah. Interesting. So now, you don't let yourself get too settled, huh? "

I shrug. "I just don't like the feeling of being tied down too much. I like being able to live out of a duffel bag, and not need much. I like feeling like a hotel room is more than enough."

Amalia sips her tea, looking like her mind is turning. "You never dream of living in a house like this one?"

I scoff. "No way. I'd get lost. Literally."

She chuckles. "Reed throws a lot of parties here. The house serves him well. Although, I admit, now that Georgina lives here, it feels much less like a 'venue' and more like an actual home."

"I didn't realize Georgina lives here. Wow. That was fast."

Amalia nods. "It was. But I have no doubt it's a wonderful thing for them both."

"How fast did she move in?"

"That's personal, I think, Adrian."

"Sorry."

"That's okay, dear." She pats my hand and smiles.

"Just tell me one thing. Was it faster than a month?"

Amalia's dark eyes sparkle. "Yes, it was."

"*Whoa.*"

Amalia lifts a brow and sips her tea, almost like she's acknowledging she just "spilled the tea" about Reed and Georgina. Or maybe my drunken brain is imagining that little sass in Amalia's expression.

I ask, "Do you live here with Reed and Georgina?"

"During the week, yes, unless there's a big party or event on the weekend, like today. I have a place of my own, where my children and grandchildren come for dinner on Sundays."

"I bet you're an amazing grandma. What do your grand-children call you?"

"*Abuelita.* Or Abu, for short."

"I love Abu. It's like the monkey in *Aladdin.* Can I call you that, too?"

She flashes me a smile that makes me blush. "I would love that, Adrian."

"Cool." I sip my tea again. "Hey, Abu. If you ever get sick of Reed—because, come on, there's a lot to get sick of there—then will you come work for me? Don't let anyone else hire you away from me, okay? Once you kick Reed to the curb, you're mine."

She flashes me a chastising look. "Don't speak ill of my Reed, Adrian. I love him from the depths of my soul."

"Yeah, but you have to know he's a prickly motherfucker."

"*Adrian.*"

I flash my most charming smile and by the look on her face, I know she can't resist me.

"Where would I work for you, anyway? I'm a housekeeper, remember? And you just got finished telling me you don't even have a house."

"I'd buy one, so you could keep it for me, my beautiful Abu."

"Oh, my. What an honor. But, like I said, I love Reed with all my heart. He's like a son to me and I'll never work for anyone else."

"Aw, come on, dude. Never say never. Even if you love Reed, you never know what might happen in life. And I've got lots to offer you."

"Like what?"

"Well, like I said, I have the maturity of an eighteen-year-old. What grandma could resist taking care of someone like *that*?"

She giggles. "You're quite the salesman."

"Also, I'm *amazing* at singing grandmas to sleep. Has Reed ever done *that* for you?"

"No, I can't say he has."

"Ha! Also, I'll happily play gin rummy with you, or any other boring card game. *And* I'll even suffer through watching *Sing Your Heart Out* with you, if that's your jam."

"No wonder Mimi adores you, with all that to offer. And no wonder *Sing Your Heart Out* hired you to replace Hugh. I can tell you're quite the charmer, my dear."

"Yeah, I can turn it on like a light switch when I want to impress someone." I wink.

"Clearly. Do the powers that be at *Sing Your Heart Out*

know they've hired a judge who has to 'suffer through' watching their show?"

"They sure do. It's why they wanted me so badly. 'Cause I'm too cool for school."

"I see."

"A little secret, Abu? Everyone wants what they can't have."

"Ah. Well, aren't you smart."

I tap my temple.

"Is your grandmother excited about you being on the show?"

"She's *ecstatic*. It's her all-time favorite show. She even watches reruns, for reasons that escape me."

"I watch them, too. They're on every night after *Jeopardy*."

I laugh. "But why watch reruns of a singing competition, when you already know who won that season?"

"I like already knowing the outcome and seeing how my favorite contestants blossomed throughout the season. And in later seasons, I absolutely love watching Aloha being her sassy little self. She's my all-time favorite judge."

"You mean besides *me*."

"You haven't been on the show yet. Once you've appeared on the show, then, yes, you'll become my new favorite."

"Thanks, Abu. Unless, of course, my girlfriend edges me out. Something tells me Laila's gonna give me a run for my money this season. She has a way of making people fall hard for her."

Amalia puts down her mug, her face contorting with affection for me. "You two make a beautiful couple. In a way, you remind me of Reed and Georgina. You're both so attractive together. Two obviously strong-willed individuals who seem so sweet together."

"Well, *I'm* sweet. But make no mistake about it: Laila's a holy terror."

Amalia giggles.

"Lucky for me, I don't like my girlfriends to be sweet."

"No?"

"Well, I mean, I like 'em sweet, down deep, as long as it takes a whole lot of effort to get to the sweet stuff. Like going on a treasure hunt or getting to the tootsie roll inside a Tootsie Pop."

"That sounds like a lot of work to me, Adrian."

"Nah. I like a good challenge or else I get bored. Ever seen the movie *Mean Girls*?"

"It doesn't ring a bell."

"It's a comedy, set in high school. The lead girl is the 'new girl' in school. That's the one we're supposed to be rooting for. But I don't even remember her name. The villain, on the other hand, that's Regina George. She's the leader of the popular girls known as The Plastics. We're not supposed to like Regina. We're supposed to hate her because she's so 'mean.' But guess who I've always wanted to bang, Abu?"

"*Adrian.*"

"Have sex with."

Her nostrils flare. She truly can't resist me. "Regina?"

I nod. "*Reginaaaaa.* My biggest childhood crush."

Amalia giggles. "Do you talk this way with Mimi?"

"Of course. She loves it. She says I'm a . . ." I scratch my head and mutter, "What does Mimi always call me? A hoe? No . . . a '*rake*'!"

Amalia loses it. She laughs and laughs, so I join her, enjoying my best laugh of the night. When we quiet down, we take long sips of our tea, now that it's finally at a perfect temperature.

Amalia asks, "Why do you think you prefer the mean villain over the nice new girl?"

"I have no idea."

"Hmm." She sips her tea again, and her body language suggests she's holding her tongue.

"Well, spit it out, woman. If I'm going to be completely myself around you, then you've got to return the favor."

"I don't want to overstep."

"You couldn't possibly. Come on. Spit some knowledge at me, Abu."

She replaces her mug on the table. "Well . . . you said your grandmother raised you?"

I nod. "From age twelve."

"If you don't mind me asking, is that because your mother passed away, or because your mother needed to work long hours, or . . .?"

"It was because my mom didn't give a shit about me and didn't have a maternal bone in her body."

Amalia nods. "I'm sorry to hear that."

"It worked out for the best. Mimi was the shit. Why did you ask the question?"

"Well, this is nothing but amateur pop psychology, of course, but I think you prefer Regina in the movie, and also in your love life, because you feel abandoned by your mother. You prefer women who present a challenge to you, women who are hard to win over, because that way, when you finally *do* win them over, you experience the pleasure you never got to experience as a child. Namely, the joy of winning over a woman the same way you always wished you could have won over your mother."

I'm speechless for a long moment. But, finally, I whisper, "And they call *me* Savage."

Amalia winces. "Did I overstep?"

"Not at all. You just blew my mind! Tell me more, Abu Dabu. What else do you see in your magic crystal ball? Can you see my future?"

Amalia winks. "The only thing I see in your future, my dearest Adrian, is that you've got a big day tomorrow and you're very drunk and you should probably get some sleep now." She motions to my mug. "Finish your tea, dear, and let's get you to bed."

I do as I'm told, drinking the rest of my tepid tea down in one long gulp, and stand. "It's been amazing talking to you, Amalia. Thanks for the psychoanalysis."

"You're very welcome. Goodnight, dear. Best of luck to you."

I stop walking. "Does that mean you're not planning to see me again?"

She chuckles. "No, not at all. I'll see you in the morning at breakfast."

I exhale with relief. "Cool."

I resume shuffling toward the exit of the kitchen, feeling worlds lighter than when I entered the room, but stop and turn around in the doorway. "Amalia? Sorry, but I just remembered why I came in here." I grimace. "I have no idea which room is mine."

Amalia bites back a smile. "No worries. It's a big house. I'll show you again."

She leads me out of the kitchen toward a dramatic staircase with wrought iron railings, saying, "Do you get drunk like this often, dear?"

"No, not at all. The last time I was drunk was . . . Oh. Last night. But before that, it'd been well over a month."

"Good. Let's keep it that way."

"Don't worry about me. I have a rule I don't drink to drown my sorrows. I wasn't intending to break my rule tonight. Tonight was supposed to be a happy occasion. A 'last hurrah' before I'm not allowed to drink for the whole season."

"Oh?"

"The producers made it part of my contract. They think I make 'bad choices' when I 'drink to excess.'"

"Are they right about that?"

I snicker. "I'll put it this way. My dick is *still* trending on Twitter, a full twenty-four hours after I got drunk at a birthday party last night."

She can't resist giggling. "Oh dear."

"I wouldn't normally drink two nights in a row, either. But, like I said, tonight was supposed to be my last hurrah, so . . . Fuck it."

"Well, I'm glad you had fun tonight."

"I didn't. I hated tonight, actually. Except for talking to you. You're the best part of my night."

"Thank you. I enjoyed talking to you, too." She stops in front of a doorway at the end of a long hallway and motions. "Here we are. Nighty night."

I enter the room—a guest room decorated in elegant hues of white—and Amalia follows me inside, telling me where I can find additional blankets and towels. She points out this and that amenity, and, lastly, asks if I need anything further or have any questions.

"I have one question," I reply.

Kendrick would tell me I'm an idiot for what I'm about to ask. But I don't care. I can't lie in bed under the same roof as Laila Fitzgerald and not at least *try* to finally get to eat that woman's pussy.

I smile at Amalia. "Could you tell me which room is Laila's? I think I'll shower and get ready for bed, and then check in on her to make sure she got to her room, safe and sound."

I tiptoe out of my bedroom, wearing nothing but a midriff-baring T-shirt and undies, and creep down the dark, quiet hallway, headed to parts unknown. And that's where the "brilliant strategy" portion of my quest ends and the "winging it" portion begins.

Crap! Why didn't I ask Amalia which room Savage is staying in tonight? Stupid Laila! This house is as big as the hotel in *The Shining*, and I literally have no idea which door is hiding Mr. Smoldering Pouty Pants.

Unfortunately, I was stupid and/or naïve enough to think I could resist him. Not only tonight. But for the entire season of the show. What I didn't count on, however, is how horny I get when I drink. And how freaking hot Savage is when he's jealous. Good lord, put the two together, and the boy is like crack to me.

As Savage sat in that dark corner of Reed's patio earlier tonight, watching me getting hit on by Colin, I felt so turned on, I could barely keep myself from sprinting over to Savage and launching myself at him like a missile. Despite all the reasons not to do it, I decided, right then and there, I'd invite

Savage to my room whenever he *finally* approached me again. I imagined myself leaning in and whispering to him, "Come to my room later, so you can finally eat my pussy 'from every angle.'" I imagined myself saying it to him in a sultry, breathy kind of whisper—the kind that would have made Savage pop a boner, right on the spot.

But then, the jerk never approached me again at the party! On the contrary, he got up and marched into Reed's house, without even *glancing* at me! Which royally pissed me off, I must say. Savage is the one who screamed at me in that laundry room that we needed to remain in character at all times, whenever anyone else is around. And then, what did that hypocrite do? He sat in a dark corner, all night long, looking like a crazy person, not interacting with his supposed girlfriend, at all, and then waltzed out of the party, without even saying goodnight to me—the supposed love of his life! What kind of dickheaded boyfriend would leave a party without even saying goodbye to his girlfriend? Not mine, that's for sure. Or if he did, he wouldn't be my boyfriend for long. So now, I've decided to find Savage, wherever he is in this massive house, and give him a piece of my mind.

I stop in the middle of the hallway and look around. Which of these doors is hiding Mr. Sexy Pants Crazy Man? None of them look on the cusp of singeing, due to Savage's proximity. For all I know, Savage's room is in an entirely different hallway. Or maybe even on the first floor.

Not knowing what else to do, I pick a random door and press my ear against it, hoping that, miraculously, I'll hear Savage's voice behind it, or maybe detect some kind of supernatural Savage-infused vibration humming from inside the room. But, no, the room is silent and the air doesn't feel super-charged with rockstar electrons in the slightest.

"Savage?" I whisper, ever so softly, my lips brushing the

wood of the door, my voice as soft as flapping butterfly wings. But, sadly, perfect silence answers me.

I tiptoe to the next door in the hallway and repeat the same exercise. But again, I'm met with the same result. When I move away from the door this time, however, I notice a frozen figure at the far end of the long hallway, watching me.

I inhale sharply. *It's Savage.* Wearing nothing but dark briefs. His chiseled, gorgeous chest is heaving visibly. His nipples are two perfect dimes. His abs cut and taut. And, hot damn, his dark eyes are two lustful laser beams taking in the sight of my barely clothed body.

For a half second, we both stand, silently drinking each other in from opposite ends of the long hallway, our chests rising and falling in synchronicity. Finally, Savage wordlessly points toward a doorway to his right, nonverbally inviting me to enter. Or was that a command? Either way, I don't hesitate. My pulse thumping and my skin hot and alive with tingles, I glide down the length of the endless hallway, and finally walk straight past him into the room with both my head and chest held high.

Savage follows me into the room—a bedroom decorated in hues of white—and quietly shuts the door with a soft click. After turning from the door, he glides up to me, slides a palm to my cheek, leans in, and, without hesitation, presses his mouth to mine—instantly provoking a long and shuddering exhale of excitement from us both.

Savage kisses me tenderly at first. Like he's savoring a first mouthful of expensive wine. But after initial entreaties, when I realize he doesn't taste the least bit like cigarettes, but, instead, like toothpaste and lust and the remnants of whiskey, when I open my mouth and enthusiastically invite him to take me in earnest, Savage's warm tongue breaches my lips and begins leading mine in swirling, sensuous strokes, an increasingly voracious dance of our tongues and lips that quickly sets off a breathtaking barrage of fireworks inside my core.

As a torrent of arousal slams into me, I slide my arms around Savage's neck and begin devouring him enthusiastically. In response, he slides his arms around my torso and deepens his kiss, until, soon, I'm jerking and jolting in his arms, gasping for air as shockwaves of pleasure and arousal throttle my every nerve ending, but especially that pulsing bundle of nerves between my legs. If there were surveillance footage of this white-hot kiss, I'm positive there'd be visible sparks flying off our bodies in this moment.

As our kiss deepens and intensifies, I inhale him, savoring the taste and scent of him. In addition to the delicious scents I've previously detected, I smell soap and shampoo now, too. And, still, not even a trace of cigarettes. Savage smells nothing but clean and delicious and sexy. *Perfect.*

"You didn't smoke tonight," I gasp out into his lips.

Savage nuzzles his nose against mine and smiles wickedly, brushing his bulge against me down below. "I knew my fake girlfriend wouldn't kiss me if I did—and I was going to get this kiss tonight, if it killed me."

I inhale sharply at the implication—that Savage consciously decided, hours ago, to forego smoking a cigarette, solely to kiss me later in the night. And at my obvious excitement, Savage kisses me, even more passionately than before, this time grabbing my ass cheeks firmly in both palms and pushing me into his hard bulge. When I moan with pleasure, he leans his body away from mine, slightly, enough to be able to slide his hand into my underwear. He reaches between my legs and moans when he discovers how wet I am, how swollen and aroused, and immediately begins fingering me in a way that elicits a loud growl.

As he massages my hard, swollen clit while finger-fucking me, I'm absolutely at his mercy. I begin buckling and growling like I've put my finger into a light socket, immediately hurtling toward an orgasm that's sure to make my knees give out.

"I have to lie down," I gasp out. "I can't . . . keep going standing up."

Without hesitation, Savage drags me to the bed, lays me down on my back, yanks down my underwear like they're gravely insulting to him, and dives right in with a loud and shuddering exhale of excitement. As he licks me, he groans and moans, and then pushes open my thighs as wide as they'll go. He licks and laps at me, at first, with a wide and greedy tongue. But, in short order, he zeroes in on his meticulous work, devouring my clit with precision.

I clutch the bed covering and writhe as Savage decimates me in the most delicious way imaginable. And when he adds his fingers to the mix, it only takes a couple swipes at my G-spot before my body explodes with an orgasm that sends me groaning loudly with deep relief and pleasure.

I sit up, eager to return the favor, but Savage stops me. His breathing ragged, he pulls off my shirt, and then his briefs, letting his big, thick cock spring to freedom. And just when I'm about to ask him if he's got a condom, he flips me over, rather forcefully, pulls me onto all fours, and starts eating me from behind.

"Condom," I choke out.

"Don't need it," he murmurs. "I'm only gonna eat you."

I'm shocked to hear it. But not disappointed. I relax into it, now that I know he's not planning to plow into me, uncovered. And quickly, my body ramps up, again. Savage is voracious back there. Fucking me with his fingers while licking and eating and biting and sucking every inch of me with his mouth. And by that, I mean, really and truly, *every* damned inch of me.

It takes me a little while to get there again, simply

because it seems like he keeps pulling back, right when I'm about to release. Over and over again, he gets me right to the edge of orgasm, and pulls back. Is he doing that intentionally? Teasing me? Torturing me? Finally, thank God, he brings me right to the edge, yet again, but this time, exuberantly pushes my pleasure overboard. And when I finally come, something unexpected happens to me. Something that's never happened before. Fluid squirts out of me during my orgasm. As intense pleasure grips me, I scream, unable to contain the rapture I'm feeling and way too drunk to care if someone in this big house might overhear me.

When my body-quaking, squirting orgasm subsides, Savage turns me over onto my back again, looking positively feral. Breathing hard, he lies next me on his back and pulls at my arm.

"Sit on my face," he commands breathlessly.

"Savage," I gasp out. "Get a condom. I want you to fuck me."

"Sit on my face, Laila. *Now*."

Trembling, I do as I'm told, and when I lower myself onto his mouth, the pleasure feels supernatural. I lean forward as I ride his face, stroking his gorgeous, hard cock with my hand, and he moans his appreciation underneath me in reply. I look down and see his chin as it moves. My eyes drift to his chest and abs, and then to the tip of his cock peeking out of my hand. It's dripping with arousal now. So, I lean forward, slowly, allowing his mouth to keep up. And then, as he continues eating me from behind, I take his hard, dripping cock into my mouth and get to work, causing him to jolt and jerk and groan with pleasure.

We're absolutely going for it. Both of us. Losing our minds. Not holding back. And when I finally have an orgasm against Savage's mouth, he growls and has one, too—gushing his release into my mouth in a shockingly warm and salty torrent that fills my mouth to the brim.

My brain understands it's time to swallow him down, of course. But, as it turns out, commanding my throat to swallow while having an orgasm isn't in the cards. At least, not when the volume of Savage's release is this big.

As my eyes roll back into my head and my body warps with violent waves of pleasure, Savage's cum dribbles out my mouth and down my chin, and then, partially, onto his stomach. When I'm finally released from my rapture, I lower myself down and lick up my mess from his stomach, like a kitten licking up spilled milk off the floor. And when I'm done, and all traces of Savage's orgasm are gone, I continue licking and sucking on every inch of him, simply because he tastes so damned good.

Midway through kissing his abs, I freeze, suddenly feeling a dramatic shift in my body's equilibrium. When the room tilts sharply, I get up and stand at the edge of the bed, trying to right the ship. But it's no use. I think I'm gonna be sick.

"Come here, Fitzy," he coos. "I'm not even close to done with your pussy yet."

Murmuring something incoherent, I turn and bolt to the bathroom, drop to my knees before the toilet, and lose the entire contents of my stomach into the bowl: however many tequila shots and beers, a lovely meal of chicken, rice, and grilled vegetables . . . and a shocking deluge of salty cum I sucked out of the famous donkey dick attached to the sexiest man alive, Mr. Adrian Fucking Savage.

THIRTY-ONE
SAVAGE

"Oh, honey," Aloha says as Laila shuffles into Reed's expansive kitchen in the late morning light, looking like dogshit that's been stepped in twice. And it's not hard to surmise what's elicited the reaction. Laila's sandy hair is a mess on top of her head. Her normally glowing skin is pale and lifeless. She's got dark circles under her eyes and her sultry lips, usually dewy and sumptuous, are dry and pinched with her misery.

Yet, still, even like this, the woman does crazy things to my body. Involuntary things. Indeed, at the mere sight of Laila's raggedy ass shuffling into the kitchen, my entire body instantly perks up. My heart rate elevates. My skin tingles. Even the memory of Laila barfing at the end of our tryst doesn't dampen my body's attraction to her. Apparently, I'm an addict now. Addicted to a drug called Laila. And there's no turning back.

Weirdly, I didn't really mind the barfing part. Not that I have some kind of weird barfing kink. Obviously, I would have preferred that part didn't happen and thought it was totally gross. But I can't deny when it happened, and I held back her hair, so it wouldn't dip into the toilet bowl, when she whimpered pathetically in gratitude at my gentle touch, my heart kind of skipped a beat. I already knew I was attracted to Sassy Laila. To Bitchy Laila. And, of course, to Sexy, Squirting, Screaming From Ecstasy Laila. But in that moment, I discovered I kinda dig Broken, Pathetic, Needs Me to Hold Her Hair While She Barfs and Act Like Her Knight in Shining Armor Laila, too. I mean, not too often, please. But now and again, sure. It turns out, I'm down to volunteer as tribute for that job, occasionally.

When Laila was done being sick, I helped her wash up, led her to the bed, tucked her in, and held her close while she whimpered and groaned. When she swore she was going to die, I stroked her hair and kissed her cheek and assured her she wouldn't. And, to my surprise, in between telling me to fuck off and to stop correcting her, she actually snuggled me, thanked me for taking care of her, and whispered my name like it was a little prayer. And the best part? She didn't steal my wallet or take a single surreptitious photo of me and post it on Twitter.

But that was then, and this is now. When I woke up this morning, Laila wasn't there. And when I went to her room and peeked inside, there she was. Fast asleep. Looking like road kill. And, instantly, I knew why she'd left my bedroom and staggered back to hers. Because a drunken tryst in the middle of the night with an asshole like me is one thing, according to Laila's Rulebook. But waking up in the morning, and seeing me lying next to her in the light of day, is something else entirely. Right then, I knew we might as well have been back on tour. That she'd drunkenly fucked me in the middle of the night, the same way she'd done on the night of the hot tub. And that now, she was going to pretend it had never happened, the same way she did back then.

Laila croaks out a pathetic "good morning" to the small

group at Reed's kitchen table as she enters the room. Along with Aloha and me, the "second wave" of people eating breakfast this morning is comprised of Aloha's husband, Zander, Fish and Alessandra, and Reed's fiancée, Georgina. And of course, as the group eats, Amalia is puttering away adorably on the other side of the kitchen.

Moving like molasses, Laila grabs some coffee and a muffin from a breakfast spread on the counter and then takes a seat next to me at the table.

"You look pretty," I say sarcastically. "Like a Picasso."

"Shut up," she murmurs before laying her forehead onto the table.

"And they were stupid enough to hire *you* to be *my* babysitter?" I say to her lowered head. "Pfft. I want a discount."

Laila flips me off without lifting her head.

"Thank God there's a professional hair and makeup person here today, eh?" I say. "Hopefully, she's a good one. She's got her work cut out for her with you."

"*Please, shut up*," she murmurs into the table. "I'm trying to die over here. Which is okay, I've decided. I've had a good run. Tell my mother and sister I love them."

Aloha addresses her husband. "Babe, will you make Laila one of your hangover miracle smoothies?"

"You bet."

Georgina offers to assist Zander, saying she was a bartender in college, and he cheerily accepts her help.

As Zander and Georgina begin whipping up the concoction, Aloha's phone rings, and she heads off to take her call, which prompts Fish and Alessandra to head out of the kitchen, too, hand in hand. And, suddenly, Laila and I are sitting alone at the table, side by side.

"I'm gonna die," she murmurs.

I rub her back. "You're not gonna die."

"Don't tell me what to do."

I laugh.

"Have you taken some Ibuprofen, Laila?" Amalia asks from across the kitchen.

"No, ma'am. I couldn't find any."

"Poor baby. I'll get you some."

"Thank you, Amalia," Laila croaks out.

"You're the best, Abu Dabu," I call to Amalia as she leaves, prompting Laila to turn her head, placing her cheek flush onto the table with her eyebrows furrowed, and say, "*Abu Dabu?*"

I smile. "Abu is a cute name for grandma. Abu Dabu is my spin on it, because Amalia's like a fortune teller with a crystal ball. Crazy smart, that one."

Laila pulls an adorable face that practically screams, *What the fuck?*

I shrug. "Amalia and I bonded last night. The woman just gets me."

Laila chuckles and then groans with pain. "Don't make me laugh."

"Aw, you feel like a shit stain, huh—not even good enough to feel like the actual shit?"

She grimaces. "Exactly."

I brush my fingertips against her high cheekbone. And then, against her lower lip, reliving our first kiss last night in my mind. Damn, that was an amazing kiss. The best of my life. I didn't even know a kiss could be that exciting. I'd put a lot of stock into finally kissing those mesmerizing lips of Laila's, and yet our kiss exceeded my most enthralling fantasy.

She whimpers. "Last night was supposed to be a last hurrah. Not *suicide*."

It serves you right for ditching my ass last night and

trying to make me jealous, I think. But what I say is, "Poor baby," while rubbing her back.

"That feels nice. Thank you."

"Even shit stains deserve a little mercy."

She sticks out her lower lip. "That's the sweetest thing anyone's ever said to me."

Zander appears and places a hideous green smoothie on the table in front of Laila, as Georgina takes the seat on the other side of her.

"Oh my God," Laila says, beholding the monstrous-looking concoction in front of her.

Zander says, "Drink the whole thing down within five minutes, and I promise you'll be magically back to normal within an hour."

Laila makes a face I'd expect to see on a person who's been dropped into a snake pit. She says, "Is this a *prank*?"

Zander chuckles. "I know it looks heinous, but, trust me, it works like a charm."

Georgina encourages Laila to drink it, so Laila finally picks up the glass, takes a tiny sip, and then winces comically, making everyone laugh.

Amalia returns with pills for Laila, and then heads out to work in another part of the house.

Zander leaves after a bit to find his wife, which prompts Georgina to say she's going to find Reed. And, suddenly, I'm alone at the table with Laila and her nasty-looking smoothie.

"What's in that thing?" I ask, as Laila takes another recalcitrant gulp.

"I have no idea," she replies, wiping her mouth. "Whatever it is, it tastes like *ass*."

"Well, if it tastes like *your* delicious ass, then sign me up."

She flashes me a snarky look. "I knew you'd bring that up, the first chance you got."

"You want me to pretend last night never happened, like on tour?"

"I do, actually. Thanks."

"I'm not doing that again, Laila. Especially not when we're going to be living together for the next three months. Last night happened, baby. Deal with it. Especially since it's going to happen again and again and again, every night for the next three months."

"Don't confuse my desire for a drunken booty call with my desire to jump into some kind of three-month-long arrangement with you."

"Why *wouldn't* we jump into an arrangement while living together? It's not like we can mess around with anyone else while we're pretending to be in love. So, let's have some fun."

She sniffs. "You smoke when you drink, and I fuck Adrian Savage when I drink."

I roll my eyes. "So, are you planning to be celibate for the next three months? Because I'm sure as hell not." I lean forward. "Especially when I already know how good you taste."

"Has it escaped your notice that *both* times we've fooled around, we've *both* been shitfaced drunk?"

"That's not why we fooled around, and you know it."

"I don't know that. When I'm sober, I'm not stupid enough to find you irresistible."

"Booze doesn't make you stupid, Laila. It makes you *honest.* And booze certainly isn't what makes me irresistible to you."

She snorts.

"Why would you even want to resist me, when I'm so damned delicious?"

"Candy is delicious, too, Savage. But too much candy isn't good for me."

"But you don't *expect* candy to be good for you, so there's no false advertising. You eat candy for instant gratification. Because it's delicious and *fun*." I smile. "Come, Laila. Let's have some delicious fun together."

She twists her mouth like she's genuinely considering it. But rather than speak, she brings her hideous smoothie to her lips.

I'm a shark smelling blood. A bloodhound on the scent. She's losing her resolve. I can *feel* it. "Come on," I coo. "When you know, going in, you're bingeing on candy, then nobody can get hurt." She purses her lips, but doesn't say no, so I forge ahead. "Whatever made you want to hunt me down for a booty call last night is still there now, even without a drop of alcohol in your system."

"I didn't hunt you down for a booty call last night. You hunted *me* down for a booty call."

"Oh, *really*? What were you doing creeping around in the hallway in the middle of the night in your underwear, if not hunting me down for a booty call?"

She bats her eyelashes. "I got hungry and wanted a snack."

I snort. "Laila, I saw you pressing your ear against a door. Obviously, you were trying to figure out which room was mine."

"Maybe. But not for a booty call. I wanted to chew you out for leaving the party without saying goodnight to me."

"In your underwear?"

"I didn't think about what I was wearing. I was too drunk and annoyed. You're the one who said we should always stay in character, whenever we're not alone. And then, you left the party without so much as a wave goodbye to me? Ha! Would a real boyfriend leave a party without saying goodnight to his girlfriend who supposedly rocks his world? No way!"

I can't help smiling. I should have known Kendrick

would never steer me wrong. The guy is a king. I say, "I left without saying goodnight because I didn't want to bother you while you were obviously having so much fun with your friends. Plus, the only people left at the party at that point were good friends who were associated with the show, so I knew you were in good hands."

"You're such a hypocrite! That's exactly what I said about Colin!"

I bite back a smile. Pushing her buttons is so damned fun. "Let's not rehash the Colin thing, okay? The bottom line is you flirted with him last night to make me jealous, because you're evil, and it worked because I'm stupid and predictable. Can we agree we're both idiot-assholes and move on, please?"

She looks extremely pleased with that response. "Yes. As long as we agree you're *more* of an idiot-asshole than me, then I'm prepared to move on."

"No. We're tied."

She pauses for a beat before exhaling and saying, "Fine."

"Thank you. Now, admit you were creeping around the hallway in your underwear last night because you were looking for a booty call."

"What about you? What were *you* doing in the hallway in your underwear?"

I grin wickedly. "Like you said, I was hungry and looking for a snack." I lean forward. "And, lucky for me, the snack I found was even tastier than I'd fantasized it'd be. So damned tasty, I can't wait to eat it again and again, starting tonight."

She bites her lip but says nothing. And I know she's on the bitter cusp of agreeing to fuck my brains out every night for the next three months.

"Aw, come on, Laila," I coo in my most seductive voice. "Why fight it? Let's have some fun."

She exhales. "I don't want it to get confusing."

I furrow my brow. "In what way?"

She shrugs. "Won't it be weird if we're working together, living together, pretending to be head over heels for each other . . . *and* having sex every night? Doesn't that seem like a recipe for disaster?"

"For who? Are you saying you're worried you're going to catch feelings, Fitzy?"

"Of course not. I'm saying I'm worried *you're* going to catch feelings."

I scoff. "I'm not the one we need to worry about, sweetheart. I'm not the one who went on *Sylvia* and couldn't stop talking about me."

"And I'm not the one who couldn't stop talking about me to that Instagrammer."

"Oh, come on. You don't believe her stupid story. Not for a second."

"I believe every word of it."

"No way. You're messing with me. You know I said I needed to 'lay low' because of the show."

"No. I believe, with all my heart, you said you didn't want her because of Laila."

"Why would I turn her down because of *you*?"

"Exactly. Why would you do that, Savage? Tell me."

I pause, my heart racing. "I *didn't*. You didn't even cross my mind in that moment. When you're not physically in front of me, I literally forget you exist. Hell, I barely remember you exist when you're right in front of my face."

She rolls her eyes.

"Seriously, Laila. If you're worried I'll 'catch feelings' from having sex with you while I'm stuck with you anyway, then don't. I'm perfectly capable of separating fact from fiction. The real question is can *you*?"

"Of course I can."

"Even if you're living with, and sleeping with, and

working with, your fake boyfriend who's an irresistible god-among-men rockstar who's hung like a jury?"

She scoffs. "I won't catch feelings, Savage. Under any circumstances. Honestly, I don't even like you."

"Perfect, because I don't like you. We're a match made in heaven, if you ask me."

She bites her lip and I know I've got her. *Finally.*

"So, we're doing this then?" I say.

Laila pauses. "We'd be fuck buddies only. No strings. And nobody catches feelings."

"Of course. It'll be nothing but fun and a whole lot of orgasms."

She puts out her hand. "Deal."

I feel like jumping for joy but manage to maintain a neutral face while shaking her hand. "Now give me our first *sober* kiss to seal the deal." With that, I pull her toward me. And when our lips meet, the kiss hits totally differently than our drunken, animalistic kisses from last night. This time, as my lips open hers, and my tongue slides into her mouth and begins slowly tangling with hers, I feel every nuanced sensation. Every shudder of arousal. Every inhale and exhale that tells me her temperature is slowly rising, the same as mine.

As our sensuous kiss deepens, I pull her out of her chair and guide her to straddle me in my chair, and, soon, she's grinding against me as her tongue goads me on. I begin caressing her breasts over her tank top, pinching her stiff nipples, and burying my hands into her thick hair, every fiber of my body aching and yearning to get inside her.

"We've got time," I murmur into her lips. "Come to my room. Let me fuck you."

"Yes," she breathes.

But she's no sooner said the word than a voice in the doorway says her name. When we break apart, breathing hard, there's a production assistant in the doorframe.

The PA says, "I'm sorry to interrupt." She clears her throat. "Nadine sent me to fetch Laila and bring her to hair and makeup. She said we're on a tight schedule."

Laila smiles and kisses my cheek. "Rain check?" She slides off my lap and points at the noticeable bulge behind my sweatpants. "I'll see *you* later tonight."

I slap her ass as she turns to go. "Count on it, *girlfriend*."

"Don't miss me while I'm gone, boyfriend."

"I can't miss someone who ceases to exist when she's not in my presence."

"Sure, Jan."

With that, she swishes her hips with extra flair, and disappears through the doorway with the PA. When she's gone, and I know she can't possibly hear me, I sit back in my chair, smiling from ear to ear, my hard cock throbbing and my heart racing, and whisper to myself, "*Hallelujah.*"

I follow the staffer outside and across Reed's patio, heading toward Reed's guest house in the back of Reed's huge estate. Apparently, the hair and makeup woman has set up camp there. As we walk, we come upon Kendrick. He's sitting on a patio chair with a laptop on his lap and headphones over his ears.

When he sees me, Kendrick pulls down one side of his headphones and greets me. "I just got the final mixes for our album!" he says effusively.

"Ooooh!" I say. "When can I listen? I seem to recall someone saying, on day one of our tour, I'd get to be one of your early listeners."

"Absolutely. We'd love to get your feedback on the mixes. Give it a listen as soon as you can and let me know if you hear *anything* that sounds wonky to you—anything at all you think is too low or high in the mix."

"It'd be my honor. I can't wait."

Kendrick clicks on his keyboard for a moment. "I just sent you a download link."

I look at my phone. "Got it! Woohoo! I'll listen now, while I'm getting my hair and makeup done!"

"Awesome. Thanks."

"No, thank *you.*"

I say my goodbyes to Kendrick and resume following the PA to Reed's casita, where I'm immediately greeted by the hair and makeup woman. After the woman gets me settled in her chair, we talk briefly about the look we're going for today—sexpot, of course—and once we're both on the same page, I settle back, put a pair of earbuds in, and press play on the first song of Fugitive Summer's highly anticipated album.

Right away, it's obvious the first song is going to be a massive hit, although I'd personally make the bass line a touch louder in the mix. Next up, the second song begins and I quickly fall equally in love with it. How does this band do it, album after album? Every song of theirs is like crack to me. And Savage's voice and delivery is always mesmerizing. From what I understand, he writes the lion's share of the band's lyrics, which is probably why he always delivers them so believably. Say what you will about Savage, the man, being deeply flawed and mercurial, but as an artist, that boy is a true genius.

The third song begins as the makeup artist finishes applying foundation and moves on to my eyes. And, once again, even before Savage begins singing, based on nothing but the sexual, dirty beat and groove and flashes of Savage's phallic electric guitar, I already know I'm going to love this one. It's got a vibe that's reminiscent of "Come with Me," the band's most sexual song, without it feeling like a copycat or redux. Indeed, the sexual vibe of the song is reinforced, even before the first verse begins, as Savage growls out a few sensual "yeahs" to kick things off, his strained voice sounding remarkably like he's getting a blowjob in the recording booth.

Finally, as the bass-heavy beat gains momentum, Savage counts off—"One, two, three, let's go!"—and away he goes, launching into the lyrics of the first verse.

Almost immediately, as Savage sings, I open my eyes, recognizing myself in the song. Is this a coincidence . . . or is Savage singing this song about *me*?

No way.

Why would Savage write a song about *me*?

"Close, please," the makeup artist says, referring to my eyes.

"Hold on a second," I say. I quickly look down at my phone, curious about the title of this one. And when I see it, I gasp. *Hate Sex High*. That's what the song is called. Which definitely makes me think I'm not crazy to think the song could be about me. Maybe? But I've no sooner had that last thought than the song barrels into its chorus . . . and the lyrics there make my jaw practically clank to the floor.

I wander out of the house with a cup of coffee and take in the view for a moment, scratching my bare belly. I feel light as a feather right now. Like everything is clicking into place. I gotta hand it to Kendrick. The man is a genius. Speaking of Kendrick, I notice him sitting in a chair with his laptop and decide to head over there to tell him he's the man—that, thanks to his advice, I've now got Laila eating out the palm of my hand.

When I reach Kendrick, he's got headphones on, and he's nodding his head to a beat only he can hear.

When he notices me, he pulls off one side of his headphones and blurts excitedly, "Did you see Zeke sent the final mixes?"

My heart lurches. "No. When? I left my phone in my room."

"Twenty minutes ago. I'm listening now and everything sounds *amazing*!"

"Oh, my God. Let me hear something!"

Kendrick hands me his headphones and I slip them on,

while Kendrick presses play on the first song—"Shockwave" —a banger that's one of my favorites on the album.

"Oh my God. 'Shockwave' sounds *so* good," I say excitedly. "Although I'd add a touch more bass to the mix. Ask Kai what he thinks, obviously, but that's my opinion."

"Yeah, okay. I'll ask him."

I listen for a long moment again, before saying, "Zeke sent the link to Reed, too?"

"Yeah. I saw Reed a few minutes ago. He was super stoked. He headed straight to his office to listen now."

"Cool. So excited."

"Same. Reed said he'll send it to some people with really good ears."

"Awesome. Is he sending it to Dax Morgan and Dean Masterson, you think?"

"Yeah, he mentioned both. Fish, too."

"Perfect. Fish's ears are impeccable."

"I know. If Reed didn't send it to him already, I would have done it myself. I sent it to C-Bomb, too. He said he'll take a listen today. Oh, and Laila, too. Just now. She's got amazing ears."

My heart stops. "Laila? You *already* sent it to her or you're *planning* to send it to her?"

"I already did. She said she'd listen right away, while she gets her hair and makeup done."

"Kendrick, no." I can barely breathe. "How long ago was that?"

"What's wrong?"

"When was that?"

"Just now. Like, ten minutes ago. Fifteen, tops. Why?"

"Where is she? Did she say where she was going?"

"Hair and makeup."

"Yes, but *where*?" I'm shouting now, as panic rises sharply inside me. "Where is hair and makeup, Kendrick?"

"I don't know. She went that way." He points. "What's wrong? Laila is totally trustworthy."

My heart is crashing. My breathing shallow. I point maniacally at Kendrick's laptop. "Quick, look to see if she's already downloaded it! If not, cancel her access. Now, Kendrick!"

"*Why*?"

"Just do it!"

"I'm doing it. Calm down." He starts clicking on his keyboard, looking frantic. "What's the problem?"

"'Hate Sex High,' Kendrick! I don't want Laila listening to that one right now. Not *yet*."

"*Oooh*." He taps on some keys before looking up from his screen, his features contorted in apology. And even before he's said a word, I know what he's going to say. But he says it, anyway. "She already downloaded it, dude. It's too late."

I take a deep breath. "Maybe not. It's only been a few minutes. Maybe Laila isn't listening to the album yet. Or if she is, maybe she hasn't gotten to that song. Where is it in the order?"

Kendrick checks the screen and grimaces again. "Third, like you requested."

"*Fuck*! She went that way?"

"Yeah. I think there's a guest house over there. Maybe that's—"

But I'm not listening. Without further ado, I sprint away in the direction Kendrick indicated, cursing a blue streak as I go . . . feeling uncannily like I'm running *toward* a ticking time bomb.

As the third song on the album—"Hate Sex High"—reaches the end of its first chorus and barrels into a sort of sing-along post-chorus section that causes my head to explode, there's a commotion at the door. A sudden movement attracts my attention, and when I look toward the doorframe, none other than Savage is standing there, his chest heaving and his eyes bugged out.

I look at him, rendered speechless, as Savage's voice continues singing in my ears . . . about *me.* And whatever Savage sees on my face in this moment prompts him to say, quite obviously, the word "Fuck." I can't hear him saying the word, but I can sure as hell read his lips, as Savage's voice launches into the second chorus of "Hate Sex High" in my earbuds:

You're falling, falling, falling, falling, falling in hate with me
I'm feeling, feeling, feeling, feeling something I don't want to feel . . .

. . .

Savage begins walking toward me, and when he mouths the word "Laila" before me, it's coincidentally at the exact same time he sings my name in the song, in the post-chorus section where Savage sings, repeatedly: "La la la la la la la la la *Laila Laila.*"

I rip out my earbuds, just in time to hear Savage asking the hair and makeup artist to leave. As the woman scurries out the front door of the casita, the song continues wafting from the earbuds in my hand, now sounding compressed and tinny, but otherwise clear as a bell.

Savage's voice in the earbuds sings: "And I'm feeling, feeling, feeling, feeling . . . *something I don't want to feel.*" And Savage before me inhales sharply and jolts in response.

"It's not about you!" Savage blurts, his face flushed. "I know how it must seem, but it's, you know, creative license. Pure fiction. Not about you."

Pure fiction? That seems highly unlikely. Partial fiction, maybe. But there's just too much obvious truth, too much coincidence in the verses, for the entire song to be *pure* fiction.

I say, "*Pure* fiction?"

"I mean, there might be kernels of truth in the verses," he acknowledges. "Here and there. Tiny kernels, which I then spun into popcorn lies in the chorus."

"I get it," I say, my heart crashing in my chest. But I'm not sure I get it. It's interesting he felt the need to single out the chorus, without me mentioning it. The part where someone is *falling* into hate with Savage and he's *feeling* something he doesn't want to feel for someone.

"When I wrote the chorus," Savage says, his features tight, "I chose words that went together well. I liked the way 'falling' and 'feeling' sound together, that's all."

"Yeah, that was a cool word choice. When I write, I like putting words together that sound good, too. I'm often motivated by the sounds of words more than their meanings."

"*Exactly*," he says. "The meaning is secondary. Not even important."

There's a long, awkward pause between us, during which he looks remarkably flustered.

Savage shifts his weight. "*Maybe*, subliminally, the night of the hot tub played a small part in inspiring the song. I think I remember writing that song shortly after we got together. So, I'm sure it'd be fair to say that night gave me the initial spark of an idea for the song, but then I ran with it and it became something totally fictitious."

Totally fictitious? That's what I'm thinking. But what I say is, "I totally get it."

"By the time I got done writing it, it was almost pure fiction."

"I write the same way sometimes. Something real gives me an idea, and I run with it."

"I know you get it. You're a fantastic songwriter, by the way."

"Thanks. So are you." My heart feels like a jackhammer. "I love the songs I've heard so far. I've only heard the first three, but they're all amazing." I swallow hard. My mouth is dry. "I hope you don't mind me saying this, but I'd personally make the bassline a bit higher in the mix on the first song. Just the tiniest bit."

"I thought the same thing. Great feedback. Thanks."

"Sure. I'll keep listening carefully to the rest, if—"

"Yeah, please do. Thanks."

"Sure."

He shifts his weight again. "Cool."

The song ends in my earbuds and a new one begins. So I

grab my phone and press pause. "I'm honored to get to hear the album early, by the way. Thanks for that."

"We like having trusted people—people with good ears . . . " He trails off and takes a deep breath. "I only ran down here to talk to you because I didn't want you thinking—"

"I don't. I understand the writing process."

"The song isn't some kind of . . . confessional or anything. Don't read too much into it."

"I don't. I get it." But, still, I'm not sure I get it.

Savage breathes a huge sigh of relief and his shoulders soften. "Cool."

I bite the tip of my finger. "I mean, why on earth would I think you were 'feeling' something you 'didn't want to feel' . . . for *me*?"

His shoulders stiffen again.

"Especially back then," I add. "I know you've discovered I'm a tasty treat nowadays, and kind of fun to hang out with, if you've got no other option, but back then, we hated each other's guts. *Right*?"

"We still do, as far as I'm concerned," he says.

"Good. Me, too."

"Good."

My eyes are locked with his as I try to discern if this feeling in my belly is delusional or not. "I mean, back then, you were *way* too busy mowing through groupies in every city of the tour to be feeling 'something' you 'didn't want to feel' about *me*. *Right*?"

He pauses, briefly, before saying, "Right. Absolutely."

We stare at each other for a long beat, the only sound the crashing of my heart in my ears.

"Okay, well . . ." Savage finally says. "I'm glad we talked about this. It's a good thing you're so familiar with songwriting and the creative process, or this could have created a huge misunderstanding. Especially going into our . . . arrangement."

I press my lips together. "It's a good thing, indeed."

He motions toward the door. "So . . . should I tell the makeup artist to—"

"Yes, please. We're running tight on time, apparently, and she's got quite a bit more to do to make this shit stain look halfway decent."

"Actually, I would have thought she's already done. You look great."

"Thanks. Zander's hangover cure worked, exactly as promised. I feel . . ." Weird. Confused. Shocked. Skittish. Suspicious. Freaked out. "Remarkably good, actually."

"Glad to hear it. Okay, well, I'll go get the makeup artist for you. See you at the press conference."

"See you then."

He turns to leave.

"Actually, one quick question."

Savage turns around slowly, his facial expression saying, *And I was so close to escaping, too.*

I smile. "In the second half of the chorus, that sort of post-chorus sing-along part . . . Are you singing, 'La la la . . . *Laila*' there?"

He flushes. "No."

"No?"

"Nope. I'm singing 'la la.'"

"Yeah, I know, but at the tail end there. After the string of 'la la's,' you didn't cap it off with 'Laila'?"

"No. I sang, 'La la' the whole way through."

"Huh. That's so weird. I was positive I heard you singing my name."

"That's what being a narcissist will do to you, I guess. You think everyone is singing your name."

I smile sweetly. "Takes one to know one, honey."

We chuckle awkwardly. But, seriously. I swear I heard that part as Laila.

His face is red. His Adam's apple bobs. "I was definitely singing 'la la' there. But if you think it sounds too much like *Laila*, then I can re-record that part, very easily, to make it crystal clear what I'm actually singing—which absolutely isn't 'Laila.'"

"No need. I'm sure I was just imagining it. Thinking the world revolves around me, like you said. I'm sure when I listen again, I'll laugh that I ever thought you sang my name on that part."

Savage chuckles with me. "Yeah, that's funny." He claps his hands together and exhales. "Okay, well, I'll let you get to it. Like you said, time is tight."

"Great. Thanks."

Looking a bit out of sorts, Savage practically stumbles out the door, and a moment later, the makeup artist returns. After she's picked up her eyeshadow palette, and I've settled back into my chair, I shove my earbuds back in, restart "Hate Sex High" from the beginning, and listen to every single word, this time extra carefully:

Hate Sex High

Yeah, yeah, yeah, yeah
One, two, three, let's go

You're falling, falling, falling, falling, falling in hate with me
I'm feeling, feeling, feeling, feeling something I don't want to feel

· · ·

Saw you with him at the show
I didn't like it
I played it cold to your face
But I was on fire
He said you were his all along
And I didn't like it
Turns out I imagined it all
Went back and punched a hole in the wall

You're falling, falling, falling, falling, falling in hate
with me
I'm feeling, feeling, feeling, feeling something I don't
want to feel
You're falling, falling, falling, falling, falling in hate
with me
I'm feeling, feeling, feeling, feeling something I don't
want to feel

Lalalalalala la la
Lalalalalala la la

I shouldn't-a said what I did
Not tryna deny it
The harder I pushed you away
You wanted to ride it
I fucked with your body, baby
You fucked with my mind
You said it meant nothing to ya
But you came three times

.   .   .

*You're falling, falling, falling, falling, falling in hate
with me
I'm feeling, feeling, feeling, feeling something I don't
want to feel
You're falling, falling, falling, falling, falling in hate
with me
I'm feeling, feeling, feeling, feeling something I don't
want to feel*

*Lalalalalala la la
Lalalalalala la la*

*I fucked with your body, baby
You fucked with my mind
You said it meant nothing to ya
But you came three times
Girl, you came three times
You came three times
You're chasing a
Hate sex high*

The song cycles through a few more choruses, until, finally, in an outro at the very end, Savage speaks conversationally over the music, his voice purring sexually above the sex-laden beat: "Did *he* make you come *three* times? Yeah, didn't think so." And I know, without a doubt, that's absolutely one of the "kernels of truth" Savage admitted were buried in the song. Unless, of course, he was making every groupie he screwed come three times, the same way he did to me on the night of the hot tub, and was also totally obsessed with his achievement in regards to them, as well.

I listen again, from the very beginning, and, once again, I can't help hearing my name at the end of the "la la la" section. Granted, Savage didn't pronounce it like he normally would, almost as if he was pronouncing my name in a purposefully vague sort of way, like he was trying to reserve himself some deniability. Like he was *pretending* to sing "la la" in that part, while *secretly* singing "Laila" with a smug little smirk on his handsome face. In fact, I can almost picture Savage in the vocal booth, smirking wickedly while recording that part, as if he thought he was getting away with a fast one.

I feel a tap on my shoulder and open my eyes.

"All done," the makeup artist mouths, and I pull out my earbuds and look in the mirror.

"Beautiful," I say. "Thank you."

"You're an easy canvas."

She begins cleaning up her station, getting ready for whoever is coming next. But I'm too lost in thought to move a muscle. Savage admitted he wrote "Hate Sex High" based on "kernels of truth" which he then spun into "popcorn lies." Like I told him, that's a concept I can fully understand, in general, since I've done the same thing in my own songwriting, too.

However, in reference to *this* specific song, a song called "Hate Sex High," in which my name sure seems to be buried artfully among a string of "la la la's"—a song about a woman chasing a "hate sex high" while Savage makes her come "*three* times"—a song about a woman falling into hate with Savage while he feels "something" he doesn't "want to feel" —I can't help wondering, in regards to this specific song: which parts are the admitted "kernels of *truth*" . . . and which are the supposed "popcorn lies"?

TO BE CONTINUED

. . .

Look for "FALLING INTO LOVE WITH YOU," the conclusion of "THE HATE-LOVE DUET."

To find out how to stream or download "HATE SEX HIGH", go to www.laurenrowebooks.com/music-from-the-hatelove-duet
And while you're there, check out tons of spoiler-free BONUS MATERIAL about Savage, Laila, and many River Records artists.

BOOKS BY LAUREN ROWE

Finding Home

I'm Caleb Baumgarten, the "bad boy" drummer of Red Card Riot.

After tragedy strikes and the toddler with half my DNA inside her
loses her beloved mommy, I get the

bright idea to hire my daughter's remaining lifeline, her "Auntie
Aubrey," as my live-in nanny. Also,

embarrassingly, as my sobriety coach, so I can fulfill the terms of
my mandatory rehab.

Going into my forced living arrangement with Aubrey in her small
town, I'm determined not to give in to

my growing, thumping, white-hot attraction. There's only a month
before the custody hearing that will

decide my fate as a father, and I'll need Aubrey to testify on my
behalf. Well, you know what they say

about best laid plans, right? Yeah. My bad.

The Morgan Brothers

Read these standalones in any order. Chronological reading order is
below, but they are all complete stories. Note: you do not need to
read any other books or series before jumping straight into reading
about the Morgan boys.

Hero

The story of heroic firefighter, Colby Morgan. When catastrophe
strikes Colby Morgan, will physical therapist Lydia save him . . . or
will he save her?

Captain

The insta-love-to-enemies-to-lovers story of tattooed sex god, Ryan Morgan, and the woman he'd move heaven and earth to claim.

Ball Peen Hammer

A steamy, hilarious, friends-to-lovers romantic comedy about cocky-as-hell male stripper, Keane Morgan, and the sassy, smart young woman who brings him to his knees during a road trip.

Mister Bodyguard

The Morgans' beloved honorary brother, Zander Shaw, meets his match in the feisty pop star he's assigned to protect on tour.

ROCKSTAR

When the youngest Morgan brother, Dax Morgan, meets a mysterious woman who rocks his world, he must decide if pursuing her is worth risking it all. Be sure to check out four of Dax's original songs from ROCKSTAR, written and produced by Lauren, along with full music videos for the songs, on her website (www.laurenrowebooks.com) under the tab MUSIC FROM ROCKSTAR.

Dive into Lauren's universe of interconnected trilogies and duets, all books available individually and as a bundle, in any order.

A full suggested reading order can be found here!

The Josh & Kat Trilogy

It's a war of wills between stubborn and sexy Josh Faraday and Kat Morgan. A fight to the bed. Arrogant, wealthy playboy Josh is used to getting what he wants. And what he wants is Kat Morgan. The books are to be read in order:

Infatuation

Revelation

Consummation

The Club Trilogy

When wealthy playboy Jonas Faraday receives an anonymous note from Sarah Cruz, a law student working part-time processing online applications for an exclusive club, he becomes obsessed with hunting her down and giving her the satisfaction she claims has always eluded her. Thus begins a sweeping tale of obsession, passion, desperation, and ultimately, everlasting love and individual redemption. Find out why scores of readers all over the world, in multiple languages, call The Club Trilogy "my favorite trilogy ever" and "the greatest love story I've ever read." As Jonas Faraday says to Sarah Cruz: "There's never been a love like ours and there never will be again… Our love is so pure and true, we're the amazement of the gods."

The Club: Obsession

The Club: Reclamation

The Club: Redemption

The fourth book for Jonas and Sarah is a full-length epilogue with incredible heart-stopping twists and turns and feels. Read The Club: Culmination (A Full-Length Epilogue Novel) after finishing The Club Trilogy or, if you prefer, after reading The Josh and Kat Trilogy.

The Reed Rivers Trilogy

Reed Rivers has met his match in the most unlikely of women— aspiring journalist and spitfire, Georgina Ricci. She's much younger than the women Reed normally pursues, but he can't resist her fiery personality and drop-dead gorgeous looks. But in this game of cat and mouse, who's chasing whom? With each passing day of this wild ride, Reed's not so sure. The books of this trilogy are to be read in order:

Bad Liar

Beautiful Liar

Beloved Liar

The Hate Love Duet

An addicting, enemies-to-lovers romance with humor, heat, angst, and banter. Music artists Savage of Fugitive Summer and Laila Fitzgerald are stuck together on tour. And convinced they can't stand each other. What they don't know is that they're absolutely made for each other, whether they realize it or not. The books of this duet are to be read in order:

Falling Out of Hate with You

Falling Into Love with You

Interconnected Standalones within the same universe as above

Hacker in Love

When world-class hacker Peter "Henn" Hennessey meets Hannah Milliken, he moves heaven and earth, including doing some questionable things, to win his dream girl over. But when catastrophe strikes, will Henn lose Hannah forever, or is there still a chance for him to chase their happily ever after? *Hacker in Love* is a steamy, funny, heart-pounding, ***standalone*** contemporary romance with a whole lot of feels, laughs, spice, and swoons.

Smitten

When aspiring singer-songwriter, Alessandra, meets Fish, the funny, adorable bass player of 22 Goats, sparks fly between the awkward pair. Fish tells Alessandra he's a "Goat called Fish who's hung like a bull. But not really. I'm actually really average." And Alessandra tells Fish, "There's nothing like a girl's first love." Alessandra thinks she's talking about a song when she makes her comment to Fish— the first song she'd ever heard by 22 Goats, in fact. As she'll later find out, though, her "first love" was actually Fish. The Goat called Fish who, after that night, vowed to do anything to win her heart. SMITTEN is a true standalone romance.

Swoon

When Colin Beretta, the drummer of 22 Goats, is a groomsman at the wedding of his childhood best friend, Logan, he discovers Logan's kid sister, Amy, is all grown up. Colin tries to resist his attraction to Amy, but after a drunken kiss at the wedding reception, that's easier said than done. Swoon is a true standalone romance.

Meet Me At Captain's Series of Standalone Romantic comedies

Who's Your Daddy?

When thirty-year-old patent attorney, Maximillian Vaughn, meets a sassy, charismatic older woman in a bar, he invites her back to his place for one night of no-strings fun. It's all Max can offer, given his busy career; but, luckily, it's all Marnie wants, too. But when Max's chemistry with Marnie is so combustible, it threatens to burn down his bedroom, he does the unthinkable the next morning: he asks Marnie out on a dinner date.

Mere minutes after saying yes, however, Marnie bolts like her hair is on fire with no explanation. What happened? Max doesn't know, but he's determined to find out and convince Marnie to pick up where they left off.

Textual Relations

When Grayson McKnight unknowingly gets a fake number from a woman in a bar, he winds up embroiled in a sexy text exchange with the actual owner of the number—a confident, sensual older woman who knows exactly who she is . . . and what she wants.

No strings attached.

But as sparks fly and real feelings develop, will Grayson get his way and tempt her to give him more than their original bargain?

My Neighbor's Secret

When Charlotte gets into her new dilapidated condo to start fixing it up for resale, she finds out the infuriating stranger who's thoroughly messed up her life is her new next-door neighbor.

Also, that he's got a big secret.

She confronts him and proposes they work together to get

themselves out of their respective jams, even though they both admittedly can't stand each other. Yes, he's let it slip he thinks she's pretty. And, okay, she begrudgingly thinks he's kind of cute. But whatever. They hate each other and this is nothing but a business partnership. What could go wrong?

The Secret Note: A Spicy Standalone Novella with HEA

He's a hot Aussie. I'm a girl who isn't shy about getting what she wants. The problem? Ben is my little brother's best friend. An exchange student who's heading back Down Under any day now. But I can't help myself. He's too hot to resist.

Misadventures Standalones **(unrelated standalones not within the above universe):**

- *Misadventures on the Night Shift* –A hotel night shift clerk encounters her teenage fantasy: rock star Lucas Ford. And combustion ensues.

- *Misadventures of a College Girl*—A spunky, virginal theater major meets a cocky football player at her first college party . . . and absolutely nothing goes according to plan for either of them.

- *Misadventures on the Rebound*—A spunky woman on the rebound meets a hot, mysterious stranger in a bar on her way to her five-year high school reunion in Las Vegas and what follows is a misadventure neither of them ever imagined.

Lauren's Dark Comedy/Psych Thriller Standalone

Countdown to Killing Kurtis

A young woman with big dreams and skeletons in her closet decides her porno-king husband must die in exactly a year. This is not a traditional romance, but it will most definitely keep you turning the pages and saying "WTF?" If you're looking for something a bit outside the box, with twists and turns, suspense, and dark humor, this is the book for you: a standalone psychological thriller/dark comedy with romantic elements.

AUTHOR BIOGRAPHY

Lauren Rowe is the USA Today and international #1 bestselling author of newly released Reed Rivers Trilogy, as well as The Club Trilogy, The Josh & Kat Trilogy, The Morgan Brothers Series, Countdown to Killing Kurtis, and select standalone Misadventures.

Lauren's books are full of feels, humor, heat, and heart. Besides writing novels, Lauren is the singer in a party/wedding band in her hometown of San Diego, an audio book narrator, and award-winning songwriter. She is thrilled to connect with readers all over the world.
To find out about Lauren's upcoming releases and giveaways, sign up for Lauren's emails via her website.

Find out more and check out lots of free bonus material at www.LaurenRoweBooks.com.

9 781964 868936